ಬ **Treasure Hunt Edition** ಚಿ

Details on page III

SHADOWORLD

Shadows Gate

Asra found himself alone in the middle of the barren sands, unable to remember who he was or how he had gotten there. Saved by a caravan of traveling gypsies, he entered into an exotic world of dancing acrobats, fortune tellers, and mystics who performed their skills for cheering crowds across the desert empires.

However, his destiny would change the day he stumbled upon a forbidden shrine to find a mythical creature entombed beneath its shattered ruins.

Promises were whispered and a dark pact was made with the ancient demon; a bond of magic that would lead him on a perilous journey to reveal his forgotten past.

Beyond the Gate...

The Shadoworld series is comprised of three separate tales sharing one common thread. There is a world of shadows which lurks beyond the edge of the light, waiting to smother its flickering flame; for it is a nocturnal creature that never sleeps, forever watching and waiting for its chance to reclaim the darkness from which it sprang.

There are those who fear the night, while others dread the day; what is left for those who walk both roads are but the gradient shades in-between. Too bright a light can blind just as equally as suffocating darkness, but it is the shadows which binds both worlds so that those dreamers among us may see the path they are meant to follow.

A Treasure Awaits

Within the Shadoworld novels there are hidden several cryptic clues, whereupon the first person who combines each and solves its final riddle will be able to locate a chest containing 1,000 troy ounces of .999 silver bullion and whom will also be entitled to an additional $100,000, including inheritance to all my art and novel royalties plus stated assets within my living will.

It's an old fashioned treasure hunt.
I've always fancied the life of adventure and pass along the torch to those brave souls who walk its path to explore its winding trail.

To collect the total monetary award, send your name and a photograph of the silver-filled chest detailing the exact location where it was discovered, including the code contained within to the publisher address or via email to:

ೞ Art@GreyForest.com ೞ

Titles by Michel Savage

Faerylands Series
The Grey Forest
Soulstorm Keep
Sorrowblade

Outlaws of Europa
Rebels of Alpha Prime

Hellbot • Battle Planet

Islands in the Sky

Broken Mirror

Witchwood

Shadoworld Series
Shadow of the Sun
Veil of Shadows
Shadows Gate

Shadoworld

SHADOWS GATE

MICHEL SAVAGE

www.**GreyForest**.com

SHADOWORLD – Shadows Gate

The Grey Forest
P.O. Box 71494
Springfield, OR 97475

www.GreyForest.com

Cover art by Michel Savage

ISBN: 978-10808481-6-4

First Edition: August 2019

Printed in the United States of America

0 9 8 7 6 5 4 3 2

Authors Note

The many titles I've created were dreamt up a generation ago when I was but a child and took many long years to put to pen so that I may share these stories. They are tales are about ordinary people placed in extraordinary circumstances, which tempts the audience to read between the lines so they might find a reflection of themselves within the characters and their struggles; for within every story is a message.

As an author, I have had the thrill of traveling to worlds beyond the stars while experiencing strange and exotic lands. Through my characters, I've seen incredible sights and wonders and had the privilege to walk in their shoes as I stood beside them to share in their trials and their triumphs.

Though these tales are woven from the golden thread of imagination, they remind me that there are those who merely sleep and those who dream of a better tomorrow; whom will one day wake to find that the sun never truly sets for the few whose ideas and imagination live beyond us.

To those rare visionaries, I commend,
and wish you well on your journey.

*Dreams are but a shadow
of something real*

ೠೞ

Chapter I
Atlantis of the Sands

A lone man sat among the dunes while the heat of the desert began to wane as the sun slowly fell upon the horizon. If grief had a scent, this man would reek with it. The welling despair could be seen in his weary eyes if only he would raise them from the grains of sand at his feet. The bitter taste of regret was sour upon his tongue, choking his words more than the dry thirst clenching at his throat. Anguish enveloped him like the warm sour sweat prickling upon the skin beneath his robes.

If one could only listen into his thoughts and the misery that wallowed within his troubled mind, you would hear but one word, "Asra."

The hot sun dipped from sight and the shadows of the shifting dunes reached out to enfold him in their merciful embrace as darkness spread over the sky above. One by one a sprinkle of stars poked through the canopy of the heavens until a river of twinkling lights filled the night. The lone man sat like a forgotten statue in an empty garden lost to time as though he were a monument to sorrow. He raised his head once to gaze upon the beautiful mystery of the stars as his ears beheld the faint calling of a distant flute.

He had little spirit left within him to rise from sand which had nearly consumed him, but the melody which caressed the wind was strangely familiar and touched upon emotions he had almost forgotten. Wonder and curiosity brought him to his feet as he fought to gain ground with every step to rise above the cresting waves that flowed across the endless ocean of sand. A soft glow illuminated the night which beckoned to him to draw ever near; lured by the tune of music sweeping across the dunes. Breaking the final ridge, his eyes fell upon a caravan of travelers busily cooking meals in the warm blaze of a campfire while musicians played in its light.

A dark-haired woman gathering supplies from her wagon saw the lone stranger as he stumbled down the hill towards the group. She dropped her basket and ran to him as he faltered and tumbled down the tall dune to the edge of the camp. She grabbed his arm to help him up only to notice the lost emptiness in his eyes. She carried him to the wagon and leaned him up against its stout wooden wheel as she fetched a waterskin.

"Where did you come from, stranger?" she asked as the gaze of his ghostly eyes seemed to pass through her.

The man in the blood-stained cloak tried to speak, but his throat was as dry as the desert air. She could see by his cracked lips and parched skin upon his face that he had been wandering the dunes for many days. Handing him the bladder, she had to help him drink as the water fought its way past his drawn lips. Taking a damp cloth, she brushed the sand from his face and helped him into a nearby tent laden with carpets and furs.

Beyond its curtain, gypsy girls danced around the fire as the tune of the musicians played on into the night while the woman helped the stranger from the desert remove his soiled clothes and let him rest upon the embroidered pillows. His consciousness faded in and out from the world around him as wild chants and swaying demons filled his mind. With a gasp of air, he lurched upright from his disturbing dreams, finding daylight streaming in from the draped doorway of the tent. Failing to recall the events from the previous eve, he knew not where he was.

A slim girl entered while he held up his hand to protect his eyes from the glare of daylight pouring in. She was alluring, with lined eyes and arms covered in intricate designs of henna that decorated her flesh. Upon her body she she wore coined necklaces and cuffs of hammered silver which jingled as she walked. She had the grace of a cat, but the tongue of a cobra.

"I see you're awake. Come, we must break camp before the hour!" she snapped at her foreign guest before she turned to exit the tent.

Still in a daze, the man looked around and found his old garments had been replaced by a set of white robes with a matching sash and length of pale linen to weave into a turban. He found his boots and leggings had been cleaned and within that moment realized that a single pendant hung around his neck. It was a strange work of artistry which appeared to be wrought of ancient metal covered in etched runes he could not decipher, yet the ornament seemed somehow familiar as was the unusual melody which had drawn him to this place. He stepped outside to notice several men who appeared to have been poised as though waiting for him to leave the tent, who swept in behind him and began hastily packing away its contents and breaking down the canvas walls.

"Over here," the woman he had seen before called as she motioned for him to mount her wagon.

The vehicle itself was wrapped with intricate designs painted from spectrums of every color. The large wooden wheels were braced with wide slats so they could navigate the silted dunes as the cart was drawn by horses of fine breeding. He climbed up to the bench where she patiently sat with the reigns in her hands as a

pair of men packed several items from the interior of the
tent and strapped them to her elaborate carriage.

"Where are you heading?" he managed to breathe in
question to the woman as she set the wagon in motion
while the other members of the caravan mounted their
various carts and steeds.

"Ah, so you do speak our tongue? Good!" She cracked
with a grin, "Who are you and what were you doing out
here alone in these barren wastes?"

He struggled for a moment trying to remember as
fleeting flashes of memory failed to fall within his grasp.

"I'm not quite sure..." his voiced faded off as he
struggled to recall the previous days which had brought
him to this moment.

"Don't let it bother you too much," she offered with a
hint of compassion, "it's likely the desert fog, I've seen it
before when men lose their way in these sands. The sun
is not kind to those who trespass upon these forbidden
lands," she mentioned, "you kept repeating a single word,
'*Az-ra*' over and over; does that mean anything to you?"

"Asra," he breathed aloud, the word being unfamiliar
but seemed to slip off his tongue as though he had said it
a thousand times before, "...perhaps that is my name," he
answered with a defeated shrug.

"Ah, good, that's a decent pet name to call you in the
meantime," she added while turning to face him, "I am
Tasha-Nell LeAir Ouswan of the Fernwood Tribe ...but
Tasha will do," she smiled.

"Fernwood," Asra recited as his hand fell back again
onto the strange pendant hanging around his neck as his
mind wandered as though its name touched upon some
lost memory.

"Yes, do you know it?" Tasha asked, "It is a lush and

vibrant land far north of the Silver Mountains, past the sacred river of Tal-eh Uum. The forests there are green as emeralds and the air thick with dew and the song of exotic birds in valleys where the hallowed white deer run free," she added with flare.

"No, I can't say that I do," Asra answered bluntly while playing with the scruff of his beard as though it had grown there without his knowledge.

"Not a very talkative one, are you?" Tasha remarked with a playful pout, "Do you remember anything about where you are from or why you were out here?"

Asra pushed himself as his mind clawed for answers to what trial of fate had brought him here to these forsaken lands, but all he could muster was a hazy feeling that there was something he must do.

"I believe I was on a journey to find something," he muttered with finality.

"Aren't we all," Tasha half-joked as she waved towards the rest of the several dozen men and women of the gypsy caravan around them as they traveled in a single line through a valley between the dunes, "...our troupe is made of dancers and acrobats, soothsayers and fortune-tellers, musicians and storytellers who seek our way to the ivory towers of Ubar."

"You are a group of performers?" Asra inquired.

"Most of us are, it is how we survive in these hard times with the border wars to the south and roving bandits who plunder what little is left. There is safety in both numbers and high walls; which is why we are constantly on the move," she granted.

"And what skills do you add to this troupe?" Asra inquired with a raised brow.

"I lead a cast of Moon Dancers," Tasha answered,

"performing the sacred ceremony of the lunar goddess as entertainment to those who can afford the price," she noted with a hint of intrigue, "...and what expertise do possess?"

"I don't quite recall," Asra responded as he looked at his hands as though they would speak for him. The lack of calluses could place one in a position of class as easily as his attire; though he felt a measure of inner confidence without knowing its origin.

"Well you look fit, so you're not a lazy lout," Tasha added as she sized him up, "and you carry yourself as those with higher breeding, even though the shredded robes you were wearing were unremarkable."

"And what of this?" Asra added as he held up the pendant which hung around his neck.

"I found that on you while redressing you, perhaps it is a talisman of some sort or a family heirloom; but it doesn't look very valuable. So you don't even remember where you got it?" Tasha asked.

"No..." he admitted as he stuffed the pendant back under his shirt.

"Well, hold onto it and maybe you'll remember. Besides, I doubt you could get a copper coin for that worthless trinket," she smirked.

Asra noticed that the rest of the members of the caravan were all wearing similar white robes, which Tasha explained that their uniforms designated them as the divine followers of Allat, known throughout these desert lands; but more commonly known as the goddess, Luna. They were just costume replicas of the temple disciples; which were usually populated by women, so she explained. They adorned them for the purpose of the theater but also aided in keeping them cool under the hot sun. Those who wore pure white in public were either virgin women or recognized as holy apostles to one deity or another, which helped them shed the air of common suspicion and mistrust that were usually held against traveling gypsies.

It was merely an act to blend in, which was a valuable talent to have in these troubled times. Animosities could flare from the border wars were tribes fought for territory either in the names of their clans or ruling sultans. High tariffs and taxes were placed upon good and transport in major cities, which is why the remote city of Ubar flourished, for it was free from such imperial levies.

The days dragged on as Asra traveled with the troupe, aiding where he could to help with the mounts and learning the routine of their camp as he regained his strength. Soon they had reached the grand city of Ubar, surrounded by it high ornate towers gilded with silver which sparkled like a beacon across the dunes.

"It's magnificent!" Asra exclaimed in wonder as they neared the desert fortress.

"It is truly a shining star among the desert plains," Tasha defined for him, "it is known as the Atlantis of the Sands. The city stands upon a natural spring which is the only source of water for countless leagues in every direction. Merchant caravans travel this far north from the coast to avoid the tolls, but none can deny it is worth the long and grueling trip to reach this remote oasis; as you will see."

His host was correct, for the high outer walls concealed the Eden which lay within. Passing through the main gate, people would pause and bow in reverence to them as they entered the sprawling city covered in colorful tiles of blue and rich with green plants. The people here wore linens of bright colors and the air of festivity was as ripe as the plump fruits piled upon the market stalls where hawkers sold their wares. Flutes and drums played as did running children who gathered to play at the central fountain were cool waters flowed.

Their architects had constructed a masterpiece of pipes and statuary which brought the water to the surface where it discharged as a fine mist that cooled the streets of the bazaar along with clear pools where people filled their water skins and jars. There was also a place where travelers could wash their dusty feet as its runoff diverted into a channel, ingeniously designed to feed the lush gardens and tall palms that shaded this desert sanctuary. Ubar was not a mere oasis, but a true paradise hidden among the vast barren wasteland.

"The full moon will be upon us in three days time, which is when our performance begins at the celestial temple," Tasha remarked, "in the meantime, help us get our mounts to the stables and secure our wagons, and I will show you around the city. Otherwise, you owe us nothing and are free to pursue your own destiny if you should wish to part ways, my friend," she offered.

Asra thanked his host for her hospitality and felt obligated to repay her for her kindness. Regardless, he had not a copper coin to his name and nothing of value but the mysterious talisman he wore. Accepting her offer, he helped to park the wagons and assist the rest of the troupe to unload their gear for the show. They set up a booth in the market square and began their art of selling potions and fortunes to those with extra coin to spare.

Tasha had disappeared into the celestial temple which was used by travelers of all faiths. It was home to many idols of gods and goddesses whose effigies lined its interior. There were many strange deities he had never heard of before, with heads of bulls and bodies of lions, serpents and falcons crossed with the bodies of men and beasts sat alongside giant tapestries that displayed the mysterious world of the dead and the hereafter, among them a giant tree with roots from which sprang all life. There were many beliefs, but all were tolerated and revered in this sanctuary of the gods.

Allat was merely one of many such deities so revered. While gazing in wonder, Asra had bumped into an old man whose balding head grasped onto what thin wisps of hair he had left. His eyes were dulled and face wrinkled with age. He stumbled and dropped his walking staff when Asra accidentally stepped back into where the fragile man had stood.

"My apologies, great father," Asra offered in respect to the elder as he bent to retrieve his staff for him.

"Ah, it's alright my son; nothing bruised but my pride," he joked with a weak voice as he accepted his rod from the stranger, "...by the way you were distracted, I would assume this is your first visit to our temple?"

"You are observant," Asra offered with admission, "it is my first time to see Ubar ...I believe," he finished as his gaze fell away for a moment to search his lost memories.

"By your attire, I would assume you are affiliated with the goddess of the moon, Al-lat," he asked.

"Well, I'm not..." Asra stumbled with his words, "I mean; our troupe of moon dancers just arrived for the lunar festival."

"Ah, well, as you can see, there are many deities to choose from," the old man offered with a wave of his arm towards the many statues, "but not all are divine. Some are mischievous and rude, some angry and bloodthirsty who thrive on vengeance!" He barked with a stomp of his staff for added dramatics, "Presented here are helpful spirits for every walk of life, from those who are served by lowly peasants and farmers to those highborn who merely worship riches and wealth; whom may, or may not, sway our fates."

"You sound like you've met them all," Asra granted with credit to the old man's breadth of knowledge.

"Hmm, heh heh," the old man giggled lightly, "I guess you could say that."

"Is this the only temple in Ubar?" Asra inquired out of curiosity, as he wanted to see more wonders this city had to offer.

"At the moment, yes," the elder replied, "however, there was a time many generations ago when the city was filled with several shrines who worshiped jealous gods, who frowned upon sharing their roof with others whom did not honor their ways," the old man revealed as he walked alongside Asra to the outer entrance where he pointed towards a walled-off building surrounding one of the shrines he spoke of, "but they were shuttered a generation ago as tensions erupted between extremists when their followers began to shed blood in the city streets out of misdirected pride for their vile gods."

"They killed one another over their beliefs?" Asra asked as though he had never heard of such a thing.

"Yes my son, untethered faith can be a powerful weapon that can twists men's minds and sway them to do terrible and ugly things," the elder answered with a mournful tone, "so the ruling Master of Ubar banned individual temples in an effort to quell the spreading of such fanatics in order to protect the people; and any similar evil deities of pride and vanity are not allowed to be worshiped within the Celestial Temple."

"That sounds like a wise decision," Asra offered, since the edict had regained the common peace that was put at risk by such radicals.

"So one would think..." the old man answered darkly.

Asra was waiting for Tasha to return from the depths of the temple which was strictly partitioned for women, who practiced their private rituals beyond the lustful eyes of men; and he remembered the trinket hanging about his neck. Pulling it out from his robes, he held it before the elder to show him.

"I was wondering if I may ask, great father, in your long years, have you ever seen such a pendant of this design or perhaps recognize what these symbols mean?" Asra inquired with sincere curiosity; hoping for a chance that the old man might hold an answer.

The elder peered closely at the talisman for a moment with strained eyes from his weak vision, but a confused expression of dread slowly spread across his ancient face. His faded eyes turned up towards Asra as his tongue trembled in his toothless mouth in a stricken gaze of doubt and fear. Without a word, the man backed away from Asra and quickly turned with shaking hands to shuffled down the steps to be lost amongst the crowd as though to escape him.

Asra stood baffled for a solemn moment, wondering what he had said to offend the old man. With a shrug of his shoulders, he knew the elderly were prone to bouts of mumbling and unfounded hysteria as their minds shriveled from age. Baffled by the man's reaction, Asra turned back to the interior of the temple he saw Tasha approaching his direction.

"Ah, there you are!" She waved with a smile as she drew near, now clad in a sheer white shawl and gauze robes which accented her figure. The women's section of the temple was lined with a private pool where they bathed and cleansed themselves before their female gods of fertility. Her hair was now woven in tight braids pinched with tiny silver cuffs and adorned a sterling tiara wrapped about her head. Covered with the scent of jasmine petals and myrrh, this woman could be easily mistaken for a goddess herself as she flowed towards him in all her radiance.

"Are you ready for a tour of the city?" Tasha asked as she took his arm and they made their way into the bustling crowd.

Chapter II
Forbidden Shrine

The busy marketplace was filled with crafts and goods of every kind as the masses inspected their wares. Also among them were several entertainers who had staked their own place in the bazaar to show such skills as breathing fire or amazing sleight of hand doing tricks for the gathering crowds. Some were acrobats with such refined balance that their audience was left gasping in awe. Here in this grand display of diverse cultures anything could be bought or sold for the right price.

They passed opium dens where fragrant scents saturated the air and thick mists pluming out from open doors as red-eyed nobles and vagrants alike stumbled about as though in a drunken stupor. Further along, their group crossed the brothels where the pleasures of the flesh were traded for riches, and love was but a masked commodity. Large men rippling with muscles stood with an iron gaze in their chiseled faces and sharp scimitars strapped to their sides; for they were charged with protecting their masters' property. Women with hungry eyes peered from behind thin veils as their seductive fingers and swaying bodies beckoned at those who passed; tempting them with promises of bliss.

Tasha commented on the giant guards, who were men that weren't men, while she explained the process as to how these eunuchs had been castrated to her companion, ending with her delightful smirk at the shiver it drew from him while the image of such a cruel kiss of a blade flashed through Asra's mind. Though the women were alluring and talented in their trade, their hearts were as cold as stone; similar to the eunuchs who were emasculated to serve but one purpose. It was a curious thought that left Asra's head swimming with questions as to why a person would sacrifice so much for a career that would forever cripple the possibilities of their future.

"Perhaps they have accepted their own fate," Tasha offered in an attempt to answer her guest's philosophical question while they passed through the market towards the gardens at the outer quarter.

"I don't see how anyone could be so short sighted unless they were forced to do so as an act of penance," Asra responded.

"Your perspective is far too narrow, my friend," Tasha answered, "I may be young in years by comparison, but I have seen the terrible parts of people and the evil they can do. It is strange to think how hardship and pain affect people differently, which can either drive someone towards the highest hopes or deepest despair. The catalyst of which can be seen as either a strength or a weakness; regardless if they are both one and the same."

Asra was left both humbled and a tad confused by Tasha's words, which left him wondering which direction his fate might turn once his own memory returned, if ever. There was certainly more to his host than met the eye, for Tasha carried herself with the charm and grace bestowed by confidence, though there was a lingering scar in her tone when she spoke to him about such subjects. It was something he could barely read about her, like ink bleached upon a papyrus by the desert sun. A shadow of something was there at the border of recognition about her, but its true meaning might well be lost to time.

They entered the city gardens where the few children present were helping their mothers gather berries and dates, as these plots were commonly shared among the permanent residence of the court. Ubar was ruled by a city master whose small council resolved differences between disputing merchants and their trade, including enforcing rules upon travelers with a fair hand. Ubar demanded neither taxes nor tariffs from its visitors and in return for their hospitality the city and its people were gifted funds and supplies by those whom could spare; promoting the proverb that if you treat people with fairness and dignity it will return a hundredfold.

It was this commonly held level of honor and respect which kept Ubar from falling into the chaos and anarchy present within the surrounding bandit tribes. The few raiders who had dared to attack this outpost over the years where overwhelmingly repelled when every citizen and traveler took arms and stood in defense of the City. An Eden is not just known by its greenery and comfort, but also by the way people treat one another. Here the happiness and joy in the air were as fragrant as the scent of frankincense drifting through the streets; it was a good place to be.

Through a system of pipes and narrow aqueducts, channels from the natural spring at the center of the city square delivered fresh water to the floral gardens. A rich display of flowers of every hue draped the garden walls and vines which climbed the citadel which housed the city master and his court. Tasha paused to reach out and savor the scent of a blossom which she cupped in her hands, then turned to Asra to ponder the fragile life of the bud which she held.

"Given the proper environment, anything can flourish,"

she noted with wonder as she gazed upon the lush foliage. It was quite true, for the protected environment of the nursery stood in stark contrast to the barren hot sands beyond the city walls.

"But it is also in their nature for any plant to bloom if given the opportunity," Asra answered in kind.

"So you don't think this flower had a choice?" Tasha asked in a curious tone to her companion.

"A blooming flower is only acting to release its pollen and go to seed, that is the very essence of its nature," Asra repeated his phrase.

"But a flower that doesn't bloom has doesn't risk being picked and withering before its time," Tasha responded with a hint of sadness in her tone.

"But if a blossom could somehow choose not to open, then the world would never be thus graced to behold its true colors," Asra granted as he picked the blossom from its stem and set it in the tiara of her braided hair.

With a girlish smile, Tasha let him place the flower in her hair and they continued on their way to the main hall where the money changers were collecting an assortment of coins from across the territories. Here, gold and silver were worth their weight no matter what king or crest was stamped upon them. Rare gems and precious stones could also be traded in kind for currency to be used for buying goods. Ubar had its own system of economy so that its population would be guaranteed fair trade within their walls to the benefit of all.

With regal pomp and splendor, the city master made his appearance in the main hall, surrounded by attendees and sensual courtesans bearing as much flesh as possible in their skimpy attire. He was an older gent, as one who had gathered wisdom from his years and applied them to good use. Though his position came with fame and wealth, he also bore the burden of the responsibilities which concerned the welfare of the city.

"Ah, welcome visitors, I see many new and happy faces do I not?" He exclaimed with a joyful tone as the city master addressed the crowd, "to those of you who are new to our magnificent city we have a special treat in store this evening. An Oracle from the lands beyond the Black Sea has just arrived from Al-Hajar, who will be putting on a special performance of her ceremonial dance to the forgotten spirits of the underworld!" the grandmaster announced with an eerie resonance to accent the showmanship he was known for.

"Well, this should be worth seeing," Tasha whispered to Asra as the gathering crowd erupted with applause. The show was to be set at the foyer to the celestial temple, and from the talk of the crowd, it was promising to be quite the spectacle. Tasha and her group of Moon Dancers usually practiced their routines before any public performance, but the members of their group always enjoyed the chance to watch and learn from other artists. Tasha departed to inform her troupe of the evening's recital while she left Asra to explore the market with her promise to rendezvous later that eve.

While shopping the stalls and exotic wares of the market, Asra felt a tinge of remorse that he hadn't done anything to repay Tasha for her assistance, and felt bound to show her a measure of gratitude. His pouches were empty of coin and he had nothing of value except the donated clothes on his back ...nothing except for the mysterious talisman that he wore. Hesitant to pawn off the only item that offered a hint to his forgotten past, Asra wandered the fringes of the market in search of any extra labor that he may provide for a minor fee that he may trade for a small gift to present to his host.

Asra eventually exited the market and found himself roaming the back alleys of the city while making his way aimlessly past the urban section of the desert outpost. This area was unusually quiet and there were few peasants to be seen as most of the commoners were attending the marketplace and preparing for the evening festivities at the central arena. Before he knew it, Asra had stumbled upon the edge of a deserted courtyard of an abandoned temple, one which had once been dedicated to a jealous god. Asra recalled the words of warning from the old man he had met in the Celestial Temple about this forbidden shrine which had once been occupied by bloodthirsty fanatics.

Asra was about to turn around and backtrack his way to the market, only to realize he was quite lost in the maze of mud-brick houses. He turned corner after corner to no avail when he suddenly saw a small boy dash between the buildings. He called out to the young street urchin for directions to get back to the central square, only to find the child in rags passing a nervous gaze his direction before disappearing between a pair of iron bars which had blocked access to the closed temple. Asra made his way to the locked gate to find one of the bars had been pried loose from its fastenings; which now swiveled on a single bolt and allowed the child to squeeze through.

Asra felt responsible for having scared the child which led him to enter the forbidden grounds, and against his better judgment, pressed his girth through the small breach in the iron-clad gate. He wasn't thinking about what the penalty might be for trespassing upon the hidden shrine, for it was clear that it had been abandoned for many untold years. The small courtyard within was lined with a tall iron gate topped with jagged spearheads, while it appeared that over time the city had continued to build around its border; enclosing it with several walls which had bricked over its original causeway. Here, ruins of statuary and elaborate carvings were left broken and scattered as discarded remnants upon its foundation while a chilling silence filled the yard as memorials to a time long past.

A scuttle of feet and scattered stones caught his attention as Asra looked up to see the boy gazing at him once again from the doorway of the ancient temple. With an unsettled look in his eyes, the child turned and squirmed his way through the crack in the giant door which had fallen off its hinges, and made his way to the inner sanctum. This did not bode well, for Asra took a moment of thought to the risks of entering this cursed place; but the guilt of leaving the child behind in this decaying structure went against his conscience. He approached the tall archway and struggled through the crevice as the giant door groaned with a ghostly moan.

The interior of the shrine was cast in cobwebs and shadows, making it all but impossible to see but for the scant rays of light leaking in through the broken stonework. The child was nowhere to be seen among the carved pillars lining the dark sanctuary.

"Boy, come out into the open, you're not supposed to be in here," Asra warned as he spoke towards the shadows.

Another scuffle of small feet led him towards the main altar where the black shadow of a large idol fell across it. As he stepped into the thin rays of light leaking in, Asra looked up towards the ghoulish sculpture towering above him. It was a dreadful sight for a sober man, one that would scar his memory for days to come. The forgotten god these fanatics worshiped was a four-armed giant; its twisted face bearing tusks from its broken lips with a gaze that made his blood run cold.

Each hand of its four arms bore an item of terror. A curved khopesh sword was raised to strike, and another which hand grasped a severed head, the third held a honed kris dagger; its long and wavy blade snaking its way from the hilt to its needle-sharp tip, and finally, in its extra appendage it grasped upon a spear covered in etched flames upon which crest sat the pinched iris of an eye. The menacing figure sent a shudder through his bones, disturbing his calm. Following the stare of the imposing effigy drew Asra's gaze down into the dark well of the altar before him where there sat a single knife.

It was hard to see at first, for it appeared to be camouflaged by the stone itself, its blade hewn in a manner to replicate the very grain of the masonry. A glint, then another of several blood-red gemstones set within its decorated hilt beckoned to him as Asra reached out to pick it up. A moment of hesitation fell over Asra, wondering why such a valuable object would be left behind; though presumed it had been abandoned in haste when the temple had been barred generations ago. In the darkness the glinting light from its jewels reached for thirsty eyes, luring him to take it; for the bejeweled dagger would certainly fetch a decent price in the market, which he could trade for coin and acquire a gift for Tasha; surrendering to the impulse which had led his path to this very place.

The frightful chill he had felt moments before quickly evaporated and were replaced by a sense of luck and fate which brought such riches within his grasp. Asra picked up the ritualistic dagger and found it oddly warm to the touch. It was unusually heavy for its size and the handle possessed a strange texture like the scales of a snake. The rubies set within the hilt flickered as though with an internal flame. As he was admiring his prize a fleeting figure caught his eye as the young boy sprang from the shadows where he was hiding and bolted past the altar.

Quick of hand, Asra instinctively reached out to catch the child by the collar of his tunic, but missed as the dagger he held slipped from his grasp between his fingers as he lurched to snare the boy. Feeling the sting of its blade upon his palm, Asra turned from the fleeing child to see that his hand was deeply cut. The red essence within him welled from the wound and a single drop of his blood fell upon the ancient altar. As it struck the stone, a thud like a roll of thunder boomed far below through dark chasms hidden deep within the earth.

Asra cursed in pain as the crimson began to flow, and quickly tore a strip of cloth from his tunic to wrap the wound. He took the knife and secured it within his sash before making his way out the door to follow the child. Once he pushed his girth through the damaged doorway, Asra was struck with confusion as midday has somehow turned to dusk. While calling out to the child who had escaped him, he fought his way through the gloom of the littered courtyard and found the broken gate from where he had entered.

Once beyond the gated temple, he traced the walls through several avenues until he heard the festivities of the market echoing through an alley. Rushing back to meet Tasha for the evening's spectacle, he found the market was now lined with colorful flickering lanterns as a blanket of stars began to dazzle under the night sky.

Asra shrugged off the unsettling feeling of confusion, wondering where the many hours of the afternoon had gone; for he had not stepped within the forbidden shrine but for a few moments.

Not wishing to dishonor himself by being late and leaving her waiting, Asra headed back to the steps of the Celestial Temple to meet with Tasha and her troupe. A large gathering had formed where the City Master had the guards set a stage for the mystical Oracle to perform her ritual dance. Drummers and musicians arrived to line the steps of the stair, along with a thick row of flickering candles which surrounded the entire perimeter of the landing. When the City Master finally arrived with his courtesans, he announced the performance was about to begin and a hush fell over the crowd.

Asra found Tasha and hurried to her side at the front of the stage just as the opening drums began to beat. The rhythm of the music was tense yet foreboding, swaying the crowd with anticipation. Gasps of surprise arose from those who saw a tall hooded creature step from the temple hall, wearing a long black cloak; its face covered in darkness except for two glowing eyes. The tall beast had impossibly long arms which waved towards the surrounding audience as though to cast its dark charms upon them.

It glided to the edge of the steps as its appendages reached towards the hems of its cloak and tore them open. From within its folds, the female Oracle sprang as if in a violent birth from its bindings and released the giant mannequin she had worn as an exterior costume. Assistants scurried to pull the puppet from the stage as the Oracle slunk towards the landing at the base of the stair; quickly snapping her head towards the gawking crowd on either side as they gazed in wonder.   The mystic oracle bore the sensuous body of womanhood; her hips wide and breasts full and firm as her naked curves pierced through her loose attire. Upon her shoulders, she wore an engraved golden mantle from which showered thin strips of red cloth, and clearly nothing more than her oil-covered skin beneath its curtain; much to the excitement of the men.   Upon her head, she wore an elaborate crown of golden horns bearing candles infused with a strange mask which covered her eyes entirely.

Her exotic costume added to the mystery and awe of her presentation; capturing the full attention of the crowd. The choreography of her dance boasted her sensual body, drawing unblinking gazes and breaths of carnal pleasure from the crowd as whoops of ululation erupted from the women. Her moves and actions were precise, which only added the enigma of her blind mask. She would move and sway from one side of the arena to the other; occasionally grabbing the walking staff of an old man at the front of the crowd and stroking it as a phallic to the cheers of the crowd, while touching another patron sensually across their chest.

Man or woman, neither escaped her approach and erotic temptations as the rhythm of the music quickened. Eventually, the dancer came face to face with Asra who stood gazing at the spectacle. Her silken hands caressed his exposed chest between his pale robes as they dropped farther down to the glee of the crowd until she suddenly yanked out the ritual dagger he had tucked within his sash. Taking it by the handle, the Oracle stepped away in dance and began to slash it through the air as though in battle against invisible foes. Righting herself, the dancer ended the fray in a delicate pose and passed the blade across her tongue as the drums met their climax and the music stopped.

There was a moment of silence until the entire gathering erupted into wild applause. The masked woman then gracefully ascended once again up the stairs and into the darkness of the temple along with Asra's dagger in hand. Not knowing what to do, Asra turned to his host as she applauded alongside him.

"That was certainly an amazing performance!" Tasha exclaimed, "And where did she get that knife from?" She asked with an innocent smile towards Asra, for he had been standing beside her during the entire show.

"Ah, it must have been a prop," Asra fumbled for an excuse, not wishing to admit to its possession or having to explain where he had attained the jeweled dagger.

"Well, that was enough entertainment for one night; why don't you come join us for meat and wine. You know where our tents are set up beyond the entrance to the market," Tasha pointed towards the front of the bazaar where the stalls were now closing for the night.

Asra hastily agreed to join her, but the jeweled dagger was of significant value, and he had no intention of letting it slip away so easily.

"Certainly, but I have something I wanted to see first and will be there momentarily," Asra answered.

Asra nodded with a smile while Tasha offered to save him a seat by the fire back at their camp as they parted. He had little direction to go by but to search the rear of the Celestial Temple for any sign of the visiting oracle. Once he reached the women's sanctuary, Asra was met with accusing glares at the female priests stationed at it portal as he began to falter upon his intentions to trespass within. Not wishing to make a scene, he inquired if he could speak with the traveling dancer.

"Ah, another one..." the priestess sighed as she shook her head only to roll her eyes at her companion standing beside her, "the Oracle has no interest in being part of your harem. You can satisfy your lust at the local brothels; now be gone with you," and waved him off.

Turned away from the women's private sanctum, Asra left the temple. Not wishing to be thwarted, he made his way with stealth around the back wall to the temple grounds to see if he could find the traveling dancer and retrieve his blade. Sneaking haphazardly through the private gardens he stumbled upon a stone plaque hidden in the shadows and tripped, face first, into the mud. Lying there in the dirt, Asra froze when he heard the heavy footsteps of an armored guard approach his way.

"Who goes there?" The guardsman barked into the shadows of the foliage. He tapped his spear once again on the stone pavement and followed up with a warning, "Last chance defiler," he cautioned, and followed with penetrating his spear into the nearby bushes. Once the sharpened edge of the spear shot within a mere hands-breadth of his face, Asra jumped up from where he hid and raised his arms in surrender.

"Alright, stop ...I, I have no weapons!" Asra blurted, his once white robes now stained in mud and soil.

Asra gulped as the sentry pointed his long-bladed spear to his neck, but was also left bewildered as to the man's uniform. This warden had skin as black as night, and his layered bronze and leather armor was of a unique design. He was certainly not one of the city guards, but a private mercenary. The glare from his eyes moved towards Asra's raised arms as the guard tapped his wounded hand. With a look of surprise falling across his face, Asra was astounded by the words that came from the warrior's lips.

"Ah, it's you," The guard stated with certainty in his heavy voice, "you have been expected; come!" He snapped as he righted his spear and motioned for Asra to follow in his steps.

Clueless as to what was happening, Asra stumbled after the guard who had spared him and caught up to his pace as he weaved through the garden path to the rear of the temple. There he approached a large tent shaped like a lotus flower; its canvas covered in elaborate decor. Taking his position to the side of the entrance, the dark-skinned guard gestured Asra to enter the decorative yurt. From the folds of the curtain passed waves of aromatic incense hinting of cinnamon and honey. With caution, Asra passed through its folds to find it filled with several tables made from rich exotic woods, each covered with polished trays covered with dozens of glass vessels filled with curious luminescent liquids.

Bells and prayer scrolls hung from one end to the other, circling a central cradle filled with pillows made of yak and fleece tied by intricate needlework. Around this hung several candles and oil lamps whose flames seem to burn with an intense fury; flaring in unison as if to acknowledge his arrival. Stunned as he was, Asra was further startled when a sudden movement came from the array of pillows when the dancer emerged from its plume of tapestry and folded furs. She sat up to gaze at her visitor through her blind mask as if to size him up.

"Who are you..." the Oracle asked, her voice sweet and alluring, yet strangely out of sync as though there was an echo between her words.

"I, I am Asra," he answered, as his eyes scanned the room for his stolen blade.

"...Of course you are," the dancer responded as she stood to her feet as her bare breasts pierced through the curtain of her shredded gown, "but who are you now?"

Asra was confused by the inquiry, not knowing how to answer such a perplexing question.

"I, actually, I was just..." Asra began to admit he was trying to find her, but his words were cut off as the woman interrupted.

"Your mind is distracted..." she hissed, "any mortal man would yearn for these," she answered while motioning to her breasts as she parted the strands of her dress to reveal herself to him, "but instead, you desire only *this*!" The oracle pulled a cord that hung beside her which lowered a small table from the ceiling. The system of pulleys brought the tray between them where Asra could see his bejeweled dagger now lay.

With theatrical motion, she flared her wrists as though to cast a spell and every candle in the room responded by turning a bright blue. Asra felt captivated as the oracle drew closer and waved her hands over the ritual blade as her fingers danced of their own accord. Within moments the dagger began to jerk and rattle upon the tray as though it vibrated by a power unknown. An instant later the flames returned to their normal amber hue, as did the dagger which now remained motionless.

"You took my dagger during the show ...which ah, was an incredible performance I might add; but I just came to retrieve it, and I'll be on my way," Asra stuttered through his words so that he could be rid of this enchantress.

"The claw of the great Afrite' is not your property!" the oracle snapped with an unforgiving tone, "Give me your hand!" She demanded as the dancer stepped forward.

Asra knew he had been found out, but wondered what

game this witch had planned. She was aware that this blade was not his to claim, but had been stolen from the abandoned shrine. At first, Asra raised his unbound arm, but the snarl on her lips caused him to offer his wounded hand in its place. She grasped it tightly and held it open as she peeled away the loose bindings with care. The oracle appeared transfixed as she inspected his wounded palm through her blind eyes, and snatched a small polished orb from a table and placed it within his grasp to peer through its glass as it sat within his hand.

Asra jumped when the sphere suddenly cracked and the blood from his wound began to sift through the shattered crystal. The oracle took an audible breath of shock as she witnessed the reaction while holding his hand firm. The strange sorceress quickly brushed aside the broken shards and looked once again to his palm as she drew him near to see for himself what had happened.

"Your blood has been drawn by the blade of the Djinn, and has touched the altar of sacrifice, yet you still live," she uttered with a tone of despair.

"What does that mean?" Asra asked with a tone of fear creeping into his words as he saw that the cut from the sacred blade had carved a new life-line of destiny upon his palm.

"While your heart beats, you are a walking sacrilege to the ancient Djinn, and you are but a blasphemy in their ungodly eyes," the oracle answered in cold words that drew a shiver down his spine.

Chapter III
Wishes Three

Asra was satisfied to have finally retrieved his dagger but was not too thrilled to discover that he was cursed. The oracle issued a further warning that the unholy blade was not a mere trinket meant for mortal men but needed to be returned to the creature from which it was formed. There, of course, was a catch.

"The race of the Ifrit are terrible winged demons who are a wild breed of the mighty Djinn," she began, "in a time when the world was young the spirits of the elements roamed this realm while the cosmos was still in the making."

"But I'm sure that was a long time ago," Asra shrugged, "what does that have to do with me?"

"It is told that the ancient spirits of the earth, the sky, and the waters took pity upon man who once crawled in the dust and darkness underground, and helped them steal the secret of fire so that they may warm themselves and find their path in the blurred shadows of life," the eyeless witch continued, "however, the spirits of fire and flame became angry when they found that a portion of their magics had been pilfered."

"...The jinn were these fire spirits, I presume," Asra blurted to fill in her story.

"Yesss..." she answered with a frightful hiss, "in their rage they hunted the race of men to take back what had been stolen, and a time of blood and fire blew across the lands like a hot wind. Thus, man burrowed back into their caves and hollows to escape the death boiling above, hiding from the world which they had learned to fear. But in this time they learned the mysteries of fire and used it to smelt weapons to protect themselves and defeat their immortal foe. The spirits of the world felt pity on man for the wrath they had brought upon them. The spirits of the earth gave up their ore, and the spirits of the winds breathed into their forge so they could mold their metals, while the spirits of the waters helped them cure the molten steel. One fateful night the race of men crawled from their tunnels as the spirits of wind and water danced in the sky and cast down showers to weaken the Djinn as the muddy earth grasped at their feet while men drew their metal blades and shields to defeat the spirits of fire; then bound them in chains and dragged them down into the earth."

It was quite a fanciful tale, one which had been long forgotten in the faded text and tomes hidden away from generations of men so that the world would forget. The oracle explained that once peace had returned the spirits of the world faded away as men began to worship other gods in their place. However, the Djinn still lingered, caged deep within the earth, for they could not forget the misdeeds against them. She said that they still burned with bitterness and fury, and their angry bellow could be heard whenever the earth rumbles.

"So, you're saying all I have to do is return this dagger to the forbidden temple, and I can lift this curse?" Asra asked the oracle as he stared at his wounded hand.

"Nooo..." the witch answered in her drawn tone, "your life must end on the altar which has tasted your blood," she confessed, "or everyone you know will suffer."

Asra stared at the strange blade lying before him and struggled against either heeding the words of this strange witch or ignoring her entirely and just selling it for a few coins instead and forgetting about all this superstition. Such gifted tellers of fortune were not to be scorned so easily, but tromping off back to a forgotten temple to slit his own wrists wasn't in his plans for the evening. He could always hawk the elaborate dagger to a street vendor and pass the curse along for some other fool to deal with; so he nodded in agreement to the masked sorceress. The oracle then picked up the knife and slipped it gently across the tip of a black candle lit beside her, coating the blade with its wax; and then promptly wrapped it in the same bloodied strip of cloth which had once bound his hand.

She handed it over to him to take, but as Asra grabbed the handle she continued to grip onto the weapon with resistance as her other hand shot forward and pressed upon his chest in the very spot where his talisman laid beneath his tunic. As she pressed harder, Asra started to feel a burning upon his chest as the pendant began to sear his flesh. The oracle drew closer with a sultry resolve and licked her lips as if it were an act of seduction.

"Though you think me blind, I see your intent," she breathed to him in warning and released her hand from his chest as she ripped off her mask. Though her lips were luscious and her cheeks smooth and enticing, Asra faltered in shock as he saw that atop the perfect body of the Oracle sat a ghastly sight. Where her eyes should be were burnt holes, horribly scarred by some dreadful wound. He could see the raw bone of her skull beneath, now stained as black as coal. The sight of her unsettled him as he pulled the dagger from her grasp in his haste to escape the tent and fled into the night.

"Do not defy the Djinn, or you will face the Tali-ma as I

once did!" She screamed from the folds of the tent as her words followed him beyond the garden path.

Asra stumbled through the darkness as both his pace and the beat of his heart quickened. Shaken and out of breath, he wandered into a clearing where the light of the lanterns from the market fell upon him. Hurrying his way back the camp of the caravan, an uneasiness fell over him as he looked into the heavens above and felt a strange disquiet overwhelm him as though the very stars were watching his every step. Asra finally passed the walls of the outer market and stumbled into the firelight of Tasha's camp.

"Asra, where have you been?" Tasha announced in welcome, though her tone changed to one of worry when she saw the color had been drawn from his face, "Are you unwell ...you look as though you've seen a fright."

"I, ah, I'm fine," Asra stuttered as he quickly tucked the stolen dagger into his sash beneath his robes.

"Here, have a sit. Quickly, bring us the waterskin," Tasha asked one of her crew as she helped Asra take a seat by the fire pit.

"Uh, perhaps some wine instead?" Asra inquired of his attentive host.

"Wine instead," Tasha corrected with a shout as she gave a shake of her head towards her troubled guest left ruffled in his soiled robes.

Asra settled down after getting a plate of spiced meats and glazed fruits into his stomach. Tasha had noticed how nervous he had been while eating as his hands shook and brought him woolen caftan to keep him warm. Asra tried to come up with an excuse to where he had been, but not wishing to dishonor himself by admitting he had met with the Oracle. The exotic dancer had made quite a commotion among the men and jealous women during her performance, and Asra didn't want to appear like a sex-starved letch.

"I was wondering if you might know any stories about the ancient gods and spirits," Asra inquired to his host.

"Well, there are many fables told throughout the seven kingdoms," Tasha admitted with a hint of curiosity as to why he would ask, "were there any in particular you were interested in, my friend?"

"Do you know any about the Jinni or the Tal-ee-ma?" Asra asked as he repeated the last words of the Oracle which still haunted him.

Tasha poured herself a cup of wine and took out a leather pouch tied to her sash. She emptied its contents into her hand and stared into the colored stones as they reflected in the firelight.

"There are many stories we are told as children we thought to be nothing more than fanciful tales; but as adults we learn the principled lessons behind such stories; especially so when we discover their words etched upon the walls of ancient mosques and inked upon tattered scrolls," Tasha answered as she took a seat before him on the ground and drew a circle in the dirt between them, "it is said there were once mystical creatures known as the jinn who ruled the world through fury and fire, but that men learned to defeat them by using their own magic."

"You mean fire itself?" Asra inquired while Tasha clasped the colored stones in her hands and breathed upon them a single whispered question. With a toss, she let them fall into the circle where they scattered.

"Exactly," she answered as she turned to gaze into the dancing flames of the campfire beside them before looking down at the seer stones cast before her, "though there were gods of the mountains and the sky, it was the alchemy of fire that changed the world of men so completely," Tasha noted with finality as she read the fortune before her in the sand.

"What does it say?" Asra asked with curiosity as he tried to decipher what she was reading in the divining of the stones strewn before them.

"It says you have a hard decision before you..." Tasha explained as Asra swallowed the knot in his throat, "in the world of men we seek answers to the unknown and try to cheat our fates in the process. This gives fortune tellers a chance to peek into places mortals were not meant to see. They cast stones such as these or throw bones if they wish wisdom from the dead; or glean hidden knowledge from cards or crystal balls, and even tea leaves if they are able," she added while holding up her wine cup and swirling her finger within its rim for theatrics, "but messages can be distorted and the future misread. I for one, see mystic fire in your future, Asra."

Tasha picked up a stone with the elemental symbol from the center of the circle and held it before him to see. It was etched in the shape of a pyramid. She handed it to him while he gazed at the triangle carved into the small stone and began to hand it back to her when she refused.

"Keep that as a reminder of this moment in hopes that it may serve you, friend," Tasha offered, "the element of fire is known as the great cleanser; and as for your interest in the Tali-ma, it is from the language of the underworld which means; '*what comes next.*' Where did you learn of that saying?" Tasha inquired with an inquisitive glare over the lip of her cup as she took another drink.

"Oh, I ah, I don't quite remember," he lied while reaching for an excuse, "it may have been from a storyteller in the market square weaving a fable of the jinn; and I was just curious," Asra finished.

"Ah, well then, there is your answer," Tasha granted, "our troupe has a long day tomorrow to practice our dance for the ceremony of the moon, so I must get my rest, as should you. Leave your soiled robes by my cart in the morning and we will be meeting back here before sunset for a meal before our show at the Temple. I hope to see you then."

Tasha got up and walked to her tent as Asra remained alone with a wineskin in one hand and the fortune stone in the other as he stared blankly into the flickering flames. His mind wandered as it became lost in the dancing light and his thoughts brushed upon the burdens of fate which had recently befallen him. Tasha's divination was accurate; he had to make a difficult choice to face what follows, as the words of the Oracle now made sense. His wounded hand still ached as he clutched onto the divination stone while Asra lay down by the fire to sleep; hoping to wake to find that his cursed dagger had vanished and that this day of ill-fortune had been nothing more than a bad dream.

As fate would have it, Asra would have no escape from his troubled nightmares that eve, for they were filled with visions of blood and sacrifice. Restless in his sleep, Asra twitched and shivered as he journeyed through the horrible hallucinations that left him unsettled. He awoke in a cold sweat, despite the fuming heat of the day. The fire had died and their camp empty as the troupe had set out to practice for their evening performance.

The sound of the marketplace echoed from afar as his

hand slowly fell to his sash to find the dagger he had
stolen still tucked within. With a sigh of regret, Asra sat
up and rubbed the sand from his eyes. Looking at his
soiled robes he realized he looked like a vagrant fool and
knew he had to cleanse his clothing. The runoff from the
central fountain in the city square diverted to an area
dedicated for washing while another channel fed the
lavish gardens.

Still feeling weak from his restless night, Asra stumbled
through streets of the outer market to the tubs where he
came upon several women washing clothes and bolts of
turban cloth. He found an open spot and removed his
white outer robes to scrub away the dirt, now seeing that
the rune-stone Tasha had given him was caked with
blood from his wounded hand. He set it in the water out
of sight but as he did so the dagger from his sash fell
loose and plopped into the channel beside him. Several
of the women around him became startled when a red
stain tainted the waters where the dagger sat; as though it
was bleeding into the canal.

Cries of concern began to erupt as the women around
him hastily pulled their laundry from the waters and
stepped away, with several yelling in fright. Not wishing
to be found with the forbidden relic, Asra hastily
clutched his wet robes, which were once white but now
tinted with the unnatural crimson stain. Bumbling
apologies to the alarmed women standing near him, he
grasped his belongings and fled the baths. Asra hurried
through the back streets to escape the accusing howls
behind him, only to find himself lost once again in the
labyrinth of narrow alleys which wove through the
forgotten hovels near the blighted temple.

Asra breathed heavily as he glanced behind him for fear

of being followed. Exhausted as he was, Asra wandered until he found a familiar passage which led to the gated shrine. Pressing his way through the busted gate, he stumbled through the abandoned courtyard and beyond its broken doors.

Once within, a sudden chill fell over him as he was met with a distressing sight. The heavy stone altar, from which this string of grief had begun, was now shoved askew as though the giant four-armed statue towering over it had pushed it aside with an enormous hand. With bated breath he stepped closer, dreading what he may see the nearer he drew. Once at its lip, Asra found the altar had covered a stairway descending into the suffocating darkness below.

His mind raced as he considered nothing more than to discard the ritual dagger upon the surface of the altar and flee this accursed place, but as he ripped the dagger from his sash and held it above the stone slab a piercing light bloomed from below his feet. Several lanterns lining the walls flared to life on their own accord, lighting the path of the circling stairway beneath the temple. Whispers from ancient voices drifted from the void below, luring him to follow. Asra knew that even if he abandoned the unholy blade and deserted the temple that this curse would follow him till the end of his days; so he took a deep breath and made the choice that was to be his fate.

Grasping the dagger tightly in hand, he stepped down into the awaiting passage and into the underworld below. The circling stairway was draped in carvings of an ancient tongue long forgotten from the world he now knew. The deeper he drew the flare of the oil lanterns grew louder as though to call him with their flickering light. Each lantern was unique, and appeared to be cast from gold and adorned with precious gems; causing him to wonder why such treasures would be left abandoned in this forsaken place.

 During his decent, Asra stumbled upon a breach in the stair wall which had shattered.   With caution, he navigated the ruptured stairwell as he gazed out into the void beyond the broken stonework which revealed an immense cavern below the temple. Snaking up through the center of the subterranean grotto was a natural column formed by eons of mineral growth; its exterior glistening with moisture from the natural spring contained within as it channeled to the surface above. Asra came to realize that this natural pillar was the source of the water that fed the central spring in the city square, revealing the city of Ubar had been built directly above this massive cavity within the earth.

 Asra skipped down the last few broken steps onto a pile of debris scattered across the landing. An overwhelming feeling of despair washed over him as he stood alone in the darkness. Before him lay a narrow bridge between the cavern wall where the staircase was secured and the tower of stone at the center of the subterranean chamber. Asra struggled to grab the very last lamp sitting within reach at the edge of the broken stair and made his way towards the monolith which towered before him.

 The golden lamp he held burned brightly but began to flicker wildly the closer he approached the column of stone.   Water leaking from rock cascaded down its surface to splash around its base upon the floor.   The masons who build the platform surrounding the central structure had imbedded its surface with a grand mosaic of colorful tiles filled with mystical symbols and ancient text. As he stretched out his hand to touch the cold wet rock a band of runes on the lantern he held began to glow a vivid blue.

Asra almost dropped the lamp but fumbled to recover his grip, as losing its illumination would only serve to leave him in the smothering darkness of the cavern. He paused when he noticed that a large section of the stone column was also glowing in rhythm with the lamp he held. Drawing closer to its source, Asra wiped away the silt and glaze layered upon the smooth rocky surface and took a step back in shock when he saw what it held. A giant being had been encased within a transparent crystal set deep within the stone pillar.

Its head was adorned with spiraled horns above its gaunt face. It was an enormous beast with rippling muscles and spiked wings piercing from its back. The creature was frozen in a pose of agony and anguish within the prison of the colossal gemstone. Asra stood in awe, wondering what he should do.

"You have come to give your blood, but dare to face the reason of your sacrifice ...impressive," A deep voice rang through the room.

Asra wavered as the glowing eyes of the entrapped beast snapped open. Though it was held fast within its glassy prison, the creature's gaze seemed to follow him.

"Why ...why should I sacrifice myself?" Asra stuttered as he regained his posture.

"It has been a long while since I have heard the harping of the A'ra and the mindless chanting of their priests," the beast rumbled, "but I have tasted your blood, mortal. Look here, upon the depraved alchemy that binds me to this tomb," it spoke as its fiery eyes turned upward.

Holding the lamp higher, Asra could now see the vast networks of pipes which led from the altar above which snaked down into a giant cauldron. From its end a tap splayed across the surface of the crystal. The tarnished pipes were stained with a deep crimson. It took his sharp mind but a moment to realize that the vat above was used as a reservoir to collect sacrificial blood.

The bizarre story he had heard from the blind oracle now made sense. This was one of the murderous Djinn who had been trapped eons ago, held in check by the magic of earth and water mixed with the blood of men. It had been generations since the custodians of this shrine from the temple above had been left it abandoned and forgotten, and the basin had finally ran empty. Only a single drop of his blood had made its journey down to this forsaken vault, and without fully draining his life essence the fragile bindings of this ward would fail.

"What exactly would happen if I don't give my life to the altar?" Asra dared to ask the monster.

"Hah, then the apostles of A'ra will take your life if you resist," the jinn answered with mirth as if Asra's suggestion was in jest. After judging his lack of reaction, the creature's tone turned sour as the jinn began to grasp upon the mortal's worrisome look, "That is ...unless the priests of the Temple of A'ra are no more?" The jinn came to realize that the wardens of his prison were no longer a threat, and all that remained was this cage.

"In place of my life, I instead could end yours..." Asra came to realize as he contemplated the dire warnings from both the Oracle and his friend, Tasha; who had reminded him that the choice of destiny was his to make. Holding up the ritual dagger, Asra considered the alternatives at hand. He would no longer be cursed by the demon if he rid himself of it. The creature was held here petrified and helpless should Asra wish to do it harm. Killing this beast seemed like a viable option and he could rid the world of its evil existence.

Seeing the dagger in his hand, the jinn became stricken with worry for though it could not be mortally harmed by mortal weapons, it was vulnerable to a relic made from its own origin. The beast saw the talon of the afrite' Asra wielded and recognized it for what it was. The jinn knew the danger it was in, for this stranger before him was ignorant to the ways of the old gods. This creature had been caged long ago, but men were warned by the elemental spirits that to destroy one of the ancients would upset the balance of the world.

"Be warned that the thought of killing an ancient will only end in tragedy for the domain of men," the jinn cautioned, for doing so had consequences between all realms, "however, if you release me from this prison I will grant you your heart's desire in return."

Asra contemplated the offer for a long moment as he weighed the possibility that the words of the Djinn were merely an attempt at trickery. He could either plunge the dagger into the heart of the crystal and kill this monster, or gain some advantage from what he might attain. As Tasha had said, he had a difficult decision at stake upon the crossroads of fate; to die now, or sculpt a new life. At least it wouldn't hurt to hear what the demon had to offer.

"How do I know you possess such powers to do anything for me?" Asra pondered as he began to pace before the trapped beast, "You're obviously powerless to even help yourself escape from these bonds," he noted with a grin as he tapped the blade upon the crystal cage as the jinn growled in defiance.

"I am a creature of the eternal!" The beast roared in anger as the ground rumbled in response, "Of all the elements that make this tiny world, my nature is tied to the planes of chaos. Long ago, selfish men stole my magics not knowing the powers they beheld, but I have had a great deal of time to contemplate this bearing over these endless eons and recognize that my grudge is not with those puny mortals whose insignificant lives are but a spec; but with the ancient elementals who rallied them towards the cause of my woes," the jinn answered with a sorrowful tone.

"But if I did take you up on your offer, what would keep you from merely killing me and rekindling your murderous rampage upon mankind if I freed you?" Asra inquired with a raised brow.

Silence filled the air of the chamber as the Djinn considered the possibility of being released and the cost of pride it would sacrifice to see that end. The beast had grown weary the countless centuries as its physical body had been slowly consumed while imprisoned within its crystalline shell. The Djinn only wished to return to the planes of chaos to recoup its strength and could return to the world of men and enact revenge when this mortal was gone and would be free of his oath. The lifespan of men were but a breath to the eternal jinn, and the demon could suffer such a small patience for the reward of regaining its freedom.

"The oath of an Eternal is sacred and unbreakable," the jinn granted to Asra, "upon the divine Trinity, I will grant you three prayers to be fulfilled if you release me."

Asra had many yearnings as of late, for he had awoken in the desert having lost the memory of who he was. This fortunate twist of fate could return the knowledge of his past and guarantee his future. With a mere request, he could have the riches of a kingdom or the greatness and glory any man could hope to obtain. He could be forever remembered throughout time, and all he had to do was speak any wish he desired, and it would be so.

Asra's hungry eyes turned up towards the savage beast who had played on mankind's foolish lusts for power and wealth which so cruelly separated the souls of men. They were petty creatures, whose hollow lives were insignificant and filled with selfish and superficial ambitions. He could not foresee anything this tiny mortal could ask for that could stifle his retribution.

"I do have a question," Asra asked with a scrunched brow of confusion, "you could have merely granted me one request or even a hundred ...but why merely three?"

"It is the nature of being," the Djinn explained in a defensive tone as though such sacred knowledge was common wisdom, "as there is birth and death, and what exists as life in-between. As there is light and darkness and the shades that dwell within. As between the green fields of paradise and the scorching halls of hell, there lies limbo; as much as chaos is to order, and their influence on the world of men," the beast explained, "it is this eternal triad is the balance that binds us all."

Asra weighed the words of the eternal creature and began to understand. To free the ancient jinn from its confinement he would be privileged with three blessings; no more, no less.

Chapter IV
Eyes of the Blind

Asra considered it prudent to discuss what he had found imprisoned beneath the forbidden temple with the Oracle and gain her insight before accepting such a contract with the Djinn. He felt the glare of the demons burning eyes upon his back as he climbed back up the broken stairway and made the long ascent to the shrine above. Once he was there he set the golden lamp he had taken upon the altar and found it strange how the string of lanterns set within the walls snuffed out the moment he stepped away from the shrine. Making his way out of the Temple grounds and weaving his way through the narrow alleyways; Asra raced back to the spot where he had spoken with the blind mystic.

Having hopped over the stone barriers and trudging through the temple gardens, he came to the place where the oracle had been. However, to his astonishment, her elaborate tent was now gone and the ground where it had stood was untouched as though it had never been. Asra saw several women wandering through the protected gardens which were, of course, closed to men, all except their servant eunuchs. Waiting until he found one of the neutered attendants, Asra popped out from the foliage where he was hiding and caught up to the man.

"Oh, hi, excuse me," Asra called from behind, though softening his voice in an effort to sound emasculated, "is the Oracle from the north still here on the temple grounds? I noticed that her tent is gone."

"You must be mistaken," the eunuch answered, as he

lowered his serving tray full of ripe fruits, "the Oracle never set camp upon the terrace."

The servant passed Asra an odd look, as he was wearing his stained and tattered robes. By chance, the eunuchs adorned fine silken tunics woven of a rich maroon color gilded with gold threads; so he assumed that Asra was the ill-suited attendant of an impoverished master.

"But you see, I was on duty last night to my Mistress," Asra stumbled into a lie while acting overly feminine, lest he get caught by the temple sentries and castrated for real, "...and thought I saw her large tent right over there, along with her dark-skinned warrior," Asra added as he pointed to the empty section of the yard.

"The visiting oracle never set quarters upon the temple grounds, but had left that very evening after her show," the servant admitted to Asra's confusion, "...I have not seen you before, who did you say your Mistress was?"

"Oh, um, she just arrived; and I have to get back my duties or face the whip, you know," Asra fumbled for an excuse while trying to act cordial, but only making a fool of himself in the process, "but I do thank you for your time," Asra bowed to the servant, not knowing if it was appropriate, which only procured a strange look from the temple serf.

Asra hastened away from gardens while doing his best to look inconspicuous and circled around to the front entrance of the Celestial Temple. He was left perplexed by the claim the eunuch had made which led him to question his own sanity. Asra considered bringing what he had witnessed to the attention of the City Master but feared that admitting to having trespassed upon the forbidden grounds of the banned temple might end with his neck meeting the sharp edge of headsman's axe. That might be especially true if he was found with the stolen dagger in his possession.

After entering the main hall, Asra took the effort to locate Tasha and her troupe. After inquiring with several guards and temple servants, he was left waiting at the steps of the shrine without any clear answers. The ceremony of the Moon Dancers would take place the hour before midnight within the city square at the fountains, and there was little he could do but wait until the performance so that he could speak with Tasha again for her advice on this turn of affairs. Left sitting alone in his stained and tattered robes, Asra wondered what he should do.

The wound on his hand began to throb painfully so Asra removed the cloth binding to examine its condition; hoping it hadn't become infected. He nearly jumped in shock when he watched the cut from the ritual blade appeared to move, further weaving its bind between his fate and life lines upon his palm. Asra quickly bound the wound once again, feeling further distressed. He gathered his courage to reveal this situation to the City Master and hoped that a measure of mercy would be granted for his honesty.

Marching towards the grand citadel, he found himself barred by the city guards at the inner courtyard while seeking an audience with the leader of the stronghold.

"Hold there, what is your business?" the sentry demanded with their spears crossed to block the path to the inner citadel.

"I need to speak with the Caliph on an important matter," Asra tried to explain nervously, "of an issue of great import to the safety of the city and its people," he added.

"The security of the city is our job," the sentry added as he motioned to himself and his fellow guardsmen, "whatever information you have you can report to us," he demanded with finality.

"It's more of a private matter, and I would rather discuss it with the City Master, himself," Asra offered in defense, since telling his tale to pair of grunt warriors who lacked any measure of wisdom, his wild story might get him nothing less than being thrown into a dungeon cell for being a raving lunatic.

"As you wish," the guard answered to Asra's relief, "but the Master only accepts public audience an hour before sunset, and for the Caliph's safety, you will be checked for any weapons before being allowed to enter," the watchman advised as he pointed to an enormous gilded hourglass set within a nearby niche, "you may return then, but the waiting lines get very long, and you may not get your chance today. Otherwise, you can bide your time at the benches along the inner courtyard."

Asra turned away feeling spurned, for he was in no mood to wait for such a vast period of the day. Even if he had been allowed inside to see the Caliph at this time the sentries would have found the odd ceremonial dagger hidden in his sash and might think him an assassin. He was growing hungry but didn't have any coin to buy food from the vendors or the many inns speckled across the city. With Tasha and her troupe out of reach, he didn't want to misplace her trust by rifling through the carts where her caravan had set their camp.

Asra sat upon the bench that faced the inner terrace, feeling depressed and alone in his affair as he watched strangers pass through the grand halls of the fortress. An elderly man bumped into him as Asra pondered over his strange situation. Looking up, he noticed the man was blind and carrying a tall walking staff. He shifted his weight over on the bench as the senior was feeling around to take the seat next to him.

"My apologies, elder, I wasn't paying attention," Asra mumbled through his thoughts of despair. The old man reached with a jerk of surprise, having not known Asra was there.

"Oh, I did not hear you, I thought you were part of the stonework to be so silent, my boy," the elder announced as he tenderly found a spot for his fragile body to rest, "you must be of heavy mind to be so distracted in such a place as spirited as Ubar."

"You can say that again," Asra sighed under his breath, but his words were caught by the elder settled next to him as he placed his withered hand upon Asra's shoulder to steady himself.

"Hmmm, even here you can smell the fragrant flowers of the gardens mingle with the rich incense from the traders shops," the elder tried to smile as Asra noticed the old man was nearly toothless and his eyes were glazed over with a white sheen, "you seem like a strong, fit man, why aren't you out attending to your harem?" He joked with a labored laugh; "Unless you are as ugly as an ox..." he continued to giggle.

Asra didn't know how to react to the insult but realized the elder was simply trying to make lighthearted conversation. It was odd how the egos of men became either humbled or eccentric with age.

"I'm just waiting for the Caliph to talk about a serious matter," Asra blurted, but realized that he might be saying too much.

"Ah, well, I'm not the great caliph, but I'm more than

thrice his age and have seen more of the world than he ever has ...at least before I went blind, that is," the elder postured with a lick of his toothless lips in thought of his self-grandeur, "perhaps I can offer you some insight, or at least share some interesting conversation between two philosophical men. A man gets lonely after his children leave and his wives pass away, and is left to wander these busy streets day by day. Come, help an old man feel worthwhile, even if for a few moments," he added to brush upon Asra's sympathy.

"*Wives* huh?" Asra added with a dubious reply.

"Yeeesss, many, many voluptuous wives who were once at my every beck and call. Maybe you think not to look at me now, but I was quite the stallion!" The old man spouted with a puffed chest and raised fist as though to reenact his vigorous youth.

Asra couldn't help but burst out laughing, despite the insult to the old man's virtue. The elder turned towards Asra at first with a ghastly look drawn upon his face by the rude taunt, but it quickly faded away as he too began to giggle at his amusing words.

"Ah, hah, well now, I haven't laughed so hard in years," the elder wheezed as he begged to catch his breath, "...but I *really was* quite the stud in my youth," he added to save a sliver of his dignity.

"Yes, I can imagine you were quite the breeder," Asra added with a chuckle.

"Well now, I have shared a bit of my past with you, my friend, why don't you tell me how I may be of help to a troubled soul," the elder offered.

"Hmm, well imagine for a moment if you were able to be granted anything your heart desires, what would you wish for?" Asra asked the elder, who seemed to take his question to heart.

"Oh, well now, I've made ten thousand wishes during my lifetime," the old man replied after deep reflection, "I've chased after women and riches and the respect of others, and I've also sought to make my enemies pay for their misdeeds. Then again, I've also had many regrets of my own I wish I could somehow undo or forget entirely should I ever have the chance; for bitterness is the heaviest loadstone to carry into the sunset of one's life, my boy."

"But now that you've seen the width and breadth of what life has to offer, what would you choose?" Asra begged for an answer he could grasp onto.

"Ah, well one might think that I would wish for a return of my youth, but alas, I would only relive the pains of age once again," the man answered with a note of surrender creeping into his voice, "if given the chance, most would desire riches beyond their dreams; but eventually they would find that a too high a price to pay, for you may eventually find yourself looking down upon everyone else as a servant or slave, even upon those whom deeply love and care about you. I once had the chance to ask a new and wise king of the Far East how wealth had changed him, and he said that prosperity only brings out what you already are inside. If you are generous at heart, then wealth will allow you to be even more so; but alas, those who are evil and selfish would become evermore vile and malicious."

"Wise words indeed..." Asra added in note.

"Now others might desire power above all else, but my years have taught me that there is a thin line that separates loyalty and obedience, for a tyrant sees no difference in the two, but views allegiance as one and the same from his followers," the elder explained.

"And how would one know the difference?" Asra asked.

"By the act of giving, young man," the blind man replied, "a selfish man expects devotion where a kind soul will seek to earn the trust of others."

"So in all your life, what is it that you might seek to change if you ever found the chance ...the return of your youth, your eyesight, honor among men, or would you desire the riches of a kingdom?" Asra challenged him for a straight answer.

"Ah, my child, I have seen many wonders in my lifetime, and also much ugliness in this world," the elder began with hint of sadness, "I fear if I had my eyesight back, I would only be cursed to see the worst in men; thus, my blindness is a blessing. If I had my health back, I would likely ignore the wisdom of my years and retrace the steps of my reckless youth. If I had riches and a kingdom of my own, I might become a selfish tyrant surrounded by fake friends and those who would only have envy in their hearts. So I am happy to be humble in my last days here, and find a simple measure of peace each day I awaken."

The blind man's words were branded with modesty, for he had grown tired of the struggles of men and found his own serenity as his reward, and was thus satisfied with that small triumph. Asra could not grasp onto such a prize, for his mind struggled with his forgotten past, not knowing whom he truly was or what he had done to deserve such a cruel fate that left him abandoned in the desert to die. The elder knew that one's fortunes can change with the wind and that destiny can take on a life of its own. In his lifetime he had learned the value of joy and the meaning of regret, and that untamed ambitions will always leave a scar upon oneself and others.

"What if you could have the powers of a god and live as an immortal?" Asra offered as an answer to this enigma.

"Ah, so you think that endless time would allow you to correct any mistake or cure any disappointment?" The old man argued as Asra nodded at the possibility only to realize his gesture went unseen, "The wealth of time is not always a blessing, my friend, as you can see by my wrinkled face," he chuckled, "but by example, even the many gods by which men worship, their deities have never found peace among themselves," he offered to illustrate the futility of Asra's question.

"You may be right," Asra answered as he reflected on the old man's perspective.

"We come into this world crying, my boy, it would be best not to leave the same way," he offered in return, "...oh my, the day grows cold as the warmth of the afternoon fades. I can hear the music from the market as the festivities of the eve begin."

"Yes, it appears the sun is falling," Asra answered the blind man.

"Well, it was good to speak to someone, and I thank you for your time, young man," the elder offered, "perhaps we will meet again, ah ...I did not catch your name?"

"Oh, I am called, Asra," he offered in return, as that was the title Tasha had claimed for him. However, the old man seemed to find the label amusing.

"Hmm, an interesting name indeed..." he smiled with strange delight which left Asra confused, "one that I have not heard for many years."

"And what should I call you, elder?" Asra inquired as the old man got up and began to hobble away while tapping with his staff to make his path.

"Oh, my name is not important, my friend, for my time to be remembered has passed," he offered in return before turning away and disappearing into the crowd.

Asra was left bewildered by his reply but presumed the addled mind of age was nothing that should concern him. He sat alone for some time while a line of people began to form at the entrance hall to the inner citadel. Asra stood to take his place among them so that he may talk to the Caliph about the demon entombed beneath the city, but as he did so the cut in his palm began to burn fiercely, forcing Asra to grip his hand in severe pain. Passerbies turned to notice his sudden cries of agony as he tried to cover the wound, wondering why it would not heal.

As he turned away from them to inspect the dressing, the jeweled dagger slipped from his sash and clattered to the tiled floor. While curved blades of khanjar were commonly worn in the lands of the Oman Empire, such unsheathed daggers were eyed with great suspicion; especially so within the court of the Caliph. This brought the attention of the guards who heard the rattle of steel and the whispers from the crowd that Asra had an open blade; which was strictly taboo upon the grounds of the citadel. Asra cursed his luck, knowing that this did not bode well for him in the presence of the city guards.

Asra hastily apologized to those around him and snatched the dagger from the floor as he swiftly made his way into the bustle of the outer market while clutching his hand in pain. He barely managed to escape as the guards who pushed their way through the doorway and stood glaring out into the crowded bazaar from the entrance of the keep. Asra ripped off the bandage to find the gash from the blighted dagger was moving again, creating a deeper furrow upon his palm; forcing him to stifle a cry of agony. Seeing that his wound was not getting better, he set out to find a local healer for a cure and medicine to help suppress the pain.

Asra stumbled through the crowd, trying not to bring attention to himself as he coddled his injured arm. Asra stumbled across the abode of a healing shaman by the sign of a lotus above the door and quickly made his way inside. The shop was riddled with clumps of hanging herbs and vials filled with mysterious substances of every hue, and he was soon greeted by a woman of large girth who bridled herself with a collection of charms and trinkets of her trade. The art of healing was not merely just for physical conditions, but also combined with the mystical beliefs in the occult.

"Aye, what ails you my prince?" she huffed with heavy breath as she waddled in from behind a curtain of beads and plopped herself onto a stool before a wide rattan table, "here, here, have a seat and let me take a look at ya," she ordered as she patted the bench.

Asra sat down and laid his wounded appendage on the table while the woman unwrapped the binding.

"Oh my, well this is a nasty cut, but not too bad that Gartha can't fix," she noted with pride to her name.

After shuffling about the room she brought back several items and an assortment of ointments while she gathered a tight bundle of dried herbs and lit them to wave the resulting smoke over his wounded hand while chanting to herself all the while. Gartha seemed intent on her remedy as she clasped her eyes tightly shut and mumbled her mantra with fierce emotion. As though in shock, she suddenly stopped and gasped for air as her eyes flew open as if in surprise. Her reaction was so violent that the countless shells and beads sewn into her dreads clattered together as her hair flung back.

"Ah, there ya go, boy. I have expelled the infesting demons and you will heal right up as good as new," she exclaimed to Asra's bewilderment. He had wished she was being serious and had cured him of his curse, but his hoped faded when he realized that she was just performing theatrics for coin.

"Ah, what ...that's it?" Asra inquired.

"Well, it is a strange cut, but a touch of ointment will dull the pain, as will some time at the opium den at the end of the row," Gartha mentioned as she motioned to the end of the market stalls.

The large woman smacked her lips as her eyes darted between the many salves and powders on her tray and began to mix them at random. She took the paste and smeared it onto his laceration with the tip of her long decorated nail. When she was done, she turned her fat face up towards her patient with a wide smile plastered across her cheeks.

"That will be four silver coin. Three, if you have any opium to spare ...perhaps?" the healer demanded with a tinge of hope trailing in her voice, revealing her private addiction.

Asra was about to concede that he didn't have any money to offer, nor did he understand what viable remedy she had performed from her rancid concoctions when another wave of pain pierced through his arm. Asra grabbed his wrist to hold himself steady as Gartha leaned over to inspect the strange fumes coming from his wound. Her eyes popped open as she witnessed the batter she had set in his palm start to froth and foam away from the laceration.

"That is very, very strange," the healer whispered as she

gazed at the bizarre reaction to her herbal paste, "don't move; just give me a moment..." she pressed while excusing herself as she shuffled her way beyond the beaded curtain and returned with a large dusty vial wrapped with parchment and cords.

"What is that?" Asra asked through the flair of pain as Gartha popped open the cork top with its broken wax seal, and promptly took a swig of its contents. She swallowed the first gulp then paused to answer him.

"Oh, this..." she nodded towards the bottle of alcohol after licking her quenched lips, "this is called 'Sura'; a powerful magic!" The healer spouted with conviction and took another swig of the aged liquor, then swished it around in her mouth. Asra was taken aback with slight disgust when she leaned forward spat the extract into his open hand. The results were almost instantaneous.

A ball of green suddenly fire flared up where the elixir touched the wound, causing them both to lurch back in shock. Asra watched in horror as the cold turquoise flame that was left raced across his palm. He jumped up to pat the flames out while knocking over the table in the process and sending several dishes of powders and bottles smashing to the floor. Gartha also jerked back in fear, screaming like a desert banshee.

"Ahhhh! You are cursed; an abomination! By the nine demons of night, be gone with you!" The fat woman continued to scream as she flailed her arms, then her wild eyes turned to the mess he had made while Asra was hastily wrapping his smoking hand. The unpleasant aroma of the smoldering concoction filled the small room as Asra quickly danced his way towards the doorway.

"You have to pay for this mess!" The healer called after him as Asra escaped outside and into the crowd, wondering what the crazy shrew had done to him.

Asra raced through the crowd, but only when he stopped to catch his breath did he find himself once again within sight of the forbidden temple at the edge of the city. The nearer he approached the dark shrine, the less his hand ached. It was then he realized that he could not outrun fate or would have to lose his hand to do so.

Chapter V
Ceremony of the Moon

His conviction grew with every step towards the shrine; knowing what he must do. He would run the ritual blade through the heart of the Djinn as it lay petrified within its crystal cage; Asra could see no other way. This strange ordeal he had been drawn into had unsettled his mind and began to consume his every waking moment.

Asra had experienced a streak of bad luck since he had stumbled into that unholy temple and he wanted nothing more than to have this nightmare come to an end. After pushing his way through the broken doorway, Asra found a disturbing sight. The heavy stone altar had once again been placed back over the stairwell, sealing it shut, while upon it sat the small boy he had followed into the temple before. Most disturbing of all, the stone deity which towered behind it appeared to have taken on a different pose; one which now held a posture of defense against his arrival.

Asra crept forward with a measure of caution while his previous resentment and anger began to bleed away as a cold aching fear crept into his soul with every step. The small boy in his ragged clothes turned his head toward him and Asra could see the voids of his eyes were filled with nothing but sinking darkness.

"Have you come to sacrifice yourself before the A'ra?" the boy inquired with a deep and ancient voice. Asra would have turned in fear and fled in terror at that moment if not for the bizarre sights he had witnessed over the previous day.

"There has to be another choice," Asra finally answered after searching his words while testing his sweaty grip on the ritual knife held tightly in his hand.

"Ah, so instead you come to seek the demise of our captive," the child remarked in its unholy voice, "we know death well and you reek of it, craving its deliverance..." the possessed child added as Asra glanced down at the cursed knife he held, "be warned, you cannot upset the order of the world and not pay the price!"

"Why can't I..." Asra began to argue before he was hastily interrupted.

"What ...kill the demon and lift the curse?" the child replied smugly as Asra awaited his answer, "Many before you have asked that question over the endless eons. Priests and their acolytes who have sought such answers to rid the world of all its wicked beasts. However, before you give your life, we will offer you a small secret which has been hidden from the realm of mortals who do not even wish to acknowledge the truth they already know in their hearts ...for it is the lineage of Men, themselves, who *are* the monsters that blight creation."

The words hit Asra like a stone, realizing the legitimacy of such a revelation. As fleas to a wolf, was not mankind merely a parasite to the eternal spirits that shaped this realm? It was the acts of men which had thrown the world out of balance, but instead of taking accountability for their misdeeds, they imprisoned the Djinn whose wrath had merit. Mortal men had stolen magic that was not rightfully theirs, and the world was worse for it.

There were countless gods from across the lands, many of whom may be nothing more than mere flights of fancy or pure fabrication; but the legends of the primal elementals were chiseled into lore as the first beings to walk this earth. From them, all things sprang as life struggled to survive. Asra, however, would not lay down his own life so easily. He knew not of his past but was determined to make his own future. If it was his destiny to die here, it would have to be another day.

"The jinn offered me another choice," Asra breathed coldly as he contemplated his next move.

"The Djinn are tricksters, they will spread any deceit that suits them," the boy replied with a casual shrug, "the followers of this temple have suffered ten thousand lies from this fiend, and none have faltered; for it is our sacred duty as wardens to protect this eternal prison."

"So, you're saying your followers were also extended false vows by the demon in exchange for its release?" Asra inquired.

"As many as the grains of sand upon the vast desert dunes," the possessed child replied.

"And how is it that you knew the Demon's pledges were false...?" Asra channeled back to the boy upon the altar.

Asra's words were followed by an uncomfortable pause by the youth haunted by the ancient voice. The acolytes of the temple had been charged with the duty to protect their captive but had never once considered that there was a grain of truth in the demon's pleas. Over time their followers had become too impassioned with their ceremonial sacrifices which eventually led to their sect being disbanded and left forgotten within the walls of the this oasis. Now a lone trespasser had asked a question they had refused to ask themselves.

"The Djinn are hateful and malignant spirits, and cannot be trusted!" the child finally rebounded with a reply.

"Why don't we ask the beast himself?" Asra taunted the temple guardian.

Michel Savage

The will of the A'ra had been weakened over the many years their temple had been left shuttered and abandoned. Without their routine ritual offerings of blood, the mystical bindings placed upon the trapped jinn had depleted. The beast itself had also weakened, but had seen an end to its suffering in Asra's eyes; for a man with no past knew not who he was or what he was capable of, even if the fiery elemental did.

"You will not be allowed near the demon, again," the child threatened, "you know not what dangers you provoke, mortal!"

It was clear to Asra that the child possessed by the guardians of this temple had no intention of allowing him to fulfill his act of retribution. The ghosts of the temple wanted his life, while the jinn wanted its freedom, and Asra had a desperate choice to make. He took a bold step forward and addressed the child with the black eyes by the point of his dagger.

"I will not be a martyr for your cult," Asra warned as the possessed child climbed to his feet upon the altar.

"You will upset the equilibrium this sect has kept for your own selfish ambitions," the child charged as he backed away, "we have kept our pact beyond the tethers of death to keep the Nocturnal at bay!"

Asra wasn't swayed by the confusing words of the child, not knowing what this 'Nocturnal' might be it had referred too; but he was not just going to lie down and die for the sake of some archaic ritual by a forgotten cult. Asra called the bluff of the unholy child, seeing that it had no power to stop him. The boy put his arms up in defense and there was a sudden flash of darkness in the sanctuary as the air itself seemed to flow with murky shadows. Asra struggled through the dark wind and placed his hands upon the altar as he tried to grab for the child.

As his bloodied hand touched the table, the stone block moved; revealing the stairway below; while the row of golden lanterns set themselves aflame, lighting the way. The child dashed beyond his reach to the protection of the columns, calling out to Asra from the shadows.

"Beware the misery and anguish that will be wrought by your selfish deeds," the ancient voice warned as Asra stepped down into the stairway beyond.

Asra turned once, seeing that the spirit that possessed the child failed to pursue him. He descended the crumbling steps until he once again reached the bridge which spanned the open rift. Grabbing the familiar lantern upon the passage wall, Asra wondered how it had been returned to its alcove from the altar above where had left it before, while he made his way towards the imprisoned beast. The demon did not stir, and Asra was only met with a calm silence covered by the soft sound of cascading water from the spring as it flowed over the stone pillar encasing the great beast.

"What, nothing to say, demon?" Asra shouted with anger towards the monolith which held the creature, "No last words before I end your torment and send you back to the hell from which you sprang?"

"So, the little man had decided his destiny; and a poor choice it was..." the jinn answered, "you could have anything that you could dream within your grasp, but instead you choose death."

"If I rid this world of you, I also free myself from this curse," Asra responded as he held up his injured hand, baring the wound which moved with a life of its own.

"Small fool, it is not I who has cast this hex, but the

priests of A'ra, who mean to use your lifeblood to keep me bound. End me, and they will hunt you down to the ends of the world to exact vengeance," the jinn conceded, "it was I who had opened the altar gate to invite our first meeting and granted you passage to my presence."

"Merely for the purpose of using me as a means for your escape from this tomb, Trickster!" Asra quickly responded with insult.

"The guardian of the temple will not allow you to leave this sanctuary, which has now become your prison as well," the demon granted, "you have only one option left that will free us both ...release me from this vault and I will grant you what was promised."

Asra's attention was distracted by the howling wind moaning from above when he saw the lights of the lanterns began to slowly flicker and extinguish as the haunting tempest descended the stairwell towards them.

"You must act quickly, mortal; for the guardian of the temple pursues you, and once these mystic lanterns are smothered, we will both be locked in darkness forever," the Djinn warned him.

* * *

At that same moment high above in the courtyard, night had already fallen upon the city and the lunar ceremony was about to begin. Tasha and her moon dancers had spent the day getting into costume and prepping for the evening show. The stage was set beside the central fountain along with several flaming braziers surrounded by flowing banners. As the full moon rose ever higher into the evening sky, Tasha had wondered where Asra had disappeared too as she had not seen him since she had left him asleep at their camp early that morning.

As midnight approached a procession of musicians

made their entrance and began to play; each dressed in pure white robes with their faces covered by ivory masks. They flowed like ghosts in the evening light as the music began to the delight of the gathering crowd. Many had never seen the famed Moon Dancers from the jungle valleys of Fernwood, and those who had knew it was a spectacle not to be missed. The blessings of the lunar goddess, Allat, was bestowed to all those who attended, and the people of the desert welcomed such superstitious invocations with great earnest.

Travelers of the sands held immense respect and reverence for the gods and their charms, for fate and destiny were as elusive as trying to capture the flowing smoke of incense in one's own grasp. Every person present, be they child or elder, had dreams of their own to pursue; either towards love or happiness or fame, or all three if they were so blessed. The people of Ubar did not live in envy of another but saw life as an opportunity and death but a door to the great adventure. Though many had a reverence for the customs of their forefathers and what greatness the curious and the bold could achieve.

As the music swelled too high notes and the tempo of the drums rose like thunder, the sudden quiet introduced the first of the belly dancers to flow into the light of the stage. In succession, several women swirled into a wide circle as a number of men with armed with polished swords stepped into the arena to form a half-moon. Blades clashed as they swayed between one another, the women barely missing the blades by a hair. Each of the dancers carried a pair of candles, expertly balanced as they turned and weaved in serene synchronicity, as though representing the stars in the heavens as they chase across the night sky.

Tasha then entered the stage, a single dancer dressed in silken black, representing the new moon. Drums beat and tambourines rattled with each step she took as she pranced around the square in light-footed acrobatics. She stopped in the middle of the stage and drew a single rod from her woven braids; allowing her hair to drop and flow freely about her shoulders. Twirling the scepter she held above her head unraveled the fine sash about her waist to which it was anchored; sending the stream of silk to fly about her body in constant orbit.

Few had ever seen a ribbon dancer, as the fine fabric trailed in impossible paths as it braided through the air. The spectators were spellbound by her artistry and skill as the sash snaked around her as though by a mystic wind at the direction of her wand. As the rhythm raced to its pinnacle, the music suddenly stopped as Tasha spun the ribbon one final time, to wrap itself around her waist only to disappear upon her ebony attire. Once again the dancers in white encircled the stage and drew ever near to the solitary woman in black at their center.

The pulse of the drums renewed as a double flute hummed an ancient tune of renewal as the women in white met the girl representing the shadow of the moon. There was a sudden sigh of wonder from the lips of the crowd as the dancers held up their candles, which remained floating midair as they withdrew their hands to raise the single girl in her obsidian dress. Applause in praise erupted from the audience as the hovering candles floated ever higher above the crowd, only to draw their attention back down to the circle of dancers in white who had swallowed Tasha in their folds. In a flash of music, the dancers fell away exposing Tasha now adorned in a blue silken gown finely embroidered with silver stars.

The performers dropped their pale robes, revealing a spectrum of colors layered beneath; each iconic print presenting astrological figures from of the heavens above. They pulled silken fans from their waists which billowed into ethereal clouds as they flowed like feathers in a gentle wind. Weaving between one another like the rays of the moon, they dance with the grace of the stars themselves. It was truly a magical sight to behold.

The musicians hit their climax as the body of dancers combined and with a sudden blink, the floating candles extinguished. As the assembly dropped their attention back down towards the stage, they were astounded to find that all the dancers were again draped in ivory robes as they unfolded like a lotus blossom to reveal Tasha in a frosted silver vestment holding a round orb before her; its glow emerging like the dawn of night. The drumbeat rose to its final crest, then ended with a crash; ending with the soft tune of a fading flute as gentle as a morning breeze. Tasha released the spherical paper lantern as it drifted up into the sky towards the moon shining above. After a moment of stunned silence, the surrounding crowd erupted into feverish cheer and applause.

"The full moon smiles upon us," the high priest of the Celestial Temple shouted with glee from the steps of the sanctuary as he raised his hands toward the glowing orb soaring in the sky above the audience, "...the blessings of Allat be upon you all," he cried before taking a bow and fading back into the temple.

The cheers and flattery from the people of Ubar were complimented by tributes of ripe fruits and sweetmeats and precious gifts of admiration; along with the countless clinks of silver coins and precious gems as offerings to the dancers and their lunar goddess. Visitors of every station could be seen stepping forward to remove engraved brooches and jeweled rings and treasures from their person as tithing for the blessings of the moon spirit. Such was the tradition of the children of the desert and their reverence for the divine.

The smiles and joy of the crowd fell into a sudden silence when a low rumble surged through the city. The people of Ubar were stunned by the strange event as whispers of concern began to rise like a tide from the frightened crowd. Tasha and her group were leaving the stage when Asra came bursting through the mass of people surrounding the square, wearing his crimson-stained robes as he waved for her attention.

"Tasha ...Tasha!" he yelled with tired breath as he pressed to reach her.

"Asra, what is it? You look troubled," Tasha replied with concern as she stepped aside with him from the view of the crowd.

"I ...I've done something terrible!" Asra responded with a look in his eyes that scared her as he grabbed her shoulder, "We need to get everyone out of here!"

Tasha looked down to see an object he had cradled within his arm was a golden lantern gilded with a string of runes which were glowing as fiercely as hot coals. Suddenly another rumble coursed through the city, shaking the ground beneath their feet. Voices of concern soon turned to cries of fear as the quake persisted. Baskets of fruits tumbled and stalls began to crumble throughout the market as the tremor quelled, only to resound stronger than before.

"What is happening?" Tasha asked with dread creeping into her voice as the quakes continued.

Screams of terror could be heard echoing through the

city as clay tiles and stone supports began to fall into the city streets, blocking passage to some while injuring others in their wake. Women cried aloud, wailing that the gods had forsaken them while one stood above them all and pointed towards Tasha still dressed in her silver gown. A look of irrational anger boiled upon the woman's face as she pulled a dagger from her belt.

"You are the cause of this, Moon Dancer - a blasphemy to our temple," the woman shouted as several members of the crowd rose to join in the feverish accusation. Tasha's dismay turned to despair as she looked back towards Asra and his glowing lamp while several antagonized members of the mob drew curved knives and sabers in their fear they were suffering some superstitious reprisal by their gods.

Mere moments before the ceremony, Asra had been trapped beneath the forbidden shrine, whose guardian had pursued him into the vault beneath the temple. With the knowledge that if he had killed the Djinn he would not live through the night; Asra had chosen to take his chances by releasing the demon from its cage. Using the cursed dagger, he had cracked open the crystal binding and released elemental spirit from its living tomb. The soul of the jinn escaped through the rift to reclaim the flame from the lantern from which it drew power, only to be absorbed into the vessel itself.

Asra had lost the ritual dagger, as it had remained wedged in the crystal cage, and was now left unarmed. Seeing several members of the angry crowd with drawn weapons, they both retreated back into the Celestial Temple as the gathering mob began to cry for Tasha to be sacrificed. They raced through the halls past the statues of many gods who seemed to glare down upon them with contempt as they struggled to keep their feet through the aftershocks created by the shattered wards that once caged the demon deep within the earth below their feet. With a violent rumble, they fell upon the prayer rug in the central chamber as the angry mob drew ever near.

To Tasha's dismay, Asra grabbed his gilded lamp and began to shake it and calling out to it for help. Thinking he had gone mad, Tasha began to back away, wondering what she should do to escape this situation as the building shook while mosaic tiles of the temple began to rain down upon them.

"Wake up! You had better keep your promise!" Asra shouted at the lamp as he rubbed the falling dust from the glowing runes etched around its rim as he spoke to it, "I command you to take us to safety!" Asra barked again as Tasha's eyes turned worrisome at the loss of his sanity. As she was deciding if she should flee from him, a deep cold voice forming in the very air around them, and Tasha froze in shock.

"If that is your desire?" was all it asked in response.

"Yes, yes ...take us to someplace safe far away from here!" Asra called back over the clamor of falling rubble and screams of the people outside.

Tasha flashed a look of dismay towards Asra as he paused to look at her, the crazed look in his eyes were like that of a wounded animal. Her attention quickly turned towards the few stragglers who had chased them into the temple to exact their revenge, for they had presumed Tasha was somehow the cause of this calamity as the result of her ceremonial dance.

"The gods are angry and must be appeased ...kill the heretic, and it will calm their temper!" One of the men shouted to the other fanatics surrounding him.

"Witch, false priestess; you brought this upon us!" Another voice from the crowd called towards her.

A radiant glow began to spill from the strange lantern Asra was holding, issuing a stream of light which seemed to swim through the air like a current. It fanned out between them both and seeped into the rug at their feet; appearing as though its radiance was weaving itself into the very threads of the tapestry. With a sudden heave, the rug curled up upon its edges, entrapping them both within its folds and suddenly hurled them into the air. Members of the angry mob gasped in fear while others formed signs of protection with their hands as the large rug heaved their quarry above their heads and soared out through the hall entrance.

Both Tasha and Asra had lost their footing on the unsupported rug and had tumbled into one another while their limbs intertwined. Gathering her balance, Tasha look out from the flapping folds of the carpet at the dreadful sight below as cracks in the earth fanned out across the city while people ran for their lives. She shuddered as one of the tall ivory towers faltered and collapsed, crushing hovels and market stalls beneath its marbled stone. Fires broke out from toppled braziers and broken lanterns igniting several blazes which fanned throughout the doomed city.

Left in a state of shock, it took Tasha a sobering moment to realize that they were flying through the air like a soaring hawk. The night sky was speckled with stars as the full moon blazed down upon the tragedy unfolding below them while they drifted over the outer walls and across the cold desert dunes. A lone camel had broken from its tether and fled through the shattered gates as the walls of the city began to crumble. The unfortunate beast had nearly made it to a distance of safety when the ground beneath its legs suddenly gave way and sucked the animal below the surface as though the desert floor had turned to quicksand.

Asra had regained his balance and sat beside Tasha while they both watched in horror as the bedrock upon which the outpost had been built collapsed into the cavern hidden beneath its foundations. The wellspring contained by the massive stone column which once housed the imprisoned Demon had been shattered; splintering the support upon which the desert fortress had been erected. Fate is a fickle mistress, for the natural spring which had fed their fountains and given the city life, had also been the very cause of its doom. As the two companions were whisked away into the night, their breath caught in their throats while they watched the pillared walls of Ubar fall as the city was swallowed by the hungry earth.

Chapter VI
Isle of Limbo

It felt like forever until the carpet began to slowly descend upon the shores of an island oasis in the middle of a dry lake bed. The small isle was surrounded by an immense flat of white salt as far as the eye could see. Several trees of strange shapes littered the small bluff which was once surrounded by water. The rug came to rest gently upon the ground as the weave of fabric unfolded to release them.

"Where are we?" Tasha asked as she glanced around the lonely landscape.

"I, I don't know," Asra replied, still shaken from the events of the evening which had ended the lives of so many innocents, "where have you taken us, Jinn?" Asra spoke towards the golden lamp in his hands. When he did so a turquoise mist poured forth from the tip of the lamp and flowed into the corporeal form of the demon he had freed from beneath the city.

"Someplace safe and far away," the ancient being answered.

Tasha fell to the ground in terror behind Asra, looking up at the elemental spirit tethered to his lamp by a trail of smoke. The beast cast a malicious grin towards the mortal girl who cowered before him. It was a feeling of satisfaction he had not enjoyed for a thousand years.

"What is this forsaken place?" Asra demanded once again to the Djinn.

"It is an isle of limbo known as the Partition, a seat of purgatory between the timeless realms of paradise and damnation," the jinn answered.

"But why did you bring us here?" Tasha dared to ask while trying to grasp for an ounce of sanity to explain this creature which had materialized before them while she regained her feet.

"I fulfilled my first charge to this mortal within the bounds of his command, who made no clear distinction where he wished to find sanctuary," the jinn answered in a curt tone, "I now have but two duties left to render as repayment for my release from our pledge."

Tasha turned an accusing gaze towards Asra, wondering what mischief he had dragged her into.

"You made a pact with this fiend?" Tasha exclaimed.

"I found this Djinn trapped beneath the city within the ruins of a sealed temple, but its guardians were going to take my life for trespassing upon their sacred shrine," Asra answered with heavy guilt, "so I released this demon from its prison to save myself ...there was no other way."

"Only at the cost of the lives of my friends and thousands of innocent people who died because of your poor decision," Tasha snapped back with tears welling in her eyes, "how could you be so selfish and cruel?" She broke down and began to cry, remembering the fearful screams of the people as their lives had ended.

"I ...I'm sorry, Tasha, I had no idea what would happen," Asra tried to explain to no avail as Tasha pushed away from him. Asra could now see in her eyes that *he* was the monster she considered far more hideous than the wicked jinn looming above them.

Tasha couldn't come to grips how her entire world had been turned upside-down in the span of a single night. Thousands of happy people who were enjoying the pageantry and festivals were now left buried in a mass grave; all because of the actions of this one man. Tasha began to blame herself for having ever saved him from the desert sands. She had shown compassion for Asra, but now carried the weight of guilt for her good deed.

The jinn seemed to relish in her grief, for his glowing eyes showed delight in her pain. The demon had been held captive for countless centuries and the taste of revenge was sweet indeed. Furthermore, these mortals blamed each other for the demise of the city and its people, adding to the flavor of his retribution. Merely two more duties left to fulfill his sacred oath to this pathetic mortal and his reign of terror could begin.

The destruction of the walls of his prison and all its inhabitants was a good start, and the jinn felt satisfaction from the resulting aftermath. Though Asra held the lamp which contained his weakened essence, the Djinn was confident it wouldn't be long before the small man would use up his remaining requests and the elemental would be free to remove the life from his coil of flesh and bones. It was no mistake that the demon chose to deliver them to this place of purgatory, for the malicious creature had anticipated that his mortal master would require another wish to be spent to rescue him from this desolate place. It would be an entertaining game to see what he would do next.

"I demand that you take me back!" Tasha ordered towards the misty demon that appeared to ignore her with flagrant intent, which only served to set her fury a rung higher as she turned towards Asra.

"There is nothing there to return too," Asra tried to console her, "you saw the entire city sink beneath the sands..." he lowered his eyes with the shame of what he had done.

"Then return me to my valley in Fernwood..." Tasha began to whimper through her welling tears as she grieved her fallen friends, but her tone withered as she realized that she did not wish to bring the same blight upon her childhood home which would surely transpire in the presence of the vile demon, "no, never mind. I, I don't know what to do... I should have died with my friends back in the city!" Tasha began to lament.

Not knowing what course to take either, Asra knew not of where to go, since a vast part of his memory had vanished like Ubar itself. He had two deeds of the demon's oath left to his tally and did not wish to waste them. The first one he had used in haste to save his and his companion's life. Perhaps he could make this right by ordering the Djinn to bring back the city to the way it was and inquired so with his hideous servant.

"One cannot simply wish back the dead," the Djinn answered with a grin of its pointed teeth.

"Why not?" Asra demanded.

"It is a rule of nature for the Trinity," the jinn conceded, "as mortal life itself exists between the planes of both order and chaos."

The words of the Djinn made it clear that its powers were limited in such things. Asra's hopes fell, realizing that the harm he had done was incurable. Though he had saved his own life without fully knowing the dire consequences of his decision, the knowledge of it now did not diminish his personal shame. They were both now trapped in a desolate place where the living should never be, and they had to escape back to the world they once knew.

"Where do we go now? There is nothing here." Tasha

breathed as she regained her dignity to gaze upon the desolate island among the sea of salt. She had survived the unthinkable and did not wish to die here in this accursed place.

"Demon," Asra snapped towards the misty beast to get its attention, "you called this place the Partition, the limbo between the heavens and pits of hell; but I see nothing here," he granted with a gesture of his arm across the landscape.

"Ah, as is common with mortals, little Master, they're vision is so narrow that they notice nothing they are not looking for," the Djinn answered, and with a wave of his clawed hand a veil of light was lifted that pierced through the mirage before them.

Asra and the girl turned to see a giant temple of ancient stone materialize before them; its cracked surface covered with moss and lichen with thorny vines that weaved through its fractured surface. The towering monolith was covered with imposing sculptures of gargoyles with vicious tusks and wide-eyed beasts. There was but a single doorway set at its base before which sat a great basin. As they stepped towards the open vessel they felt an overwhelming urge of fear telling them to flee from this place.

"What is inside that shrine?" Asra asked with dread creeping into his voice.

"The one thing that mortal men fear most in their lives... *Judgment*," the jinn answered with bitter enticement.

"We should investigate within to see if we can find a way to escape this place," Tasha whispered to Asra as she drew near with a suspicious glance towards the jinn looming above them. Asra was hesitant at first but owed her that decency to abide by her wishes in this moment.

He agreed and turned back towards the jinn, wondering how his immense girth would fit inside.

"We should search inside the shrine for answers," Asra announced to the demon, who responded with a stout grimace to his choice of action.

"Be warned that once you cross the threshold I cannot aid you within the boundaries of this sanctuary," the jinn advised his temporary master.

With a nod of understanding from Asra, the genie collapsed into a cloud of mist which was drawn back into the golden lamp. He and Tasha stepped past the empty basin and entered into the pitch-dark gate of the ancient mausoleum. Several steps in from the doorway they turned to find that the entry was now a hundred paces behind them as daylight flowed through the open door. They turned to one another with rising concern as Asra held up the lamp and its glowing runes to light their path.

Though they remained upon level ground, the length of the temple's interior had by far exceeded its exterior dimensions. The toll of a distant bell resounded through the darkened bowels of the shrine, its volume climbing higher with every breath they took until it became a thundering roar causing them to clasp their ears as the air itself seemed to shake from the clamor. A sudden silence gave them relief, and as the two companions opened their eyes and uncovered their ears they found an old man in a ragged cloak standing before them. In his hand he held a long river pole with a small bell attached to its tip by straps of worn cord, and with but a single finger he stilled the ringing of its chime.

"The pier is closed," the elder mumbled through his shaggy beard, "but you may choose your destination."

Tasha and Asra both appeared puzzled by the stranger's

statement.

"We're a little confused by what you mean, honorable father," Asra offered with respect.

"I am *not* honorable," the old man stamped back abruptly, "I am Kharon, the boatman who provides passage to the afterlife," he answered as he reached out his hand, palm upward, "regardless, a toll is still in order," he ended with a sniffle of greed.

"We, ah ...didn't arrive by boat," Tasha offered in lieu of fee that was requested.

"I assumed as much," the old man smacked his mouth with its missing teeth, "my boat went adrift long ago. Yet, I still have a duty to fulfill here granting passage, even as mere toll keeper."

"What exactly *is* your duty?" Tasha dared to ask.

"The salt flats you see outside extend to every shore of the world, and it was my duty to ferry the dead to their place of eternal rest ...for a price, of course!" he finally added while twitching his eager fingers for payment.

"But... we are not dead," Asra answered to the old man's dismay; who slowly stepped towards him.

As he came closer, Asra could see that his eyes were entirely white, containing no iris within, and the man hesitated with each step as though blind. When he reached him, the elder tapped his hand against his chest and seemed shocked when his fingers met resistance. Noticing his guests were of the flesh, his posture became stout and the expression on his face turned angry.

"How did you arrive at this sacred place?" He demanded with a jolt, "It is my sole duty to convey the lost souls to these gates," he spat with a measure of ire as he motioned behind him at which three tall arches appeared; their rims glowing with an inner light. He then sniffed the air and his own fingers which he had touched Asra's robes, "You did not wash yourselves at the font before entering the temple," he accused, "you have tainted this temple with the breath of your sins!"

"What is this *font* you speak of?" Asra inquired, truly confused at the accusation.

"The large basin set before the door of the temple, you dolt; you can't miss it!" The old man barked.

"But the bowl was completely dry," Tasha replied as the man gave a stumble of disbelief.

"Impossible!" he barked back at her, "The fountain has never run dry... but then, maybe that's why no one has passed this way of late," the old man exclaimed, but fondled his beard in thought as he contemplated their preposterous claim.

"The sea surrounding this island is dry as dust as well," Asra offered as an explanation.

"Oh, it is not an ocean, but a river," the blind man snapped back with irritation, "but even the great wasteland it has left behind serves as a border between the underworld and the living; which reminds me that you two never answered my question."

"We flew here," Asra replied with minor hesitation, not able to believe it himself.

"First you trespass upon the isle of limbo and then defile this shrine with your foul tarnish of life, then proceed to insult me?" Kharon barked in exasperation.

"We had the help of a j*...." Asra began before Tasha quickly elbowed him in the ribs and interrupted what he was about to confess about the jinn.

"I know it's hard to explain, but we are here nonetheless and would like to return to the world of the living beyond this desolate isle," Tasha intervened as she silently signaled to Asra not to mention the lamp or the demon to the blind ferryman for fear of reprisal.

"Well, since I no longer have a boat, I've been reduced to the post of a gatekeeper; and since you're here you might as well make your choice and I can air out this unpleasant stench of the living you've dragged in here with you," he answered while waving his hand in front of his wrinkled nose, "pick a door and your final fate, and be gone with you," Kharon brushed them aside with a curt tone as he gestured towards the gates.

Both Tasha and Asra stood in awe at the trio of tall archways standing before them, not knowing which to choose. The longer they stared at each of the gates, one archway began to turn shades of gold and ivory, while another appeared to bud with greenery and flowers, while the last flecked with ash and hot, glowing cracks. They were pretty sure which one to favor, but wanted to be sure before committing. Making a mistake here could lead to a disappointing end.

"Where exactly do each of these gates lead?" Asra finally asked the ferryman.

"Ah, not so stupid as you appear..." Kharon answered with a sly grin, "and here I thought you were just going to skip through one of the gates without a word."

"I imagine one leads to paradise and other to the abyss; but where does the third one lead?" Tasha asked innocently.

"*Three* arches you say?" The blind ferryman inquired with a raised brow, "Hmm, well there used to be seven. Well, regardless, one will take you to your idea of Utopia, or Eden, if you will; and the opposite would be to the inferno of Hell and eternal torment, in whatever form you might imagine it," he granted.

"...And the middle door?" Asra asked as they considered the only choice left undefined.

"Well, that would likely be rebirth, a second chance to relive life; which I can imagine would be the far worst choice of the three," Kharon answered with a bitter smirk of satire curved upon his lips.

Tasha was immediately leery of the options at hand, for anyone in their right mind would see only one logical choice, so this situation left her puzzled.

"It's such an obvious choice, so what's the catch?" She asked the ferryman.

"I'm just the boatman who delivers passengers, and the former gatekeeper, who has disappeared to who knows where, was the one who offered judgment to the lost souls who arrived," Kharon conceded with a shrug.

"In what way," Tasha inquired, "how were they judged by this ah ...this missing Gatekeeper?"

"Oh, I think you misunderstood me, young woman," Kharon replied, "the sentinel did not pass judgment upon them, but *offered* it to them, as I said; or weren't you paying attention?" The old man snapped back.

The two companions found the ferryman's statement perplexing since they had assumed that after death one was judged by their grace or misdeeds in life and sent through to their befitting reward or damnation. What Kharon had suggested was that the destination in the afterlife was one's own choice. That was certainly an enlightening revelation; so she pressed to affirm if it was the Gods themselves who chose the fate of men's souls, since every story she had ever heard had claimed thus.

"So you're saying each mortal chooses their own destiny and not the Gods themselves?" Tasha dared to ask.

"Oh my, and here I was beginning to think you were the

bright one of you both," the old man answered with a sigh as a slight towards her, "the gods, or goddesses, or outlandish creature of whatever form you may worship, are actually the indentured servants of men," he answered to their utter surprise, "without praise or worship such deities are forgotten and eventually fade away; thus, they are reliant on mortals for their own existence."

That admittance took a load off of Asra's shoulders, for he was certain that when he died he would have been cast through Hell's gate to spend his eternity in a realm of flame and brimstone for his recent offenses.

"But obviously, everyone would choose the gate to Paradise," Asra mumbled with certainty as he gazed upon the three portals.

"Oh, well, one might think so," Kharon responded with a wrinkle of his brow, "but seeking eternal pleasures can become boorish. You would be surprised how many choose damnation purely out of personal guilt, knowing it is deserved ...at least in their minds. The idea of rebirth appeals to many who wish to try their luck again; as though they felt they had missed some revelation to the meaning of the universe or simply desire another attempt at a better life ...which philosophically, is merely another form of guilt if you spend as much time as I've had to think about such things," the blind ferryman offered as consolation.

"So, what will happen if we go through any of these doorways?" Tasha inquired.

"I am not privy to such secret knowledge," the old man admitted, "I am just the ferryman."

"We just witnessed a thousand people die, so why do we not see anyone else in this place seeking their eternal destiny?" Tasha asked.

"Look at me, young woman," Kharon instructed her as he motioned to his cold blind eyes, "the living cannot see the dead, nor do they notice you in return. Since the river of delivery dried up ages ago the wandering souls of the dead take time to reach this final sanctuary at the crossroads of the world ...though, unfortunately, many lose their way," he confessed with a bitter tone wrought with mild indifference.

"So you can see them with those blind eyes of yours?" She inquired.

"I do, in a way, and the trail of them is never-ending ...though oddly, I have not seen a single soul since you both arrived," the ferryman admitted.

The uninvited guests to the Temple of Partition had wondered what they should do. Giving up her life and entering Paradise didn't seem like such a bad choice to Tasha, but Asra was torn to take the opposing gate to face torment. He held a great measure of guilt for his crimes against the people of Ubar; he also considered that a domain of fire might give the Djinn in his lamp greater powers. He did have two more requests left upon his contract after all, and didn't wish to squander them.

Taking Tasha back to her tribe in Fernwood began to seem like a petty waste; and he had no other particular destination in mind, having forgotten his past. Asra broke away from Tasha and headed for the gate to damnation. If things on the other side didn't go well once he breached the gate, he could wish his way out by use of the jinn. Tasha passed him a strange look, wondering what he was doing, but felt that he would deserve what he got for the harm he had done.

"I'm truly sorry about what happened, Tasha, it was not what I had intended ...I hope you will forgive me," Asra spouted with remorse towards her before he marched off with intent as he proceeded towards the last portal. However, to his surprise, he smacked into it as though it were a wall of thick glass.

Seeing this result, Tasha cautiously held out her hand to test the gate to Eden before her; but noticed that it too was blocked to her physical body and would not allow her to pass through.

"Ah, well that's interesting, but not surprising," Kharon stated with a smirk as he heard his two guests trying in vain to penetrate the portals blocking their passage, "well, you know you could always go outside the temple and kill yourselves, then trot back in to try again," he proposed.

Though it was a logical approach to their dilemma from the old man's perspective, the two living mortals still found the ferryman's callous suggestion held a defined lack of tact. Perplexed as to what they should do, the two companions considered asking the Djinn about the situation, since the eternal being might be able to provide some insight. Though, after handling the lamp in his attempt to entice the jinn to answer his hail, there was no response forthcoming. Asra then recalled the warning that the jinn had given them prior to entering the Temple that it would not be able to aid them within the walls of the sanctuary.

The two of them made their precarious journey through the darkened hall back to the entrance at the empty basin to consider the situation. Asra again attempted to invoke the genie from the lamp, which spiraled out before them but now appearing far more human than its previous demonic form.

"How may I serve, master?" The Djinn inquired, though

Asra was a little stunned by the jinn's new form and tone of servitude.

"I tried to conjure you inside the Temple, but you wouldn't respond," Asra responded.

"As you were thus previously advised that I would be unable too, Master. I am not materially endowed to exist in such a place where domains converge, for it would upset the delicate balance that binds them," the jinn answered, "thus, I require a vessel to pass through such places unscathed."

"We weren't able to transit through any of the gates within," Tasha intervened, as she felt less intimidated by the jinn's new form.

"Only the dead may enter the gates of Partition for passage beyond, and that is not something I am able to do for you directly," the jinn replied, "however, if the master of the lamp should wish to expend another desire for another means of travel, I will attempt to comply within the scope of my powers."

Asra had growing suspicions that the demon was not actually all-powerful as he had claimed and that it was currently in a weakened condition since its physical body had been left behind in the crystal capsule buried beneath the shattered city. The lamp he held was the container of its spirit now which had left the creature with strict limitations. For Asra, fate had taken a cruel turn, leaving his shoulders heavy with guilt and remorse. At the moment, he would consider anything to help him alleviate the burden of his recent offenses and harm he had caused towards Tasha.

"You owe me two more prayers to fulfill before you are released from your vow," Asra commanded towards the jinn, whose pale sapphire skin mirrored that of tales of immortals from the eastern lands across the Arabian Sea.

"I do, my master," the demon in disguise answered.

"And what will you do once my wishes are satisfied?" Asra dared to ask.

"I shall return to the planes of chaos far beyond the breach of this realm," the jinn responded, "and I am eager to do so after spending a millennia in bondage."

"And if I so desired, I could request *anything*...?" Asra coaxed the elemental for a direct answer.

"Respectively..." the Djinn answered.

"What does that mean, exactly?" Tasha inquired into the conversation between the two of them.

"It means I can manipulate the binding elements of this plane proportionately," the jinn responded harshly to her interruption, "if my master here wished for a mountain of gold, such things cannot be created from nothingness; but must be drawn from what source already exists."

His statement clarified that the powerful demon could only manipulate the elements of this mortal plane.

"So if I requested unending wealth, where would such riches be funneled from?" Asra got more specific.

"From others who possess what you seek, wherever they exist; but only by means that are possible within the limits of this realm," the misty servant answered.

"So the product of such desires are not created, but acquired," Tasha whispered aloud in afterthought.

"Exactly," the jinn granted towards her.

"But your powers gave us the ability to fly through the air on a carpet to bring us here," Asra countered.

"The prayer carpet upon which you stood was empowered by the worship of men, and it was the delicate dance of the desert breeze which allowed you to be carried upon the wind," the jinn replied, as though the answer would make complete sense to his audience.

"So you are saying I can only request my desires within certain limitations of your ability to comply," Asra noted as a statement, "thus, I could request riches and fame and a harem of women to my heart's desire..."

"But of course," the jinn answered in a shrewd tone to appease such greed, "you could ask for gold and jewels and a kingdom of your own, or the admiration of those who would serve you willfully, or you could pursue the pleasures of the flesh until the end of your days."

It was that final statement which caught Asra's attention, for if he had only two choices, he could clearly not combine all three. The demon was manipulating him to make a tough decision; casting the pettiness of men's desires upon the table for him to choose. However, the Djinn had failed to include the power of knowledge and the gift of eternal time. Asra could live out his days with all that common men desired; riches, companionship, and influence over men; but those were mere shadows to the untapped potential he could conceive.

"And what if I chose immortality?" Asra goaded the elemental to answer.

"This is not within my powers to grant in your current form, for your anatomy simply would not endure such a transformation, and you would cease to be," the demon answered with a shrug as to the absurdity of the notion.

"Then perhaps there is another way to seek such an end," Asra answered, "what if I chose to be granted the power of the Djinn?"

Chapter VII
Stolen Magic

At first, the demon scoffed at the idea of a mere mortal demanding the powers of the jinn, but all too soon an expression of worry crossed the cyan face of the ancient elemental. When pressed for a definitive answer, the Djinn admitted it would have to keep its oath if such a thing was actually possible. By doing so, Asra could attain everything he could desire and more, without being fully limited to the obligations of the fire spirit. He had seen petty magicians and illusionist play tricks on their audience, but having real powers over the elements on any level would place him far above other men.

"What you now ask has never been done, and an outrage to the sacred beings who have formed this world," the Djinn spouted, "to gain such skills they would need to be siphoned from another elemental!"

"But you would have to comply nonetheless if I so requested as part of our bargain," Asra confirmed with a glare towards the mystical beast.

"...I would, Master," the jinn scowled in defeat, "but I am the only such being on this plane, as the others have long since retreated to their own realms."

"Your powers will do," Asra replied in a tone born of greed as the jinn glared back with contempt.

"Be aware that I must retain enough primal energies to survive, and cannot grant more than what might destroy your mortal body," the Djinn offered to the delicacy of such a transference.

The demon had more than one reason to be afraid of

this sudden twist of fate; for there were consequences he could not afford to let this contemptuous little man become aware of. Asra had been right about one thing; that knowledge itself is the ultimate power. The demon considered the consequences of doing what Asra demanded and the weakened condition it would leave him in. The Djinn could not kill this mortal outright for his insolence, but Asra would likely end up destroying himself while meddling with such arcane powers.

The bound jinn contemplated the results of such an ordeal which would leave him drained, but he could recuperate to his full power within his own realm and return to enact his vengeance. It was feasible that his bound master would be unable to control such energies and end himself in short order; leaving the jinn to escape from this earthly realm. While the other elemental spirits who created this world had more leeway, the element of fire itself had defined limitations which the Djinn were forced to obey. The demon recognized he was only momentarily enslaved to the will of this mortal until his obligations were completed; and knew the mystic powers of the jinn would eventually consume him.

"What are you doing, Asra?" Tasha asked with concern, "Such powers are not meant for mortal men to possess!"

"But I could find a way to make things right, why would you stop me from doing that?" Asra snapped back, having shed his guilt in exchange for this mantle of absolution now unraveling in his mind.

He could change the course of his destiny and free himself of this burden of remorse which had been forced upon him. Deep inside Asra's soul, something abruptly twisted out of place, and a decision of who he was to become solidified in his resolve. The mystery of whom he may have once been no longer seemed to matter; for he could carve his own path and no-one could stand in his way. The elation of obtaining such control began to consume him, and the demon grinned as he watched this curious transformation take place.

"This is not the way to make things right, you know that in your heart, don't you?" Tasha pleaded.

"I don't even know who I was, Tasha, and have no ties to tether me to my past, and I can now see that for what it truly is... *a blessing*," Asra offered, but doing so with an unyielding tone which scared her.

Tasha had traveled most of her life and seen many cultures and people of all creeds and nations. One thing she had learned was how to read people and see them for whom they were no matter what mask or veil they wore to conceal themselves. Many did so because they were afraid of being judged, but others were disturbed and dark in their views with poisonous intentions. Tasha could now see that dim shadow beginning to stain Asra's mind and buckle his spirit. It was the detached look in his eyes she feared the most; for it was the hollow gaze of a man who could no longer see the light of virtue.

Everyone has their own definition of what corruption is, but the Djinn knew it well, more so than most, and Asra began to reek of it. Over the long centuries, the demon had witnessed countless improprieties committed by these earthly mortals. There were always those few who craved to be better than their fellow man; usually based upon social conditioning, but a majority was due to the surly condition of their race itself. Mankind was deeply flawed, and the race of men were well aware of those flaws but continued to commit them regardless.

Elementals viewed the world in a completely different

context, for existence relied on the balance of all things. There were, however, those few mortals who accepted such harmony usually separated themselves from the massive communal hives which men created. Their prophets hid in isolation, for they saw the consuming distractions within these civilizations which men had created for themselves. In the eyes of the Eternal spirits, the race of men were nothing more than pets, while the Djinn, however, viewed them as irritating pests.

A mortal posessing the powers of the jinn could upset the balance of this world; but such an outcome was not yet decided, so the demon was bound to fulfill his promise heedless of the danger it posed. Regardless, the demon was confident that Asra would come to an untimely end by his own hand once he dared to attempt controlling such volatile magics. Such a transference was possible, but not without inherent dangers. The ancient demon found himself beginning to despise this little man for his reckless arrogance.

"I will fulfill your desire if you wish it so," the jinn advised, "but to do so we must retreat to an area beyond boundaries of this island."

"For what reason?" Asra asked with suspicion.

"Such a delicate process is not exact and could possibly leech into other objects without direct focus. The island of Perdition would create too great a distraction for such magics to be guided into a mortal frame, and would quickly bleed away," the Djinn offered as an explanation.

"Where would be the safest place to commit to this?" Asra asked.

"I could take you to one of many sacred sites across the world that would suffice if you so wished?" The jinn answered.

Asra saw what the demon had done with the baiting of his words, and realized that the elemental spirit had brought him to this place far out of reach of civilization so that he would be forced to dispose of another request against his tally. His first wish had been expended in the desperation of the moment, and Asra wasn't going to fall into that trap again. The contempt the demon held for mankind had not gone unnoticed, and Asra had found the perfect way to weaken the jinn from enacting retribution against the world of men. Asra wasn't entirely confident that he could survive such a process of leeching the demons magics, but he had already put on a good performance as he spoke to Tasha in front of the Djinn to make his demand convincing.

Scanning the wastelands beyond the dry shores of the island, Asra saw a way to escape his dilemma.

"Will these arid salt flats suffice instead?" Asra suggested as he motioned to the barren plains.

"I suppose we could try," the demon answered with a tone of contempt for being deterred so readily.

The two companions climbed down the steep banks and marched across the dry bed into the open basin as the sun began to set. Feeling they were a decent distance away from the isle, Asra summoned the genie from the lamp to do his bidding. The misty jinn looked around nodded its approval to his master and Asra placed the lantern upon the course pale brine and took several steps back. The jinn then motioned for Tasha to stay behind him during the transition that was to take place.

"Demon, for my second wish, it is my request that you gift me with the powers of the jinn," Asra stated boldly, "so that no one else can harm me," he added for safe measure in case the Elemental had alternate plans.

"That is your desire?" The genie responded.

"It is," Asra answered with slight hesitation.

The jinn clapped its hands together as it closed its glowing eyes and a sphere of fiery light manifested between them. Tasha peeked out from behind the jinn to see what was happening as tendrils of blue flame began to trail through the air. Wisps of light flicked like falling snow around the sphere as the Djinn began to mumble in a strange language as ancient as the stars which began to glitter fiercely upon the sky above. The bellowing chant dropped to a deep hum as the salt plain around them began to glow with a vivid teal hue.

Tasha gasped as Asra was slowly lifted off his feet and his eyes were filled with a brilliant light. She turned to either side to notice that crystalline spears began to grow from the salt itself, creating a small translucent forest around them as the unbound magic began to trickle away. Asra struggled for several moments and suddenly began to cry aloud in pain as the flow of energy filtered from the jinn into the shifting orb and finally to his body. With a sudden clap of the Demon's hands, the transference halted with the resulting boom of thunder shattered the crystal formations surrounding them into fine splinters.

Asra's body fell to the ground in a heap while a smoky mist of residual energy drifted from his closed eyes. Tasha ran out to help him, only to fall up short as Asra began to stir. His face and hands were now cracked and fractured as if he were made of dried mud, and his skin had turned an unpleasant shade of gray. Afraid to touch him, Tasha stood back with her eyes wide in dread when Asra began to rouse.

"Are ...are you alright?" Tasha stuttered in a tone of concern; though still afraid to touch him for fear of the malady which had overtaken him.

"I feel strange," Asra mumbled as he began to rise.

It took several moments to gather his strength and regain his feet and had a reaction of confusion as Asra touched his face and inspected his hands.

"What's happened to him?" Tasha shouted back towards the jinn who sat floating before them.

"He lives, which is all that matters, little one," the demon replied, apparently unruffled by Asra's withered appearance.

"But he's all..." Tasha began to relate as she motioned towards him, but was interrupted by the demon.

"Different than he was?" The jinn retorted, "Yes, that was to be expected. But he got what he wished for."

Asra stumbled away from them as he stared out across the salted wastes and the crumbled crystals littering the plain. He then looked towards the stars and back toward Tasha with a confused look in his darkened eyes.

"What is wrong with him?" Tasha dared to ask the demon as she was at a loss of what to do.

"Such forces are not meant for the mortal shell," the jinn answered in a casual tone, "he is more than what he was but far less than what he could have been."

Tasha was troubled by the Djinn's play of words as she took several strides over to Asra where he stood alone to help console him.

"How are you feeling?" She wondered.

"I can see things now that I hadn't before," Asra answered as he gazed around them, though Tasha was unable to detect what he could with his acquired senses.

"Your skin, it's all... you don't look well," she finally muttered for loss of words.

Asra stumbled back towards the jinn who was tethered

to the lamp and addressed the demon directly; feeling as though he had been tricked.

"You agreed to issue me your powers ...what is this, what have you done to me?" Asra demanded as he faced the Djinn.

"You were administered a small capacity of mystic energies until the duress became too great of a strain for your fragile body; if it would have continued a moment more you would have surely died," the jinn answered, "keep in mind such elemental forces are not meant for flesh and blood."

"Can you cure whatever this is ailment is?" Asra asked.

"It is merely a cosmetic side effect, but I could try if you so wish, my Master," the jinn responded.

"What remedy could I use instead?" He demanded, as Asra had been keen to the demon's trickery.

"There must be something we can do to treat his condition," Tasha intervened as she begged the jinn.

The demon thought for a moment to himself, knowing that he had only to weasel one more duty from this foolish mortal before he would be set free. He could not fatally harm the master of the lamp with whom he shared a sacred pledge, but perhaps a natural death by aging could accelerate his resignation. There was one place the demon knew of which could serve to that end should Asra wish to risk such a voyage. The misty Djinn turned back toward the two mortals and offered a suggestion to resolve his dilemma.

"There does exist an elixir created by the elementals long before this world took shape, which is known to reside in a city of the dead known as the Necropolis," the jinn finally answered.

Many people throughout the lands had heard tales about

such a place but were widely written off as merely ghost stories and myth. The Necropolis was a place that existed between light and shadow while sheathed in ever-consuming darkness. It was reputed to exist in the realm of men at the edge of the world. However, getting there would be a problem.

Asra knew that he could not ask anything further of the jinn in the form of a request or it would release the demon from his bond and leave him and his world at its mercy. Since he had been granted magics of the elementals, it was certainly worth a try to test them. Having no idea what these new powers might entail, he concentrated on the energy coursing through his veins. His blood felt hot, yet heavy as though they were full of lead; though it had an oddly pleasurable sensation which he began to find addictive.

With his new eyes, Asra looked towards the sky and could now see the darkness between the stars for what it was. Even the jinn himself had an aura about him in a fluttering hue of colors. His friend Tasha appeared to be spiked with a soft blush of pale lights weaving about her. Something deep within him had changed and he could feel it growing.

With an overwhelming compulsion, Asra strode over to a large shattered block of the crystallized rock from the salt bed and swept it up into his arms. He could look into the mineral and see things hidden from common mortals. He could see its uses beyond what it was and cradled the lump within his arms as he walked back towards his companion and retrieved the lamp. He glared towards the demon and motioned for it to return to the vessel.

"Your services are not required at this time, you may return to your rest," Asra stated coldly.

The jinn did not take kindly to his Master's dismissive attitude but had been drained of much of his strength this eve. With a nod of obedience, the genie dissolved into a fine mist and receded back into the lantern. Asra then reached into his sash and took out the triangle rune stone Tasha had given him the night before and placed it in the funnel as a stopper. Looking upon the glowing runes, he was convinced that it would secure the demon for now.

"That should hold him and give us a measure of privacy," Asra stated as he turned to face Tasha, who was still in a state of confusion as to recent events.

"What is it you plan to do?" She asked in a timid tone.

"When I released the demon from his prison under the city, his physical body appeared to have completely diffused and escaped through the crack I had made in its petrified cage," Asra explained, "it appeared to be drawn to the flame of this very lantern I was holding at the time, as though fire itself was its source of power it hungered for. Now that I have the gift of the jinn I can discern these runes upon the lamp were carved with powerful enchantments. I understand now that without its physical body the Djinn requires a container if it is to continue to exist in our realm, and if I ever release it from its bond, then this vile creature will only spread devastation upon all who cross its path," Asra confessed to her.

"So what do you suggest we should we do with it?" Tasha responded as she gave a fearful glance towards the golden lamp in his hands.

"We must dispose of it somewhere it can do no harm," he responded, "and this Necropolis he spoke of might suit that need."

"And what do you plan to with that lump of rock salt?" Tasha inquired with a raised brow.

"I feel ...different now, something *more* than what I was before. It's as if I can almost hear things speak to me; telling me know how they can be used," Asra answered to her baffled expression.

"Personally, I would rather return to my village; but I understand now that this creature needs to be destroyed," she answered, "so I will help you if I can."

"No, not destroyed," he snapped back, "only discarded somewhere it can never harm anyone ever again."

Asra guided her back to the temple on the lonely isle and gently placed the block of crystal into the basin which sat before it. Tasha looked on in wonder as he grasped the edges of the open urn and shut his eyes in deep concentration. Sparks began to pinch off of the salted stone until the crystal itself began to glow with an unearthly light. Within moments, Kharon the ferryman appeared at the doorway of the temple.

"What in the name of the thousand gods are you doing?" He demanded, "I order you to cease this, this... whatever wizardry you are performing at once!"

Asra stood back as the crystal slowly melted into a slag which filled the bottom of the basin while its brilliant glow subsided into a dull tone. Wisps of black smoke began to rise from the residue which weaved like tendrils into the air. Tasha was rattled to see horrid faces appear in the soot as though it was comprised of tormented spirits writhing in silent agony. The furious boatman kept his position at the doorway as though he was bound to stay within the limits of the shrine itself.

"I am opening a doorway to the Necropolis," Asra responded towards the enraged elder.

"Fool!" Kharon shouted back, "You are consuming the souls of the dead with those dark arts; you must desist from such folly."

Asra looked on, not sure if he could reverse what he had done. As he took a step forward to attempt a reprise, but the smoke became denser and began to bloom several more afflicted spirits which grew in number by the second. Tasha retreated in fear as Asra was unsure what he had released. Several moments later a section of smoke parted and revealed an open void with several steps of murky vapor leading up to its entrance.

"You would be insane to enter a torn rift," the ferryman cried as Asra turned back towards Tasha to take her hand.

With apprehension, they ascended the smoldering steps and pierced the darkened veil. With the lamp tied to his sash, Asra held an arm forward to breach the smothering blackness of the portal before them as Tasha followed in his wake. A moment later the entwined wraiths of smoke and ash exploded into a symphony of clasping coils and snapping tendrils. The violent black cords of chaos and anguish whipped through the air, only to cascade upon themselves into the void of the closing doorway.

In a moment they were gone and all that remained within the ash-filled basin was the crackling remnants of residual energy. The ferryman gazed forth with his blind eyes, sensing the suffering of the deceased whose spirits had been devoured to form the corrupted rift. Kharon new the dead well, but the place where the two living mortals had journeyed was a realm of despair. It was a land ruled by the undead which no soul could escape.

Chapter VIII
The Silent Bridge

Asra stepped through the void and immediately fell to the ground with Tasha close behind. They both turned to watch as the rift they had just dropped through folded upon itself and dissipated, leaving them stranded. While they stood to brush themselves off and gazed at their surroundings, a sharp wind suddenly whipped past as if to greet them and was gone. They found themselves standing in a lush garden surrounded by high cliffs where a lone waterfall cascaded into a clear pool before them.

"It's not exactly what I expected," Tasha exclaimed with a raised brow she stepped forward to admire the brightly hued flowers.

"I agree, this doesn't appear anything near what I imagined a 'City of the Dead' to look like; perhaps we ended up somewhere else," Asra concluded.

Tasha plucked the flower from its fragile stem to smell its fragrance, but the very moment she did so the entire flower dissolved into ash within her hands. She glanced down at her empty palm with troubled alarm, and quickly brushed her hands clean off the residue.

"Maybe, maybe not," Tasha responded, "but we should take a look around to see what is here."

Asra nodded in agreement and they both stepped through the lush field of flowers and beyond the enclosed bluff surrounding the hidden falls. They were struck in awe as they reached the peak of a hill which had an open view to a picturesque jungle filled with rich foliage. At the center of the valley stood a large sculpture shaped like a circular arch.   Reaching up from the ground directly below it was something that appeared to be an enormous tree, though inverted as though it were the tangled roots which were exposed instead of the canopy.

The pair made their way towards this structure as there was nothing else in sight worthy of note. It was a long path they had to cut through the field as the monolith was over a league away from where they had entered this strange realm. The closer they drew, they felt the ground crunch beneath their feet; but it took a while before they noticed these clumps created wisps of dust as they tread upon the injured vegetation. Halfway along Asra looked for a fallen branch or limb that he could use as a walking staff, but found none.

"Do you notice something odd about this place?" Tasha inquired to her companion.

"Well, of course... pretty much everything here!" Asra responded curtly in jest as he motioned around them.

"No, I mean something else," Tasha grimaced, "there are no birds or insects. There's nothing but silence."

Asra came to a stop and realized she was right. This strange place was devoid of life except for the thick flora. Aggravated that he couldn't find a fallen tree limb, he stepped over to a tree to snap loose a branch within reach that he may use. He struggled for a moment to break it free, only to pause when they heard a strange wind blow as it whipped through the trees.

Finally snapping it off, Asra took his newly acquired staff and came to stand beside Tasha. He was about to offer to find her one when the branch began to dissolve in his hands. The outer layer of wood flecked away in the breeze as it turned to dust. Within moments the entire branch disintegrated, leaving nothing but a cloud of ash which quickly dissipated into the forest floor.

"The same thing happened when I plucked a flower," Tasha admitted as they wondered what strange magics were at play in this place, "let me show you," she added as she stepped over to a small bush and plucked a single leaf. Within seconds the leaf faded into nothingness and she wiped the soot of it from her hands.

Looking around with a measure of scrutiny, they could not see any fallen leaves or forest litter one might expect to find. Once something dies here, it fades away. This realization left them unsettled as they continued towards the great tree which began to tower over them the closer they approached. Once they reached a great rim surrounding the immense structure they crossed a sight which left them troubled.

"Didn't the demon say there was a potion here that would help to cure you?" Tasha inquired as she dared to touch his crackled grey skin.

"Yes, he mentioned an elixir of some sort, but the jinn didn't elaborate," Asra answered as they stared across the enormous field of huddled corpses piled at the foot of the colossal tree.

It was a strange find indeed, as they had expected any remains would have vanished considering what they had witnessed thus far of this curious realm. Asra was about to step down into the massive pit to get a better look at the cadavers to examine what could have been the cause of their demise, but Tasha stopped him and pointed towards the monstrous trunk. There appeared to be thousands of decayed corpses spread across the great divide between the enormous barren tree and the border of living foliage surrounding it. The mass of them piled up upon the trunk as though they had settled there like fallen leaves.

The piles of carrion appeared to be centuries old. The skin of their desiccated remains appeared creepily similar to Asra's current condition. This thought left Tasha's mind reeling with questions as to who these people had once been and how they ended up here. The reason Tasha had stopped Asra began to make itself clear when he looked to where she was pointing.

At the base of the tree, a crack in its trunk widened and a single naked figure stumbled out, shriveled and lurching as though in great pain. It stood there for a moment and looked upward at the sky, then its knees buckled and the lifeless carcass tumbled into the great pile, becoming one with the mass of bodies. It was a ghastly sight which gave them pause, for they wondered what horrible fate might await them if they drew closer. Asra took a few steps back and unstrapped the golden lamp from his sash and set it upon a nearby stone.

"We need to find out what this place is, and how we can locate this cure the jinn had spoken of," Asra ceded.

After Tasha nodded in agreement, Asra unplugged the spout of the lantern and brushed the line of runes which circled the lamp.

"Come forth, Jinn," he called aloud.

A mist of smoke issued forth from the lantern, now quite thicker than they had seen before; as was the Djinn whose material form appeared more opaque. The blue demon appeared to be waking from a deep sleep as it materialized and gazed down upon them.

"What is your bidding, my Master?" The jinn answered in a deep tone, though within moments the misty beast had gazed upon their surroundings and a look of disdain formed upon its hideous face, "How did you arrive at this place?" The jinn demanded.

"You claimed there would be an elixir to cure this condition I contracted from the transference of magics," Asra responded while ignoring the demon's question.

"I did, my Master," the genie replied, "...which resides within the Necropolis, which this is not!"

"Where exactly are we, demon?" Tasha dared to press an answer from the beast.

"Someplace you do not want to be," the elemental answered, "before you is the Gehenna, resting at the precarious edge of the Netherworld," the jinn gestured towards the giant barren tree that dominated the landscape, "it is a place where the wicked are disposed in a reserve of everlasting serenity."

"How would one get to the city of the Necropolis from here?" Asra returned.

"This is a place untouched by chaos and without order, it cannot be tampered with by the presence of the living," the jinn replied in a stern warning, "this incarnation you see before you are the hidden roots of the world tree itself; this is not a place meant for the eyes of mortals," the demon answered in a nervous tone as it peered around the landscape with a measure of unease.

"You didn't answer my question," Asra bit back with impatience; for he had no wish to stay in this strange and unsettling realm a moment longer if it could be avoided.

"You must enter the hollow, for it is the only doorway within this domain," the jinn answered as he pointed towards the small fissure in the bark where the withered man had appeared moments before.

"And where in the Necropolis can I find the cure for this...?" Asra persisted with his questions as he held his bare forearms to the jinn; exposing the breadth of his unsightly ailment.

"The roots of the Tree of Life weave through many realms; it is an elixir made from the sap of its heartwood which you seek. However, unlike the Partition, where the souls of the dead have been parted from the flesh, the Necropolis has become the residence of the undead who are bound to their own," the jinn answered, "they are forever cursed to suffer the rot of the flesh. It has twisted their decayed minds beyond insanity and they will seek any sustenance from the living to replenish their own withering by feeding on that which possesses vitality."

"Are you saying they eat the living?" Tasha asked with a dreadful tone.

"Yes," the demon answered with a slight smirk upon his fanged lips as he motioned toward Asra and back to her, "while his condition at the moment may go unnoticed by the dead, you, on the other hand, would be a banquet."

"And once I was cured, we would both be placed in jeopardy," Asra responded to the comment.

"Indeed," the genie answered, "and would then have to find your way out of a labyrinth brimming with the undead. It is such a daunting task you face that I could fulfill within mere moments if you should so request?" The jinn offered with a graceful bow.

Asra could see what the demon was doing as it was attempting to sell him on his 3rd prayer to release him from their contract. The jinn could easily transport them there and then leave him abandoned after it had fulfilled its final oath. Asra was not so easily duped and chose another means to reach his destination. He turned to inspect the land around him with his new senses and offered the jinn an alternative opinion.

"If I can gain passage to the Necropolis through that

hollow, and once I arrive there, how do I find this potion made from the extract of the tree?" Asra pressed.

"Seek the Circle," the demon responded with a grimace that he had been deterred once again, "they are the oracles who weave the tapestry of life and fate, and it is they who possess this potion you seek."

"Then return to your vessel if you have no more to say," Asra demanded, and the jinn obeyed.

After corking the spout, Asra once again stood at the edge of the ring of death which encompassed the great tree. He gazed with mystic eyes across the landscape to see beyond what could be seen. Asra clasped the lamp to his sash and rolled back his sleeves as Tasha looked on in confusion, for they would have to wade through the zone of death to reach the hollow rift within the giant tree. She jumped in fear as Asra's hands began to glow and blue flames began to ripple upon his fingers.

Moments later the flames burst into a vivid yellow light which cast out from his arms and touched the pile of cadavers heaped upon the massive trunk. Once ignited, the fire spread until it engulfed the entire perimeter, as ugly smoke rose from the grisly stack. The stench became nearly unbearable as it siphoned into the air in thick powdery clumps of scorching soot. As the angry fire flickered, the rising heat made it appeared as though the mass of bodies writhed in agony as they were being consumed.

Suddenly, a shrill could be heard piercing the air, centered from the giant tree itself. The flames whipped up the trunk, baking the exposed bark, but finding no foliage to ignite and carry the flames higher. Tasha was unnerved to see the unreachable roots of the tree high above begin to twist and coil in a tightened grip around the giant arch that spanned its canopy. Only when the ground around them began to tremble did Asra cease his strange magics and turned back towards his companion.

"What are you trying to do?" She spouted with concern as the earth beneath them continued to shudder.

"When I took the time to view this realm with my new senses, I could see how it was formed. We need to reach that doorway to gain passage to the Necropolis," Asra answered in a tired tone as though the expense of such magics exhausted him, "...so I have awoken the Titans."

A sudden violent tremor nearly sent them tumbling to the ground as their attention was turned to the nearby cliffs. It was as if the rocks themselves had a life of their own. An enormous section of stone lifted from the earth, tearing up plants and soil as the beast below it exposed itself to the world above. The entire cliffside had concealed a sleeping giant, one of impossible proportion.

It appeared to move slowly as the monster lumbered to its feet, destroying huge tracks of land and foliage in its wake. Enormous trees and patches of soil cascaded down its body in a deadly rain of dirt and debris. Even Asra stepped back in nervous fright of this goliath he had stirred. Once it gained its stance, the being stretched as though roused from a great sleep, then turned its stony gaze directly towards the two tiny mortals.

The creature looked angry, as though displeased by this interruption in its eternal rest. It bent down to one knee, causing a shockwave to shake the ground beyond. It then stretched down its arm towards them; its sheer immensity swallowing up the sky above as it drew ever near. Fearing they were about to be crushed, Tasha turned and began to run.

"Do not move," Asra warned her as he grabbed her arm

to stop her.

She shot back a look of pure terror as her eyes turned from his towards the looming monstrosity bearing down upon them. Tasha tried to yank herself free from his iron grasp as fear overwhelmed her, but could not break his grip. Her breath caught in her throat as the colossal hand wavered over them for what seemed like a lifetime before it came to rest several feet away. The giant's hand then began to penetrate into the ground below their feet and lifted the entire patch of earth they stood upon.

The leviathan lifted the two mortals to impossible heights towards its strangely distorted face as if to inspect what tiny creatures it had captured. Tasha fought to keep her footing as the speed of the wind and choking clouds of ash wafted around them. Asra looked up at the enormous beast and appeared to say something to it, though his voice was merely a soft whisper as he spoke. Their trajectory then turned towards the colossal tree before them as the titan set their scrap of earth they stood upon by the large gap within its trunk.

A sea of burning bodies and hot embers drifted below them as they passed towards the cleft in the great tree; leaving Tasha to choke on the poisonous air, though Asra seemed unaffected by the soot. They stepped off the crumbling island and entered into the open fissure. Behind them, the giant removed its hand and dumped the residual earth upon the ground which landed with a violent impact as it crushed everything beneath it. The colossus then stood for a long moment as though in contemplation as it stared at the great tree; then turned its girth to stride away towards the horizon.

"I'm trying to get control of these magics the jinn possess," Asra confessed as he looked at his scorched hands, though they were not burned.

"What was that monstrosity?" Tasha asked with her eyes still wide with shock.

"The titans are the curators, or gardeners if you will, for the world tree," he answered, "there was a *wasting*, if you could call it that, drowning the roots of the great tree, suffocating it."

"Or, those dead bodies were being used as fertilizer," Tasha snapped back.

"Regardless," Asra responded with a shake of his head, "it all had to be burned away to disperse the sickness concentrated within its core."

"But I saw you speak to the giant; what did you say to it?" Tasha inquired.

"I merely asked it to take us to the doorway in words it could understand," Asra replied to Tasha's mounting confusion.

She was beginning to wonder what the jinn's archaic powers were doing to his mind. Asra seemed different; not just his wilted exterior, but the person who he was inside. This thought concerned her in several unsettling ways. Tasha became alarmed when the opening gap in the bark creaked and shut behind them, locking them both inside the entry which appeared to have no exit.

Only the soft glow of the magic lamp lit the interior as they searched the wood-rimmed walls for a means of escape, but their efforts were in vain. A gushing noise resounded from beneath their feet as a groaning throb could be heard pulsating through the grain of the walls. Without notice, the floor beneath them gave way and they were both sent plummeting through a narrow shaft awash in a waxy red. Tasha screamed as the tunnel channeled them through its trunk deep into the unknown.

The crimson shaft was slick with an oily residue that left them helpless to resist as they slid deeper into the depths of the tree. After receiving more bumps and scrapes than they could count, the couple was dumped into a shallow pit where they laid, catching their breath. Left dizzy and nauseated from the unpleasant ride, they found themselves lying in a mound of sour slag among several heaps of floating moss. Wiping the film from their faces, they surveyed their surroundings and couldn't believe their eyes.

Above them, large root-like strands tipped down from enormous vines woven within a chaotic lattice secured above, which infrequently dipped down and deposited bits of material among a massive graveyard of corpses. Unlike the choking stench of the burning cadavers above, the area was filled with a tart aroma reminiscent of vinegar and honey. Before them, an open archway led towards a glowing waterfall.

Stumbling their way through the debris and vermillion gravy sticking to their feet, they tested the warm waters cascading over the archway and passed through falls which gently rained down upon them. On the other side, an even stranger sight awaited them. A city of ancient stone and wood intertwined as if one; created in exotic designs of architecture. It was both compelling, yet disquieting to behold such wonders found in such a dreary and forgotten realm.

"Is ...is this the Necropolis?" Tasha wondered aloud as Asra came to her side; while noting that not only had the mystic waters cleansed them of the sappy residue, but had also removed the scarlet tint which had stained Asra's robes; which were now left bleached a brilliant white.

"I don't know, but I would rather not test the jinn's

patience again for he might create a problematic situation for us both which will merely serve his own agenda," Asra hinted toward the malicious intent of the demon as he placed his hand upon the golden lamp at his side.

"This magic you bear," Tasha turned to him to ask, "how do you control it?"

"It almost feels like a great library has been inserted into my mind," Asra began, "where I recognize many things for what they are, but I actually feel it instead ...it's difficult to describe," he offered as he shook his head to understand his own words, "it's as though I can both see and sense the connections of things, for the most part."

"What do you mean?" Tasha inquired.

"Well, it's subtle, and there are a lot of voids I can't perceive because I don't have the full abilities of the jinn themselves. It's like listening to the calls of a thousand birds within a single cage and trying to identify one by its song among the cacophony of the others   ...but every time I use these powers, I feel as though a part of me has burned away inside," Asra confessed.

"We should see what is here and if we can locate that cure for you and a way to be rid of the demon as well," Tasha offered towards him.

The curious pair set off towards the strange metropolis along the winding path beside a river of glowing waters that ended at the edge of a great chasm. An ancient bridge spanned the fissure between them and the city beyond where the gentle waters rose to a roar as they cascaded over the rim and into the abyss below. These steps were left worn over a thousand millennia as though this place had once been a great city to behold but now left in a state of decay and disrepair. Once they reached the center of the lone bridge, a cold shroud of silence enveloped them.

Asra turned towards Tasha to say something, but she could not hear the words from his lips. Calling back, she found that her own voice was muffled. She held up her hands and with a snap of her fingers, but no sound emerged. Clapping her hands produced the same muted result which left them baffled.

Against their better senses, they pressed forward into the stifled veil as even their footsteps were subdued while they crossed. Once on the other side, the cloud of silence lifted and their ears began to discern their surroundings. Tasha looked back towards the sight of the flowing rivers of light spilling into the endless gorge, but hearing nothing from the opposite side and its rushing waters. It was a surreal vision, like gazing at a moving painting of a picturesque scene.

"What was that?" Tasha paused to ask her gifted companion.

Asra closed his eyes and placed forth his withered hand, seemingly feeling the very air as his wilted fingers touched invisible threads like the cords of a lyre. For a moment she could see emotions flashing over his face, as though reliving an unpleasant memory lingering in one's past. He slowly pulled back his arms with a single tear washing down his face as he lowered his head, having identified the curious phenomena.

"That was serenity, the calm and quiet of death in its truest form," he answered as wiped away his tear and turned to join her as they continued on their path between the looming towers into the heart of the Necropolis.

Chapter IX
Fleeting Shadows

The city itself lent an appearance to a massive a crypt, though it had an eerie beauty to it. The quiet streets and dusty remains of crumbled stone and splintered wood fit the persona of a graveyard. There were no bodies or living corpses to be seen as the jinn had forewarned, which only strengthened their resolve to continue. Tasha, it appeared, had her own misgivings as to what had transpired with Asra moments before.

"Back there, before we entered the city, I saw you crying..." Tasha led on with a tone of concern.

"I didn't realize I was," Asra admitted without turning to meet her curious eyes, "magic, or whatever this power is called, has a feel to it that manipulates you as equally as the person who wields it."

"Did that hurt?" She inquired.

"Do you mean to ask if it caused me harm to reveal that silent ward upon the bridge?" Asra responded in kind.

"Yes, was it painful to recognize it?" Tasha asked.

"It was ...but not in the way you may think," he answered in short, but failing to elaborate what he meant by the strange remark.

The vast metropolis appeared to have been left untouched for countless ages, though much of the ruins were still intact but held obvious signs of decay among the shattered buildings. Neither of them was fond of the idea of running into walking corpses who fed off the living, but Asra knew the risk of releasing the jinn from its final duty would only lead to far greater despair. High towers loomed above, creaking as bits of dust and stone showered down upon the path; threatening to collapse at any moment. Large hollowed-out buildings and winding streets weaved through the catacombs; leaving them lost within its rotting web.

The odd pair found themselves guessing as to where they could find what Asra sought as they began to search random buildings without a clue to their destination. Behind them a shadow flitted through the dark streets and alleyways, following them in their tour of the silent ruins. Tasha glanced behind her several times for having caught movement out of the corner of her eye; only to find nothing when she turned its way. Asra also began to notice the odd figure that darted between the shadows and found himself questioning what it might be.

"Did you see that?" Tasha whispered in fear as they both looked towards the area where the specter had passed from one building to another.

"Yes... I thought I was just imagining things," Asra answered as he slowed his pace.

They decided to press forward and came across a small stone bridge which jumped a dry channel and made their way to the other side. Finding a spot to hide in, they found it the perfect place to catch a glimpse of whatever had been following them. They waited long moments, whispering to one another in the shadows where they had taken cover wondering if the strange shade tracking them would dare to cross. Finally, they saw a flicker from the other side and held their breath in anticipation.

The blurry phantom wavered from one area to the other on the opposite side of the channel, seemingly shy to expose itself by crossing the open bridge. With a daring start, it suddenly dashed across; but Asra stood out from the shadows and held his hand up towards it. Strange whispers of a long-forgotten language fell from Asra's lips as the phantasm was held fast. The shade appeared to struggle violently until Asra lost his grip on his enchantment; reacting as though he had been physically shocked.

The phantom dashed to their side of the empty course and melted into the dark ruins beyond. It was now among them, lurking somewhere in the shadows. Asra and Tasha backed into one of the buildings, seeking a place of refuge to cover their backs. Finding a tabled altar, they readied themselves for what may come.

Tasha jumped as the shattered shade of a man walked between them and disappeared. Asra turned to capture it with his magic, but it was gone. Moments later it reappeared but advanced towards them from the opposite side of the room. Asra once again attempted to seize it, but the wraith slipped from the grasp of his spell.

"You cannot harm me, warlock," a voice called in a tone that echoed upon itself.

They both stepped back in astonishment; not knowing what type of creature they were dealing with. Asra felt uneasy about its presence since he was unable to use his powers to stop the creature.

"What kind of spirit are you?" Asra demanded as he stood forward between them to protect Tasha.

"I am one of the unbound," it answered as the shade flickered in and out of sight, "there are many of us here who dwell within the outskirts of the Necropolis who have shed their mortal coil."

"What do you want from us," Asra demanded of the apparition which drifted ever near.

"Freedom," it answered bluntly, "as does any creature."

"Well ...ah, we can't offer you that," Asra stumbled on his words, as he was at a loss as to what the shade meant.

"This is a place where she does not belong," the phantom nodded towards Tasha who crouched behind her friend, "if you help me, I am willing to help you," it offered to him.

"What do you mean?" Tasha stood up from behind her friend and stepped to the side, "What is wrong with me?"

"The radiant essence of life within you is like the tune of a charmers flute to a nest of snakes within a basket," the wraith answered, "you cannot help but to attract the risen dead to your presence in this place."

Asra had recalled how the Djinn had mentioned something about Tasha being unwelcome in this realm, and what the spirit said next confirmed that his present blighted condition helped to shield him from perception by the undead.

"And what about me?" Asra asked the flittering shade.

"The cold mist of death surrounds you, warlock; you are like us and have no true power here," it answered.

"Perhaps we can strike a deal," Tasha intervened as Asra was lost in thought at the harsh words of the phantom, "we seek a potion to cure my friend of his condition. It was said to have been created by the elemental gods of long ago at a place called the Circle. If you can help us obtain it, simply tell us what you might want in return."

The wraith flickered in and out of existence for a moment as it considered her request. It seemed to pulse as though in a state of conflict with the subject of Tasha's appeal, but finally agreed to her demand.

"The place you seek sounds like the a great apothecary at the outer edge of the city which sits upon a vast precipice, but be warned that time has not been kind to its foundations and the edifice is on the brink of collapse into the void beyond. I can guide you there if you agree to find my physical body and destroy it in the lighthouse," the shadow replied.

Asra turned towards Tasha's confused gaze, for it seemed like a simple enough task to fulfill.

"What is this lighthouse you speak of?" Asra inquired.

"It is a beacon that flares once every cycle, lighting the way of the dead so they may find their way to it. It is the only place in this realm where my remains can be consumed and I may be rid of it forever," the shadow answered, "do that, and I will take you to what you seek."

"Sure ...take us to where your corpse lies and we will do that for you if we are able," Asra readily agreed.

"However, there is one more thing you must attend to before we can reach where it resides," the shimmering shadow replied, "first we must mask your companion from the dead, or they will obstruct you and tear her limb from limb to feed on her living flesh."

That result didn't sound pleasant in the slightest as Tasha answered with a glare of shock towards him. Asra's withered condition and granted powers of the jinn has altered his body which cloaked him from the dead, but Tasha had no such protections and Asra found his magics severely crippled within the boundaries of this realm. They knew not what she should do to protect her, so they inquired as to the means of that end. The phantom advised them of what was necessary, but its measure was far from easy to achieve.

"How may we hide her from the dead?" Asra inquired.

"She must don the armor of our grand Oracle, the dark mistress they call the Nocturnal," it answered.

Asra had heard that name before, recalling it from his

confrontation with the possessed child in the forbidden temple which led him to this fate. From what he remembered, this great oracle of theirs was someone, or something, that the followers of the A'ra greatly feared. They had been the guardians who staved off the Nocturnal, for they were delegated the duty as unholy guardians to the imprisoned demon which they held. Perhaps finding this being would grant him some answers to the trials he must face ahead.

The phantom was distrustful but knew they had to retrieve the set of archaic armor from within the temple of the Oracle before they could reach the lighthouse to obtain the physical remains of the ghost. The journey itself would not be easy, especially for them to procure the sacred armor with Tasha accompanying them. With that consideration, they agreed to leave Tasha at a secured building where she could wait in relative safety for their return. Asra and his ghostly guide ventured into the dark recesses of the city to fulfill their mission.

"How is it that you have come to be here," Asra asked his guide as they weaved through the labyrinth of buildings deeper into the metropolis, "...separated from your body where other souls are bound to theirs?"

The wraith remained silent for a long while to the point where Asra believed his question was being ignored, but was finally graced with an answer by the flickering spirit.

"The Necropolis is the place of the cursed beyond cursed, for those who reside here are shackled by the flesh and their earthly desires," the wraith began, "once in a great while there are those who see past this illusion of our rotting minds and choose to shed this material coil; but the nature of this place still binds us to it."

"So your curse was willful?" Asra asked in confusion.

"Aye, it was. However, this realm is designed to daze and befuddle our minds with decay, and we are blind to see anything but the path we have elected and can longer choose otherwise," the shadow conceded.

"Even though you have broken free, you are still bound to your body here?" Asra considered the wraith's odd dilemma.

"The nature of the Necropolis seals that bond, and only by the purification of our bodies can it be broken," the shade offered as an explanation, "thus, I remain here, cursed to wander alongside the walking dead who are bound to their rotting corpses."

The strange pair found their way into a wide avenue where Asra got his first glimpse of the undead. Their withered remains in various stages of rot left them staggering too and fro. There were those who seem whole, while others dragged their twisted limbs as they left smears of their own organs in their wake. The stench was something Asra had not been ready for, and the perfume of it nearly gagged him.

"At the end of this path lies the entrance to the Temple of our great Oracle," the shade noted, "but be warned that using your warlock magics will only bring unwanted attention to you," he further cautioned.

"And once we are inside, what should we expect?" Asra countered.

"There are powerful guardians who have dedicated their eternity to the protection of the Dark Mistress," the shade warned, "try to avoid them when you can, and if you should defeat them you must take whatever possessions they carry upon their person."

"You want me to rob the dead?" Asra spouted back in wonder as to what the phantom meant.

"Some carry coins and jewels or trinkets they once valued in a previous life. They are but tokens of what they once held dear, and removing them will release them from their servitude," the wraith suggested.

Collecting treasures from the dead didn't seem like such a bad plan, including that he would be relieving them from the burden of their wealth in the process. There was little he could do otherwise until he found a proper weapon to defend himself, for his magics in this place were severely stunted. The wraith could slip through the shadows unnoticed, but Asra had to wade through the lot of them. Choosing a path of least resistance, Asra soon found that the wandering dead could not be avoided.

He stepped forward with caution, coming face to face with their fetid stench and disintegrated flesh as the deceased among him wheezed and struggled for every breath they took. It was a nightmare beyond imagining wading among them, and he almost lost control of his stomach as he stood in the midst of the ghastly sight. Refusing to let fear overwhelm him, Asra pressed through to the edge of the grand temple at the end of the littered pathway. Once he reached the wide steps that led to the interior, he could see that the shrine was protected by several armored undead who stood guard armed with long rusted spears.

The shade had skirted the avenue as it flitted through the shadows and drifted to Asra's side. They both gazed upward at the great staircase and the set of plateaus he must ascend to reach the main structure.

"What do I do now?" Asra asked, "There are too many sentries."

"Walk past them," the shade instructed, "but slowly with your head bowed and they will think you are just another follower. Remember that they are reliving but a memory of what they once where, they recognize only threats, nothing more."

Asra took the wraith's advice and approached with his hand's clasps and head low, and avoiding eye contact with the guards; many of whom possessed none but hollow sockets in their rotting skulls. Asra began to notice a sparse few walking corpses also entering and exiting the great temple who also appeared to be reliving some forgotten past. They were but shadows of another time, recalling what they had done in life as a means of comfort in their endless eternity. Asra breathed a sigh of relief when he managed to reach the main landing, only to find another barrier set before him.

He stood by himself in contemplation for several aching moments as he waited for his guide to appear, and turned to see the shade stuck below at the edge of the flaming braziers. The phantom appeared to be blocked from entering the temple in its ethereal form as it flitted back and forth. Asra considered for a moment if he should descend down the steps to assist the wraith, but the attention of the undead guards turned towards him as he stalled. Considering the situation, Asra turned back towards the temple to complete his task which he apparently would be doing alone.

The ghostly wraith had not provided him with any details as to what this armor he was seeking appeared like; except that it belonged to the dark mistress they called the Nocturnal. At least it would be something that would fit Tasha's female form, he thought to himself. The central hall was filled with imposing figures of dragons sculpted into the stonework, along with many hooded priests among the procession who continued their piety after death.

This cursed place was far removed from the afterlife, which was reserved for those souls who passed through the gates at the Partition. The residents of the Necropolis had no choice in their extradition to this crypt, for they were the unclean. Their exile to this blighted place was the only way a natural balance in the ether could be maintained; for ugly souls must be kept in check or they would spread like a plague across the realms, corrupting everything they touched. Asra knew this was not a place he wanted to be trapped, and his thoughts began to stray on how they would be able to escape without the aid of the Djinn.

Asra had not counted on his powers being impaired and did not wish to worry Tasha so needlessly if he could help it. The guilt he had felt for his role in destroying the city of Ubar and its inhabitants started to wane, though he considered that he owed it as a debt to return her to the safety of her home village if he was able. They had both seen many strange sights which no living soul had witnessed before, and it made him consider his views of the world around him of that which dwells under the watery reflection of the living realm. He had powers that no mortal man should possess, and swore he would use them to create something fantastic and unique that would define him.

He could only use such forbidden knowledge to his advantage if they survived this journey and manage to escape this unholy realm. There was a malevolent overtone radiating from the design of the temple, for it was a filled with twisted columns and nightmarish engravings depicting demons and dragons swallowing the living. Everywhere he looked there were effigies of suffering and death, as though to remind the inhabitants of their sins that led to their fate. Once he breached the outer sanctum, Asra was met by an impassible obstacle.

The ridge of wide ascending stairs had hidden what lay beyond its crest. Below him now sat three bridges which crossed a vast chasm. The causeway to the far left had collapsed mid-section, with no way to pass. The path to the right held a growth of the strange curled wood which was prevalent in the architecture but had taken a life of its own at this juncture. Upon the center path stood two giants, twice as tall as a man and heavily armored.

They too were clearly undead, for their skin was gray and wrinkled and their armor was filled with gaping wounds as signs of previous battles. Around their feet lay the blades and armor of the vanquished, scattered like unwanted debris. Being unarmed and lacking in magic, Asra looked to the overgrown path at his best option to reach the shrine entrance on the other side. Cautiously circumventing the upper wards, he snuck his way down towards the bridge on the far right.

Donning pure white robes did nothing to help him hide among the shadows, and Asra paused in step when the rotting heads of the two giants turned his way. To his relief, however, they kept their post and made no motion to confront him. Proceeding to the overgrown bridge, Asra could now see that this path could likely have been the worst choice of the three. As he stepped forward, the barren vines twitched and tightened as though to strengthen their presentation to this wayward trespasser.

The coiling branches of the overgrowth were covered in long spines, each thorn capable of impaling a man whole. They shivered and lurched in spurts of growth the nearer he drew, which made Asra reconsider his decision. He

Michel Savage

had expected to try to climb his way through, but could now see why there were only sentries placed upon the central bridge. Picking up a bit of broken stone, he tossed it at the brambles blocking the path, only to jump back when vines lashed out at the movement as they violently poked their thorny spears at the tumbling rock until it finally came to rest.

Looking closer, Asra began to see the contorted remains of bodies within its tangles. Appendages had been ripped from their sockets where bodies where left skewered within its mass. The longer he looked, the more corpses he found intertwined within its foliage. Asra cautiously backed away and offered a wide berth to the pair of hulking sentries as he swept his way to the opposite side.

The giants glared at him through their armored helmets as he passed, stomping angrily as a warning that they could crush him like a bug beneath their heels. Their armor was of some ancient design held together by tattered bits of leather and chain. Their bladed weapons were monstrosities in themselves, being so enormous in size they could cleave through an entire squadron of men in but a single stroke. Asra skittered his way over to the collapsed bridge but the massive rift between the two sides left him in a state of despair.

As he stood on the edge of the precipice, a brazier on the opposite side suddenly burst into flame. Asra wondered what it meant and noted another pair of identical fire kettles along the opposite ridge which remained cold. Staring into the depth of the shadows, Asra noticed the ghostly figure of the shade dancing at the edges of the flickering light. Moments later the wraith appeared to him, now stationed on the opposite end of the broken bridge.

"Where did you go?" Asra petitioned the shimmering shade that stood across the void.

"The wards upon this temple are strong, and I was forced to use the shadows of the chasm for passage to this point," the phantom answered, "I can only aid you here, but I am unable to venture beyond this fissure."

"How can I cross?" Asra inquired with confusion written in his face as he pointed towards the central door, "Could you distract the giants so I could get to the entrance?"

"I am but the shadow of a man," the wraith answered, "I have no means of influence over them. However, this is only a barrier to the dead. Use your warlock powers to see this ravine for what it is."

Asra didn't fully understand what the shade meant but took his advice in mind. Asra closed his eyes and pulled at the strings of power within himself and opened them again to view the tethers of the world around him. He could now see the thin cord trailing from the wraith which tied him to his corpse far beyond the rift; he could also see the glare of the flaming brazier and how it reached out to span the broken gap between them. Looking deep into the gorge he recognized the darkness within and how he could use it to his advantage.

Asra uncoupled the magic lamp from his sash and held it before him; using the light of its glowing runes to cast a shadow of his foot as he lifted it forward. With delicate concentration, the shadow solidified and Asra found he was able to tread upon it. Step by step, Asra slowly passed above the rift until he reached the opposite side where the phantom awaited. Fastening the lantern back to his belt, Asra turned to marvel at what he had just accomplished.

"How is such a thing possible?" He wondered aloud.

"If you can imagine it so, it can be made so," the ghostly figure declared, "for dreams are but a shadow of something real."

"And the dead don't dream," Asra whispered to himself, having grasped the simplicity of the wraith's riddle.

"Thus, it is good that you are not dead, or you would have been blind to this path," the specter conceded.

Asra made his way towards the main entrance to the inner sanctum as the giant guardians grumbled and growled at him from behind for having thwarted their duty. At the doorway, Asra paused to ask for additional advice as his ghostly guide was unable to venture further.

"This set of armor you spoke of, what does it look like and how will I be able to escape this temple once I've obtained it?" he asked.

"As is the nature of armor, it will always appear to be the opposite of what it protects beneath," the wraith answered in another riddle, "and after you retrieve it, return here and find the darkest shadow and wait for me."

With that advice, the phantom flickered out and Asra was left alone. With a sigh falling from his lips, Asra turned back towards the inner sanctum to find the sacred armor of the one they called the Dark Mistress. There was little that could prepare him for what he was to discover as he delved deeper into the temple of the grand Oracle of the Necropolis. A turning point in his destiny was about to present itself, one which would forever tie him to this dreaded domain.

Chapter X
Tower of Deliverance

Asra was mildly surprised to note that this section of the sanctum was in a greater state of decay than the outer temple itself. Great troughs of fire lined the walkway to the innermost chambers, their glow illuminating the gilded ceiling above. There was a hum in the air which made him feel unsettled, the kind one hears during still nights in the desert. Here though, the brittle noise felt like a moan from the depths of the earth; like a never-ending sigh that eventually bleeds one's sense of sanity.

"I have been waiting for you..." a female voice filled the air, her tone held a biting accent like the hiss of a snake.

Asra stalled, not knowing were the source of the voice had come from; it was if the air itself was carrying her words into the hall where he stood. Most disturbing of all, she sounded familiar. Knowing he had been spotted by some mystical means, Asra quickened his pace into the depths of the temple. Passing broken stairways and toppled statues, the voice continued to follow him wherever he fled.

"I told you that your fate would turn," the female voice called, taunting him to remember where he had heard those words before, "but before you can reach my chambers you must face the trial of the Tali-ma!"

It was then that Asra recalled where he had heard that phrase before; it was the masked woman who had danced for the people of Ubar the night before the city came to its tragic end. This Oracle was the dark mistress the custodians of the unholy temple had spoken of. She was the Nocturnal this city of the dead worshiped. Asra was puzzled why a deity of the Necropolis would have visited the world of men.

"You, you were the dancer at the celestial temple..." the words escaping his lips as he remembered.

"Ah, so you do remember," the oracle cackled in mirth, "your destiny has come full circle now that you have entered into my folds."

"What do you want from me?" he replied with anger seeping into his voice.

"Fate has a way of twisting upon itself, and a few words from my sweet lips helped nudge you into my trap," the oracle confessed.

Asra searched his memory for the details of that night when the mysterious dancer had stolen his ceremonial dagger and lured him into meeting. She had filled him with fearful prophecy and foretelling which had led him to release the Djinn from its prison. The demon's escape had been her plan all along for she had guided his step by manipulating his actions that fateful day. Now he found himself trapped in her domain as an expected guest though he trespassed within the city of the dead.

"You tricked me into releasing the demon, but why?" Asra asked as he continued his pace deeper into the sanctum until he reached a stone platform surrounded by a shallow pit of flame.

"In all the days that have passed, you still don't remember who you are, my pet?" she asked with her slithering voice, "Or perhaps you have forgotten what you will become. You were my greatest servant; a minion of the Nocturnal."

Her words struck him, and he began to question if the Oracle was trying to deceive him once again into doing her bidding. Doubt cast within him, since he was still unable to recall who he was or where he had been before Tasha had found him stumbling out of the desert wastelands. Was his current state of amnesia blocking some traumatic past, or was it a consequence from being cast into the world of men? Asra's mind began to wander as he delved into the prospects of her accusation.

"How is that possible?" Asra blurted out, not wanting the possibility of such a thing to be true.

"It's easy to forget that the minds of mortals are such a delicate thing to handle," she admitted, "like soft clay they are; twist too hard and they break before entering the kiln. Far too many men fracture into shards after being reborn into something new. You, however, were one of my greatest sculptures."

"What are you?" Asra demanded, though his mind was still blurred by the revelation that he and this creature from the underworld were once in league together. It was not an idea that he relished.

"I do not explain myself to a mere servants, but will indulge in this instance as your ignorance amuses me," she stated as Asra stepped onto the central platform where there seemed to be no other avenue for him to continue, "you have served my designs from the world of men for many years, bringing the vile and unworthy to my gates. They serve as a reminder to those who pass beyond the price of transgressions against the gods in all their forms."

"You lie!" Asra blurted aloud, but his tone dulled as he sought his blank memory for the truth, only to find a cold darkness there that left him wanting, "I don't recall any of what you claim."

"So you are saying what you don't remember cannot

be?" The oracle laughed, "Oh, how convenient. If only that were true; look around you little man, you have crawled your way here through impossible odds to enter my arena, and here we are reunited. Thus, a servant comes at the beckoning of his master!"

Beyond the circle of flame the grinding of stone echoed through the chamber as carved walls parted to reveal the Dark Mistress as she lay upon a pillowed alter covered in saffron silk, her body was also draped in the same material upon which she lay while her arms and legs were gilded with polished jewelry of brilliant gold. Upon her head sat a strange crown of four bladed panels crafted to form a single mask which concealed her blind eyes. Asra knew well what horror lay beneath her golden visor and had no wish to view her face unveiled. Surrounding her throne lay piles of bleached skulls, lying in disarray as though discarded from a hasty meal.

"I don't serve you, Oracle!" Asra shouted back as he faced the dark mistress stretched upon her throne. Her nude body was no distraction to him this time, for he knew the monster she was beneath her disguise.

"Hmm, well, what must a girl do when a servant forgets their place?" She chided as she picked the dark talon of her nails, "Perhaps all you need is a reminder of who owns whom, my pet."

With those biting words, the Oracle gave a flick of her wrist towards him by which several drops of blood from her hand fell upon the platform at his feet. Asra stood back in terror when hands of burning corpses lifted from the pyre as they struggled to climb upon the stone terrace before him. Asra turned, but the pathway to the circle had been removed; leaving him stranded. A pair of smoldering undead turned to greet him with an unearthly fire glowing in the sockets as more dead behind them toiled to gain their footing upon the stage.

Asra was unarmed and had no way to defend himself from the onslaught bearing down upon him. He grasped to his waist to take hold of the magic lamp, only to struggle with the thought of discarding it into the fiery pit to be finally rid of it, or if he would be forced into employing his last wish to defeat these foes. Asra knew his powers were limited in this realm but remembered what the wraith had said about modesty and that the minimum use of magic can be just as effective given the situation. As the burning undead approached ever closer, Asra closed his eyes and concentrated.

Mystic fire was the element of the Djinn now embedded into his being, and as he held out his arm a scimitar materialized from his hand. The conjured blade glowed with a blue flame licking upon its length. He held up his sword in defense the very moment a rusted cutlass arched at his head from the first of the dead to strike. Blocking the blade, Asra slashed back and the cadaver ignited in a blaze of cobalt heat as it backed away and shattered into flaming ash before his eyes.

The adversary to follow attacked him with a spear, which Asra parried with his enchanted blade; also sending the undead antagonist into a pile of glowing ash. The dozen undead which crawled from the pit met the fate of the ones who came before, unable to resist the primal elemental flame of the jinn. Asra began to feel as though he was indestructible, but his vanity was short-lived as the number of undead rising to greet him soon doubled and tripled in number. Knowing he would be pressed back by overwhelming numbers, Asra sought a means of escape from the arena of fire and ash.

The shadow steps he had used before to cross the rift would not function in these conditions. Asra glanced behind him for a chance to withdraw from the fight and flee, but his glaze turned back towards the terrace where the Oracle lay in her gilded mask and knew he would not have a second chance to achieve his task. With magic tendrils pouring from his hand he raised the piles of ember and ash of the dead and constructed a path above the encroaching horde. As the bits of burning cinder and dust wove together to create a bridge to the balcony upon which she sat, the Oracle stood to her feet with an expression of bewilderment and anger.

"What sorcery is this?" The oracle demanded in defiance, "I did not grant you such powers!"

Asra rushed forward upon the bridge composed of ash beyond the reach of the dead to stand before the Oracle above the circle of fire. Asra expected the dark mistress to defend herself with magics of her own but was mildly surprised to find that he could breach her defenses so easily. He leapt atop the stone alter upon which she had laid and held the edge of his flaming scimitar to her throat. The oracle appeared frozen with fear as the flames licked at her exposed flesh, burning her.

"Stop this!" Asra ordered as he held her in check.

The dark mistress made a motion with her hands and chanted ancient words as Asra turned to watch the fiery undead crawl back to their smoldering grave. By then the bridge of ash had dissipated into flecks of dust that drifted upon the hot coals surrounding the stage below. A tinge of confusion pierced his thoughts, considering that the goddess of the underworld could control the dead with the wave of her hand, but yet appeared to be as mortal as he. It then occurred to him that the Oracle needed her enchanted armor to mask her from the army of undead which inhabited her realm; for she too was a living soul.

"Do not harm your Mistress, or you will face the wrath of every cursed soul in the Necropolis," she warned in an attempt to regain her dignity as she withdrew her neck from the burning blade.

"I do not serve you, witch!" Asra barked back as he saw she was helpless without the corpses to defend her, "I am here for the armor of the Nocturnal."

"Ah, no, no," she snickered with the false mirth, as she was but a slave to her own arrogance, "I cannot allow that. I order you to return to whence you came and continue your servitude under my rule."

Asra gave the blind woman a glare of disdain, having considered the measure of her vanity. He had trespassed upon her lair within the vast city of the dead and placed her at the end of his blade; yet she still blustered with a sense of entitlement. Asra thought about killing her then and there to be rid of this conceited witch; but stalled in this act which meant that she knew his character better than himself.

"I have no intention of bowing to your will, sorceress," he spat back, "and I'll take my chances with the undead even if it means forcing you to join their ranks," Asra glared as he pressed his sword towards her once again.

Seeing that Asra had truly forgotten whom he was and the mystical powers he had acquired since they last met, the oracle motioned with her arm towards an open crypt behind her where there sat a pile of dull plate armor lying among freshly picked bones and dismembered bodies. Asra lowered his hand and the flaming blade snuffed from existence as he approached the stone sarcophagus.

"Why would you need such a thing?" The oracle countered as Asra picked up the metal greaves and bracers, each delicately sculpted to represent the exterior of a rotting corpse. Even the breastplate and helmet were carved to mirror a state of decay, with bone and sinew and writhing worms artfully encased within the dull steel.

"I will let you live this once, cursed witch," Asra warned her as he gathered the armor while ignoring her question, "but before I leave, tell me who I am?"

Even without her eyes, an expression of wonder turned to amusement as she began to cackle with her horrible voice, taunting him as he stood before her as a grim glare formed in his cold eyes.

"How could such a warrior of darkness forget that he is the eater of souls?" she laughed, "You, the Betrayer; forsaking your own vengeful nature?"

Asra backed away, stunned by her words; not knowing what to believe. He turned and jumped to the pathway below the raised deck and dashed back through the torch-lit halls; quickening his pace as though to escape his secret past. Once he arrived at the fissure with the three bridges, the wraith was there to greet Asra upon his return. The shade drifted to his side as he stood facing the bridge where the two giants turned towards him.

"Good, you have recovered the armor, we must return to your friend, quickly!" The wraith stated as they looked up to see the giants crossing the bridge to greet them.

The wraith slunk back into the shadows while Asra was left alone to face the two behemoths as they lumbered towards him, slowly swinging their weapons with cruel intent. Asra glanced towards the broken section of the far bridge where he had first crossed but had only done so with great concentration. He could see that he had no such allowance as the pair of goliaths bore down upon him. In comparison, his conjured sword was a simple parlor trick that would provide little defense against their massive strength.

Asra backed away towards the bridge entangled with overgrown vines, their barren stems covered in jagged thorns. There was little Asra could do after the giants passed to the far end and blocked him off from access to the central crossings. He turned and headed towards the mass of thorny roots as the creeping shards twisted in anticipation the closer he drew. Within moments he found himself cornered between the hulking ogres and the twitching plant daring him to come within its reach.

Asra fumbled with the loose bits of armor, trying to keep from dropping them as he considered what little options he had. It was then that he noticed the helmet itself had a moving visor with carved eye slits, which he found quite odd since the Oracle herself was blind. It then occurred that this set of armor was likely not personally created for her, but was actually an ancient relic passed down to succeeding masters of this realm. The dark mistress was but a provisional occupant of the Necropolis; a city of the undead ruled by a living queen.

The phantom drifted in from the shadows beneath the bridge and faced Asra as he prepared to defend himself. He had considered using his magic to burn away the animated foliage, but the shade offered another option.

"Use the helmet of the Nocturnal;" the wraith advised as Asra wondered what purpose that would serve, "it is an icon of power in this domain by which the inhabitants of the Necropolis regard as their crown of rule."

Taking the helmet into his hands as the giants loomed over him; Asra placed it upon his head and dropped the visor. The rotting monstrosity stopped mid-swing as the enormous rusted axe came within a breath of Asra's armored head. The beast slowly pulled the weapon away as though in a state of confusion and both giants took a respective step back. The tension could be felt in the air as Asra looked towards the wraith for suggestions on how to wield this newfound power.

"The armor itself is enchanted for use by the ruling body of the Necropolis; an ancient artifact passed down through the ages to its successors," the phantom stated, which confirmed Asra's suspicions.

"The dark mistress herself is not one of the undead," Asra noted from beneath the helm.

"Only the living can rule over the dead," the wraith answered as it looked towards Asra under his steel helmet which had been carved to imitate a rotting skull with sculpted sinew and skin peeling from its bone, "you can now command her temple sentries to do your bidding; for they see you as their rightful master."

Asra understood now the power of the armor, which not only protected the living mistress from the undead but also served as a symbol of royalty in this cursed realm. Stepping aside to allowed passage, Asra pointed towards the writhing briar.

"Clear that path," he ordered in a stern tone towards the hulking giants.

Without hesitation the pair of ogres lumbered forward and heaved their massive weapons into a woven mesh of spikes and thorns, cleaving them asunder. The unruly weed did not take kindly to such abuse and reacted violently to the attack. Vines snaked up the legs of the giants to pierce them with its spines which gouged into their rotting flesh. Chunks of wood and barbs went flying as the enemies clashed while Asra shielded himself from the flying debris.

One of the giants became entwined in a thick limb that constricted about its torso and held it fast while its enormous sword fell to the ground mere feet away from crushing Asra where he stood. The remaining leviathan hacked away at the heart of the disorderly plant as it sent long thorns lancing through hits decaying body. Bits of flesh and armor were ripped apart from their struggle until the giant gave a final swing of its axe and severed the central vine.

The foliage shuddered and curled as it collapsed while the giant stumbled and fell onto its bulky rump; weakened by the numerous injuries it had suffered in the skirmish. With little resistance left within its massive frame, the remaining giant slipped back over the lip of the stone bridge, pulling the enwrapped vines harpooned within its body down into the fissure. The first giant entangled in the coil of vines fell hard against the bridge; the impact nearly shattering the stone causeway. It too slowly followed its comrade and rolled off the surface and tumbled into the void below as the remaining branches were ripped from the walkway.

"Well now, that was easier than I had imagined it would be..." the wraith expressed as an afterthought.

Asra removed the helmet and crossed to the other side where he climbed to the upper plateau of the temple before beginning the long descent to the streets of the Necropolis. They found Tasha hiding on the upper floor of the abandoned building where they had placed her; seemingly shaken by something that left her unsettled. Asra dropped the set of armor upon the floor and came to her side, wondering what was wrong. What she had to say left him just as disturbed.

"Are you alright?" Asra inquired while he helped her to stand where she had been hiding, crouched within the open door of an antechamber.

"You were gone for so long I was worried that something happened to you and that you wouldn't return, so I began to search the outer streets to see where you went," Tasha admitted, "but that strange wind we encountered in the gardens before began to pursue me."

"Most interesting," the wraith replied, "for there are no such tempests within the Necropolis."

"What happened?" Asra asked as made their way to the bottom floor where the pile of enchanted armor lay.

"I was looking for you when a dark wind started howling through the streets. I made my way into a building when it followed me inside and began to tear up the chamber around me like a cyclone," Tasha answered as she relived the incident, "I didn't know if it was another shade or some type of angry spirit, so I ran back here. I could still hear it roaming through the streets, so I hid, not knowing what to do."

These were certainly strange happenings in a strange realm, but the wraith they encountered had no insight to add other than it might be an elemental spirit which had followed them here. They took some time to fit the ancient armor onto Tasha's torso and strapped it in place. When they were done, Tasha resembled a metal corpse in all her fashion; she even seemed to admire the workmanship of the engravings hewn upon the steel. Asra poked his head out the door to see if it was clear and turned back toward their phantom guest.

"So now you will lead us to this apothecary at the outer edge of the city?" Asra inquired as he waited for directions.

"I will fulfill my promise, but only after you release my body into the fire of the beacon," he answered.

"Where exactly will we find your remains?" Tasha asked so they could begin their task.

"Luckily for you, it is located at the beacon itself, the central tower in the middle of the city," the phantom gestured towards the midpoint of the metropolis where a lone pyre lit the air high above, "we required the armor for your companion, as the undead swarm the interior of the city to be near the beacon, for they are drawn to it like a moth to a flame."

The path before them through the broken streets and shattered buildings paled in comparison to the obstacles they were about to face. As they drew closer to the heart of the Necropolis the masses of the wandering dead seemed to thicken with every step. A grand tower stood before them as it loomed over the city where the walking dead stood shoulder to shoulder. Those with arms clawed at the sky as if attempting to capture the light of the flames above.

"What are they doing?" Asra whispered towards the wraith that flitted before them as they pressed their way through the thickening mob.

"The beacon has been here longer than anyone can remember and has become a symbol of our internment and suffering," the shade answered, "once every cycle the beacon flares and a single soul is allowed to be vanquished into oblivion to escape this damnation. Thus, as all icons of deliverance, it is worshipped."

Asra could understand the desperation of these rotting souls as he strode through these wasting corpses and the despair etched upon their decayed faces. Although he found it slightly strange that Tasha walked with them in the full set of enchanted armor of the Nocturnal, but the undead did not pay her any heed as one might expect of a ruler of the underworld.

"We have arrived, and it is there you must climb," the wraith stated as the trio reached the main door of the lighthouse. Its panels were made of bolted iron bindings, narrowly designed for but a single person to enter its primeval bowels.

They pressed past the writhing dead and approached the main door, only to find it firmly sealed. Their shadowy companion disappeared into the crevices between the seams only to reappear moments later.

"It's locked" Asra announced the obvious.

"There is a mechanism which latches the entry that I cannot operate in my current form," the shade admitted, "you must use your warlock powers to open this portal, but take care not to damage the door."

"Why the concern?" Asra replied as he brought forth his hand to concentrate on his jinn induced magics.

"If the passage to the interior of the tower is liberated without check, then you will likely be overrun by the dead seeking salvation in the sanctified pyre above," the shadow warned, "you can bypass the lock here, and here," the shade answered as he lightly grazed the iron door in two spots near the hinges, which appeared to flare to his touch as though the iron was a bane to such phantom spirits.

Asra concentrated on his handicapped powers, knowing he could only manage something meager compared to his capabilities. He touched the panel where the ghost had indicated and pressed his mind to see beyond the metal; his hand suddenly clamped to the iron door as though magnetic. With great effort, he lifted the hidden latch on one side of the portal as he duplicated the process with his hand on the other at the same time. There was an audible click as gears beyond the stone facade began to turn and the paneled door slowly opened.

"You must be quick!" the shade cautioned as it swept inside the doorway.

Tasha headed into the narrow passage beyond as did Asra to follow when dozens of undead in the immediate area began to notice the door was ajar. The attention of the horde turned as they began to swarm towards the entrance while the panels began to shutter with sluggish speed. Asra realized that they would be overrun before the door could seal and would be blocked open by the press of restless bodies forcing their way inside. He drew on his powers to stave off the encroaching mob but was further drained from the exertion.

"Stand back," Asra warned towards Tasha as she pressed herself behind him.

Azure flames began to spray from his fingers as they washed towards the gathering horde. He had thought that it would repel the undead, giving the iron doors time to close; but it had the opposite effect. The first few undead that wandered into the lapping blaze caught fire and began to writhe in pain as they were consumed by the magical flames; which, however, drew ever more of the cursed dead towards the fiery source of final deliverance from this dreadful place. Seeing this, Asra withdrew his magics and attempted force the doors shut from within.

"Stand aside and let the girl try!" The shade suggested, though the statement brought a look of confusion from Tasha as she stood in her enchanted armor.

"Ah, yes, command them to stay back," Asra instructed her to follow the wraith's advice.

Tasha stepped forward with apprehension, not realizing the powers of the ancient armor. Supporting herself upon both narrow walls of the corridor, she leaned forward to stare down the advancing undead.

"Begone with you!" She shouted with a measure of doubt that such a foolish tactic would have any effect.

Tasha stepped back as the horde continued pressing forward in the moment to follow until the foremost corpse gazed upon her helmed face. More zombies behind it also were drawn from their mindless attack to the attention of the one who wore the badge of the Nocturnal. With slow response, they resentfully pulled themselves away as though forced to obey her command while the iron doors finally sealed shut. With a sigh of relief, the trio turned to ascend the thousand steps within the narrow stairway.

"If your body is at the top of this tower, why didn't you simply release yourself into the burning pyre?" Tasha began to wonder as she questioned the floating phantom before them.

"Because I sought to cheat death as I had once cheated in life," the wraith answered coldly.

Chapter XI
Shades of Deception

After ascending several dozen floors both Asra and Tasha began to feel envious of their shadowy comrade who drifted with ease up the narrow stairway. The climb began to take its toll on their strength the higher they progressed towards the pinnacle. Asra tried not to dwell on the phantoms' words as they made their way, but wondered what he had meant all the same. After a great deal of grief, their aching muscles forced them to take a rest before proceeding further.

"This passage was not meant for the living," the shade acknowledged with a note of sympathy.

"How much longer to the top?" Tasha appealed with a huff of breath.

"I cannot say, for I no longer perceive the passage of time as a result of being entombed within the Necropolis, which is why this tower serves as a beacon of both hope and despair," the shade concluded.

"Hope can be a powerful drug," Asra conceded.

"As despair can be a potent form of torture," the shade added to his words.

Gathering their will, they made their way higher up the tower with Tasha taking the worse of it as she bore the set of armor. However, the wraith warned her not to discard it as they had yet to escape the tower and make their way to the alchemist shop at the edge of the outer borders. With great endeavor, the three allies ascended the monolith until they reach the roof which opened to expose a great cauldron filled with smoldering embers.

The pyre was filled with molten ash dancing with streaks of blue flame; eerily similar to the mystical fire of the jinn which Asra possessed.

Surrounding this enormous kettle lay several gargoyles cast from iron. As he circled the rooftop, Asra counted a total of seven horrid beasts formed in the creation of nightmares. Daring to touch one, he confirmed they were sculptures, though formed with exquisite detail. The shade drifted over to one in particular, which upon closer inspection revealed a broken corpse of flesh and bone tightly held within its sharp talons.

The claws had been wrapped around the cadaver in a deadly embrace. There was no logical way the withered body could have ended up in such a position unless the statue itself had seized the corpse within its grasp and solidified into its current state. The thought of this caused Asra to take a cautious step back as he turned towards the shade which gazed upon the horrid scene in silence. Tasha approached and caught herself with a gasp when her eyes fell upon the disturbing scene.

"Ah, is ...is that your body?" She begged to ask.

"It is," the wraith answered after a long pause, "and you must reclaim it from this ghoul, and cast it into the pyre."

"How did it come to be here in this manner?" Asra inquired with a wary tone.

"This monument has been here since the Necropolis came into being. It towers above all other buildings so the dead may gaze upon it as the symbol of absolution and a reminder of their imprisonment for their vile deeds. For those who dwell here it serves as a constant reminder of their shame for which they suffer, and that only once in a great rotation a single soul is allowed to escape this eternal torture," the wraith explained.

"So, it's like a lottery to escape this cursed place," Tasha suggested.

"Exactly," the phantom responded, "but not for anything as petty as greed, but for a prize which draws ultimate regret. The dead have no concept of time here, as I, too, stood by the lighthouse door for what seemed like an eternity waiting for it to open so that I could seek a final escape. You see, the tortured souls here do not ascend, but are forever extinguished, and are left as nothing but ash," the shade motioned towards the smoldering kettle, "however, as my mind wandered upon the evils I had done in life that led me to be exiled within this realm, the door had opened once again, but another wretched soul had wandered within that decisive moment."

"Yet your corpse is up here?" Tasha responded.

"Anguish is a powerful incentive for who had spent their life deceiving others, so rather than face further torment I chose to scale the tower and reach the sanctified flames before the chosen one had ascended there," the shade answered, "once I reached the top, each of these demons were waiting for the anointed soul who had entered; which I was not."

"Then what happened?" Asra wondered, though the consequence of that fateful day sat frozen before them.

"In my impatience, I had not considered that there would be such wards to protect this place which held their berth against the unworthy," the wraith explained, "and this iron golem seized and crushed my body, to be forever held captive within arm's length of my salvation."

It sounded like a terrible fate; for the phantom knew it would never have a chance to escape this netherworld. However, now that members of the living had trespassed into his realm, the wraith had found another chance to cheat fate. His broken body had been held within this cage of iron claws while its ethereal soul was released back into the Necropolis, unable to interact with anything of physical form. It was a torment worse than he could have ever imagined.

Through countless centuries the phantom wandered through the shadows, finding the ability to explore nearly every crevice and hollow within this cursed city. The temple of the Nocturnal was the only place veiled from his curiosity as the specter was left to wander as nothing more than a feeble shadow. Flitting among the undead as a ghost, the wraith even began to envy their pain from decay and rot; for he had forgotten all senses except the bitter feeling of regret. But he now had the chance to separate the tether from his mortal coil anchored within the talons of this iron golem.

"How can we get your body free?" Tasha considered, for the statue had his remains enfolded tightly within its metallic grasp.

"Every time the bell tolls the flames claim another soul, I return here to watch as these monstrosities accept the chosen and rip them limb from limb to cast them into the pyre; only to retreat to the hollows where they now stand," the shade answered.

"Should we try to tear you free?" Asra asked, not really relishing the idea of ripping a withered corpse apart by hand, but apparently keeping it in one piece didn't matter.

"And what is the plan after we get rid you of your mortal body?" Tasha asked as she stood at the edge of the tower overlooking the vast maze of the Necropolis.

"We must find our way through the labyrinth of streets past the mausoleum of the Collector to the edge of the rift, there," the wraith pointed out across the city, "that building at the very edge is the ancient abode of the seer of the divinities who once ruled this dark kingdom."

"You mean the god's had once resided here?" Tasha inquired with an air of surprise.

"From what I have learned in my wanderings is that the old deities once ruled this domain; one which they had abandoned long ago and left to the blighted souls of men. What was once a utopia of the gods is now but a broken and rotting graveyard of their failures," the phantom replied with a hint of sorrow.

"What is this mausoleum you spoke of?" Asra asked as he joined Tasha by her side to gaze out upon the city below. From this height, he could now see a dark swirling void which encompassed the city on all sides.

"There you will find an assortment of creatures left behind from the ancient world. Beasts from a time beyond our own placed in receptacles among its twisting catacombs," the wraith answered, "within its walls lies the remains of what were once noble creatures ...but it is now nothing more than a museum of death."

Asra stared out across the vast city, seeing no other way to reach their goal but among the winding paths through the vaults of the Collector, which the wraith had spoken of. Their route would be much easier to follow with Tasha wearing the enchanted armor to mask her from the undead and their spectral ally to guide their way. Once he had attained the elixir to cure his blighted condition, Asra considered they could skirt the edge of the rift until they made their way back to the bridge of silence whence they had come. With luck, the fortitude of his jinn powers would return on the far side of the bridge, and he could create another rift gate to return them to the world of the living.

Trying to assess how they could free the wraiths physical body from the statue, Asra considered the risks of using his powers on such an ancient ward. Waking such a troublesome beast from its rest might prove a hazard, especially if doing so stirred the other half-dozen demons from their sleep. Being torn limb from limb by a pack of metal statues, against which his meager magics would have little effect, did not bode well for their chances of surviving such an encounter. Asra had no choice left but to try since the phantom was adamant about freeing his tethered soul before he would guide them further on their journey.

"Step back and I will attempt to peel away the statue's arms," Asra warned as he began to concentrate on his powers while standing before the great effigy.

Little by little, glowing points began to appear along the burly arms of the metal beast as Asra attempted to soften the metal of which it was made. The process seemed to be working until the eyes of the beast suddenly flew open, revealing blazing yellow embers beneath, and the statue shrugged from its paralyzed stance as it came to life. Tasha and the wraith withdrew several steps, but having nowhere to retreat. Asra was caught dead in the middle of the beast's angry glare as it began to beat it arms in a tantrum and growled in rage.

The sound of its howl had a horrible hollow ring which also resonated with every step the creature made as it stomped towards Asra, who had ceased his magics and readied to defend himself. He realized that a sword of flame would have little effect on such an armored creature, and faltered in his step. Falling backward, the golden lamp unclipped from his sash and was sent skidding across the stone floor. The rune-stone stopper jostled free of the mystic lamp and sapphire smoke began to plume from its spout.

The metal beast was only slightly distracted by the mystic smoke as it spewed from the lantern, and bore down upon Asra where he lay helpless upon the stone tiles. The elemental jinn materialized at the moment the creature was about to crush Asra where he was sprawled defenselessly upon the ground. Asra held up his arms in defense, realizing it would do little to protect him from being ravaged by the metal beast. The creature's razor claws came within inches of rending his flesh when it was suddenly swept away by a deflecting forced, sending it crashing into the stone niche where it once stood.

The metal beast recovered, tossing aside the tattered corpse it held in its arms and turned its glare towards the Djinn which had defied the creature of its prey. The full temper of the jinn turned against the beast as one demon battled another. The iron beast took a swipe at the Djinn only have its claws pass through smoke as the genie was left unharmed. The jinn countered with a blast of cold fire as wind sucked from around the tower and slammed into the creature as it struggled to attack.

Frost began to form across its jagged surface until fractures started to appear upon its iron skin. After several moments the beast once again froze into place and the glowing embers in its eyes snuffed out. The genie turned as the eyes of the six other statues began to open and their bodies animate upon their pedestals. Asra's servant jinn turned to glance at him once with a disapproving glare then held his palms together and began to mumble the chant of an ancient tongue which flowed from his fanged lips.

Slowly, the statues began to cease their awakening and

their eyes closed again as they settled once more into their place of rest. Once the last beast had fallen back into its rigid pose, the whispered mantra of the Djinn faded and he turned his attention back towards the pair of mortals and their spectral friend.

"My master, you should not be in this wicked place," the jinn spouted as he folded his arms across his chest with an added scowl.

Tasha bolted over to help Asra up while the ghostly wraith drifted to the source of the jinn issuing from the fallen lamp. The mystic smoke that formed the jinn flowed around the phantom as though it were something solid as the ghost tested the strange mist. Asra stood up to gather himself and walked over to pick up the golden vessel to which the genie was tethered. He could now understand how the spirit of the wraith itself was also anchored to its mortal vessel; which left him thinking about how he could dispose of the lamp itself.

"I did not summon you, nor voiced any desire your assistance ...so why did you protect me?" Asra inquired.

"You were in danger, my Master," the jinn stated as though the answer was obvious.

"But you could have easily let me died then and there," Asra motioned to the cracked stone floor where he had lain helpless before the beast, "and you would have been released from your final charge and gone free."

"There was another danger at hand, and I would not wish to see harm come to you," the demon offered, "and I have an obligation to fulfill my final duty ...as a matter of honor, of course."

Asra flashed the Djinn a suspicious glance as he turned back to Tasha while they conferred with the wraith who was relieved that his remains had been freed from the grasp of the iron golem. Floating over to it, the phantom seemed to stare down upon the body with an expression of pity and remorse; seeing how his own decayed face had turned into something pathetic and unrecognizable. After a long moment, the wraith backed away as though to swallow its own final regrets as his pair of living colleagues in this endeavor approached to help heave the broken corpse into the sacrificial pyre. The wraith nodded towards them as a signal that he was ready for this final act to be done.

"So we just toss it into the coals and you will finally be freed?" Tasha inquired one last time as she took one end of the cadaver while Asra grasped the other.

"Yes, once it is consumed, then you will have fulfilled your pledge and I will take you to the citadel to secure the alchemy which you seek," the phantom returned.

The jinn gazed silently as Tasha and Asra lifted the crumbled corpse and heaved it over the edge of the great brazier and let it tumble into the smoldering embers. The withered remains flared as blue flames began to dance around the body, feeding upon the dry flesh and bone as fuel. Several moments passed as the cinders slowly consumed the body whole until only the skull was left turning into hot ash. Asra looked towards the wraith as it began to fade in and out of existence as the last of its remains were being devoured by the sacred flames of the ancient shrine.

"What is happening to you?" Tasha asked as they stepped away when the phantom began to dissipate before their eyes.

"I am finally free of my torment," the shade granted with a whispered sigh.

"But you were supposed to help guide us through the

labyrinth to find the elixir!" Asra professed with a tone of betrayal that the wraith was abandoning them.

"Don't be surprised, Warlock, for I had warned you that I was a deceiver; and it has been a long road to cheat death towards this final end," the apparition confessed.

"How will we find our way?" Tasha pleaded; her question directed towards the fading shade, "Where can find a way to escape this awful place with our lives?"

"Within the halls of the museum you may find your answer," the wraith replied, "for the gods that once ruled this place have left tokens for those who follow; but be wary, for we are only shown what they want us to see."

With that final word the specter melted away before them and was no more. Tasha turned to Asra, who in turn faced the Djinn which hovered before them as though to seek some measure of advice from the mystic creature. However, Asra knew that asking for any such favors from the elemental would only end in them being stranded and the jinn would be free to enact its wrath upon the world of men. Looking towards the cauldron and the sanctified flames glowing within, his curious gaze was caught by the Djinn who began to suspect that his troublesome master was scheming something unpleasant in that moment of thought.

"We have to make it through the labyrinth on our own," Asra finally admitted with a shrug as he motioned for Tasha towards the stairway to start their long descent to the streets below.

"Or, I could gather the elixir for you, my Master," the jinn offered in service.

Asra paused for a moment, knowing full well that to make any request would be the end of their contract; but also remembered that the elemental demon had rescued him without need, and such a guardian would be handy to have should they find themselves in the face of trouble again. As exhausted as they were, it was tempting to take the genie's offer but chose to retain his last request for use only if he should find himself in dire need. Asra examined the golden lamp to make sure it hadn't been damaged in the scuffle but could not find the rune-stone which Tasha had given him so that he could plug the spout once more. This minor annoyance only led him to consider that he would have to watch his words within the presence of the magic lamp.

"That will have to wait for another time, Trickster," Asra delegated, "and it would be best that you return to your vessel during our journey ahead, and will call upon you when needed."

The misty demon flashed a sullen frown and a glare of contempt, but eventually considered it would be best to bide his time until he could weasel a way to slip free from his servitude. With a final glance towards the smoldering cauldron and with a weight of worry on his mind, the jinn conceded to Asra's command. The sanctified flames of the pyre could be fatal to mortal and elemental alike, but even if the enchanted lamp was destroyed by some force he would have to find a similar container to protect him in his weakened state. A human body would not be able to survive such energies in their entirety and would thus be forced to find another means.

With hesitation, the jinn finally resolved into returning to the lamp without further debate and dissolved into a haze which retreated back into the golden container. Asra tied the lamp back onto his sash as he and Tasha marched back down the thousand flights of stairs. Even the relative ease of descending the giant obelisk took its toll on their weary legs by the time they reached the iron door at its landing. By manipulating the clasps anchored upon the hinges they were able to pry the portal open and slip outside.

What they found there shocked them both, as a large stack of charred corpses were now heaped into a pile, as though they had launched themselves upon the few undead Asra had set aflame when they had first entered the tower. The dead had sacrificed themselves to escape the eternal torment of the Necropolis. They realized now that the mystic flame of the jinn drew the undead like a moth to a flame, but did so in a suicidal frenzy. He would have to be frugal with his use of the jinn fire in this realm, for it could ultimately become a liability.

They promptly headed off in the direction of the mausoleum by using landmarks they had memorized from their previous vantage point atop the tower. Through wandering hordes of the dead, the two companions weaved their way through the streets until they came upon a massive gate of twisted bars. Strange lettering of a long-dead language graced its archway while the path beyond took on a noticeable change. This could be the entrance into the museum of the ancients that the wraith had mentioned; the primal halls belonging to the Collector.

"I need a rest," Tasha noted as she sat down upon a broke ledge, weakened by hunger.

They had not eaten since their long journey began from the festival in Ubar; which now seemed like a century ago. Asra wondered what he could do to help alleviate their appetite if there was something else to consume besides the abundance of old rotting bones. Finding a broken branch lying among the rubble in the street, Asra concentrated, knowing that moderation was the key to controlling his newfound powers. Manipulating the dead twig with his mind, a small shoot began to grow from the rotted wood as small green leaves unfolded.

Along its stem, a small bud appeared that blossomed into a white fragrant flower which was quickly replaced by a budding fruit. Tasha gazed over in awe while Asra wove his magics until a strange fruit resembling something between a fig and a pear plumbed into being. It soon ripened and then quickly began to rot before his eyes, so he halted the process with a minor effort.

"Oops, overcooked it a little," he blustered with guilt that soon turned into a chuckle as he turned to see that Tasha was watching him.

"Try it again," Tasha encouraged while Asra examined the ruined fruit.

Once again he beamed living magic into the twig and the process duplicated itself as the petals of the flower fell away and another bud appeared. Within moments another fruit materialized, though slightly different than the first he had made. He plucked it off its stem and poised to take a bite, but paused with slight hesitation and politely handed it to Tasha. She pulled off her helmet and tested the strange fruit with her nose, then dared to take a bite.

"Ugh," she grimaced, "it's bitter ...but not bad," she stated while taking a curious look to it innards before taking another chunk between her teeth.

"Sorry, but it's all I could imagine. I was trying for a fig or a mango, but couldn't make up my mind. I guess I got both," he smiled.

"But how did you do that?" Tasha asked as she gulped down the last bite, driven more by hunger than the acquired taste of the fruit, "You made life from something dead."

"The demon of the lamp said it uses what is present to weave its magic, to create something new from what is already there," Asra answered, "When I think of something, it's like I can feel it *become*; if that makes any sense?"

"Well, don't just stand there, make a few more; I'm famished!" She declared as Asra looked around for another twig to use in hopes he could harvest a slightly better variety.

Tasha sat gorging herself on the curious selection of fruits he was creating. While looking for more foliage to experiment with, Asra came across a broken skull. It looked ancient and old, though not quite human. Though it was missing its jawbone, there was something odd about its shape. With little pause, Asra began to consider something that he hadn't thought of before.

"I wonder if I can bring the dead back to life?" He whispered aloud as the bizarre idea began to take ahold in his curious mind.

Chapter XII
Necromancy

Tasha got up from where she was sitting while spitting out a few seeds from the fruits she had consumed and went to join Asra where he stood examining the bones he had found. After contemplating the applications of his powers, Asra tossed away the skull and they turned to face the dark path before them. Somewhere beyond lay the manor of the alchemist where the cure they sought lay within. Getting there would be tricky, as these braided trails contained twists and turns which could easily lead them astray from their desired path.

"Which way," Tasha asked as she stepped back to retrieve her helmet.

"From what I remember, there were several parallel avenues which interconnected halfway through passages which make up these catacombs," Asra conceded.

Leading the way, Asra tried to navigate their path the best he could while considering the thoughts he had earlier began to sprout with possibilities. If he could raise the dead back to life, that could certainly help them in their quest. It was a wild idea that was worth experimentation when he found the chance.

The lane they were on was fitted with high arches that spanned the cobbled road where the facades of several buildings joined each front side by side. Many of the structures were laced with multiple doorways while others had large open portals as though to invite observers to explore inside. Tasha was drawn to the sculpture of serpent coiled around a tall pillar outside one particular building and decided to step inside for a look. As her eyes adjusted to the gloom she could make out the skeleton of an enormous snake lying upon the floor; its jaws large enough to consume her whole. Its fangs were as long as lances though the carcass itself had been stripped of its flesh.

Sparking her curiosity, she hopped over to the building across the avenue and poked her head inside where she found a library full of scattered scrolls and battered tomes. Most were damaged beyond repair and crumbling into dust, but there were a scant few that revealed images of fantastical beasts drawn upon their faded pages. The titles and words that described each creature were drawn in a type of decorative script beyond her comprehension. Many of the beasts pictured within where of creatures she could have never imagined to exist.

"Do you think these are what the phantom was talking about?" Tasha asked as Asra strode in behind her while she pointed to the creatures portrayed within the tomes.

"I suppose so; the specter mentioned this place was a depository for some type of collection; so I guess these monsters are what they obtained for their little zoo," Asra answered with a raised brow.

Looking at these illustrations, Asra imagined that many of these beasts could be useful allies if he were able to conjure or reanimate their remains and bring them back to life. If there was a way to control such monsters he could gain greater power to help protect mankind from the retribution of the Djinn when it chose to enact its vengeance upon the world. Asra wondered if he should try to reawaken a smaller beast in an attempt to rejuvenate enough of its physical essence and fully revive its body. However, he did start to wonder though why this portion of the Necropolis was left entirely deserted by the undead?

"One thing is strange about this place," Asra noted aloud, "why do you think there aren't any wandering souls here?"

"I can only imagine that it may have been for good reason," Tasha responded with conviction.

Making their way out of the library they came upon several more statues gracing the exterior of the buildings; each one depicting unique monstrosities of frightful creatures from beyond their era. Their remains were left as nothing but parched bones and scattered skeletons upon the display floors of each stage. When they finally came across a room full of cages, Asra found what he was looking for settled within these small pens. The remains of something that appeared to be a type of bird seemed like a harmless enough subject to experiment upon; so he waited until Tasha's back was turned before he applied his magic.

Reaching into one cage he cupped the remnants of the creature within his hand while letting his power trickle into it; gently at first until he turned up the tap. Cold fire flickered into the fragile body and he watched with fascination as vessels and sinew reformed and flesh renewed. Suddenly the scene turned strange as the usual sapphire flame turned a deep red peppered with black embers. The creature in his hand began to twitched and jerked in violent seizures until it burst to life and seized upon his exposed hand.

Asra yelled in pain as blood drew from his wounded palm as the razor-taloned beast released his hand as it tried to fight its way out of the small cage. Its long whip-like tail was covered with small barbs, which shot out between the bars of the cage to thrash his arm. Tasha jumped forward to help fend off the creature and pulled Asra away. Another strike of its thorny tail lashed around her covered wrist but shrieked as its undead skin began to sear upon touching the enchanted armor.

Jerking her arm loose, Tasha felt the armor where it had been touched by the small beast which now sizzled with a strange unnatural cold. Backing away from the cage, the pest blared loudly with wild antics at it battered itself upon the bars. Becoming still for a moment, its dark burning eyes glared down upon them and then turned its attention to the small open cage door where Asra had reached inside. Within a heartbeat, the evil creature burst through the open hole and dived down upon them.

Backing away, Tasha fell over a toppled cage while Asra ducked for dear life as the winged creature grazed by him, slashing with its deadly tail. The creature climbed into the air and made its escape out the door; flitting down the street screeching its horrible cries into the darkness as it fled. It wasn't until the room had settled that Tasha got back to her feet and rushed to Asra's side to check his wounds. He bound his bleeding cut with a strip of cloth stripped from his sash became untied as his golden lamp toppled to the floor at his side.

The runes glowed and pulsated as a mist issued from the lamp; materializing into the jinn who had not been called. They looked up toward the mystic demon that gazed down upon them as he sniffed the air as though detecting something quite foul.

"I smell the stench of necromancy!" the Djinn cried, "What have you done?"

Asra got up and coddled his wounded arm with a doleful glance over to the broken cage. The genie closed its eyes and inhaled ever deeper to identify what they had encountered.

"You used the powers of the jinn to bring forth the dead?" The jinn declared with an angry eye towards Asra, "such a thing is sacrilege to the trinity. No elemental may commit such a vile unbalance upon the world, for it is a transgression to the sacred circle."

Asra was a might confused by the archaic verse the Djinn was babbling about; though he did get the gist of the incrimination. He had used his stolen powers to raise the dead, and doing so was strictly forbidden by the code of the ancient gods. He wasn't sure what kind of penalty he would enact by such a deed, but Asra was a little leery about doing so again considering the consequences he had suffered. He did, however, feel oddly weakened by the ordeal.

"Why is it forbidden?" Asra asked with mild ignorance as he revealed to Tasha what he had done.

"Life cannot be made from un-life," the jinn answered bluntly as thought that single phrase defined his question.

"But why so?" Tasha inquired, as she remembered the fruits Asra had made for them to eat.

"Magics of the Djinn draw upon what is present around us, and to draw life into a thing, life must be taken from another," the misty demon explained as he motioned towards Asra's wounded hand.

Examining it for the first time, he could see how withered it was compared to his other, as though his hand had been transplanted with one from a hundred-year-old man. His life had been literally sapped from him by reviving that little monster which had flown off into the darkness. Asra now knew what the danger was and how such a thing could run out of control. He felt ever more sapped by having used the jinn magics for such nefarious purposes and needed to gain the elixir to restore himself.

"I'm fine," Asra pulled away from Tasha's arm to grab the lantern from the floor, "you should return to the lamp until you are summoned," he ordered to the jinn.

With a grumble, the Djinn pressed his hands into a sharp clap and burst into a cloud which siphoned back into the golden lantern as the runes continued to shine brightly to light their way in the dark. Binding his palm to keep from looking at his withered hand, the couple retreated back to the streets to explore the labyrinth before them. They sought to make their way in haste, lest they too become a part of this morbid collection. Judging by the landmarks they had seen, they had a much farther to go until they reached the outer edge of the city.

Breaking over several lanes towards their target the two companions found themselves at an impasse. A great mass of bones from the remains of a colossal beast had been assembled to form a crude blockade. The reason for which was not entirely clear. Perhaps at some time in the past this avenue had been occupied by the living dead of the Necropolis but had long been left abandoned.

"We will have to circumvent this and choose another way," Asra suggested with a sigh as he gazed upon the great pile of bones before them.

"Or we could try to climb through it," Tasha suggested, "there is an opening here," she pointed.

Asra really wasn't in the mood for crawling through a pile of bones, considering they could displace at any moment and crush them into a pulp.

"I'm really not up for this," Asra whined as he tried to protect his injured hand.

"Come on, bring that light over here," Tasha prompted

while referring to the glowing lamp.

With reluctance, Asra followed her lead; not wishing to be left behind in case there was a shortcut through this mess. Unfastening the lamp from his belt, he held it high as they weaved their way through the forest of bones, trying to find a path to the other side. Hearing something that left the hair raised on the back of their necks, they both froze. The shriek of the creature from the cage had followed them into the snarl of bleached cartilage, tracking them from above.

Ushering Tasha to proceed with haste, they found themselves within the torso of an enormous beast as its ribcage lined their passage like ivory bars. The flying critter which had weaved its way through the jungle of bones found its way into the eye socket of a great skull. Once within the giant cranium, it burst into a dirty ball of black light. Without warning, the entire stack of bones began to shudder with a strange vibration.

They grappled onto the nearest handhold to keep from falling off their feet as the ground below them began to pull away. In moments they found themselves high off the ground entrapped within the belly of the leviathan's skeleton. Holding on for dear life, they slipped and slid within the ribcage of the monstrosity which began to stride through the broken streets and over buildings towards the source of their quest. Tasha couldn't but help to wonder what was happening.

"Are you playing around with your magic again?" She scolded, "You know what that blue demon said you about messing with dead creatures!"

"It's not me, I swear!" Asra replied in a tone of innocence, "I don't know what's doing this."

"Well ...can you stop it?" She pressed with urgency.

"I could try, but we are actually heading towards the place we need to go," he noted while pointing between the ribs to the apothecary at the edge of the city.

"I really don't want to be kept trapped within this monstrosity," Tasha pleaded with him, though seeing the irony of her having led them both into this predicament to begin with.

Asra securely tied the magic lamp to his sash by the handle and grabbed both sides of the monsters ribcage from within. With a note of afterthought, he turned back towards Tasha.

"Maybe you should hold on to me; I'm not sure if this is going to end well," he stated with a worrisome look etched across his face; which didn't elicit any confidence in his companion.

Asra tried to concentrate, though not trying to animate the walking skeleton, but in an attempt to siphon its strength. He was sure such a tactic would cause the entire structure to collapse to the ground but he was hoping to make it do so gently if he could. In that effort, he failed horribly. Once they were near the great citadel, the giant skeleton began to head toward the boundaries of the rift that would take them on a death run over the broken edge and into the void.

As Asra invoked his magic, several flashes of dark light exploded from the skull of the effigy and its movement began to stall. He lost his grip on the ribcage and went sprawling into the lower bowels of the beast as its pace began to fail and it started to stumble. Within moments the skeletal structure began to buckle upon itself and fall apart. Before they knew what was happening, the entire skeleton lost cohesion and they began to freefall towards the ruins below.

In a flash, a thick mist of azure smoke flushed out of the lamp tied around Asra's waist which enveloped Asra and Tasha as she held tightly onto him. They were whisked away from the collapsing mass of bones and cartilage which came crashing down upon the buildings near the edge of the rift. Several structures were crushed under its weight and went tumbling over the edge into the murky darkness beyond. The two companions embraced one another as they were enwrapped by the vapor which laid their feet gently upon the ground at a safe distance from the crumbling buildings.

The genie reformed itself from the ethereal vapor and reformed back into the blue demon they recognized. Asra looked down at the tether of smoke to his lamp and wondered again why the jinn had saved him without being directed to do so.

"You are safe now, my Master," the Djinn offered with grace as he bowed to Asra while they gazed back upon the destruction of giant bones which continued to tumble upon the crushed buildings until they finally came to rest.

As the skull of the colossus reached the ground it smashed into a dozen pieces, splitting wide open. From its cranium exploded a swarm of flying creatures which shrieked as they burst into the air.

"What was that?" Tasha inquired with her voice catching in her throat as she gazed upon the flock of flying rats with their razor claws and jagged tails whipping in the air like knives as they circled above.

"Those are butcher bats," the jinn explained as it looked towards the cloud of repulsive beasts and their horrible cries, "they were once a plague upon the seven kingdoms of the ancient world, which you have now revived," he answered as he offered an accusing glare towards Asra, "I had warned you not to use your gifted powers on such creatures."

"We were caught in the belly of some giant skeleton; how did those little beasts infuse themselves into a pile of bones?" Asra inquired with a measure of curiosity.

"Butcher bats kill their prey or infest the dead they find and lay many eggs within its host, during such time they would animate the dead body to so that it could move to a safe place to protect them while the eggs hatched. However, you had infused what was already dead with powers and created a beast born of dark magic. Such unnatural creatures can siphon such dark energies to propagate. By trying to hinder the creature you have only made the situation far worse."

"But we were only trying to escape from it," Asra responded in defense, "...and why did you save me a second time without being invoked?"

"I merely would not wish to see harm come to you, Master" the jinn answered in a dry tone which Asra found hard to believe.

Remembering what the demon had said before upon the roof of the tower that it had '*an obligation to fulfill his final duty*' to Asra via their sacred contract. He now understood that the Djinn could not let Asra simply die until he fulfilled his last wish, or the jinn would be forever trapped in limbo for a sacred pledge it could never fulfill. That meant that as long as he retained his last request, Asra could use the jinn as his personal bodyguard who would have to save him from any mortal harm. This was a twist of fate he had not foreseen, and a term of its vow he was certain the Djinn had been intentionally hiding from him.

Instead of asking the genie outright and call him on the

conditions of his pledge, he thought it wiser to keep what he suspected to himself for his own advantage. The jinn stood firm as the flock of angry butcher bats began to swarm in their direction, seeing the movement of prey. Turning behind them they saw that they had been transported over the length of the labyrinth and were now standing at the steps to the alchemist lab at the edge of the rift. The building was in questionable condition, but the wraith had forewarned them that it was at the verge of collapsing into the void.

Instead of demanding the jinn return to its vessel; Asra held the lamp with the misty demon trailing behind, half-formed in its state of appearance. They made their way into the entrance to find the building nearly half-gone. A great portion of its foundations had been left poised over the tip of the breach as several sections of the floor were pocked full of holes that stared into the oblivion below. Standing among the center of the ruins was a crystal box holding a glass container rimmed with golden horns.

"Is that what we came here to find?" Asra inquired to his misty servant.

"It is the sap of the heartwood from the tree of life blended with the waters of the eternal rivers, purified by the silver veins of the Eden leaves," the jinn answered as it gazed upon the ancient potion, "this is the antidote you seek, my Master."

The path to the altar upon which it stood was a dangerous path for them to plot, for it was riddled with shattered columns and pits into the darkness swirling below. Any tile or stone could give way and send him plummeting into the void or unsettle the bottle resting so precariously on the edge of disaster. He suspected that the jinn would rescue him if he should fall, but there was also the chance of losing the divine potion forever.

"How are we going to reach it?" Tasha wondered aloud, seeing the precarious pitfalls and stonework which could collapse upon them if it met any disturbance.

"My master," the jinn interrupted with sour news, "I must warn you that my powers are impotent beyond the threshold of oblivion."

"What does that mean," Asra responded, though the answer was quite obvious.

"If either of you should be cast into the void which braces the Necropolis in its place between the realms, you will be forever lost," the jinn answered grimly, "so I would strongly urge you to abandon this endeavor."

The demon's words hung heavily upon Asra's shoulders, for gazing into the swirling abyss beyond it was easy to believe his warning. This was a risk far greater than he thought it would be and the Djinn's own fate was also put at risk by his actions. To be reckless now might mean an end to his chances of revealing his history and escape the fate foretold by the Dark Mistress who had called him her servant. Since he had departed the Temple of the Oracle, Asra had pondered why she had called him the Betrayer, and what he may have done in his past to earn such a dishonorable title.

Chapter XIII
A Twist of Fate

Asra was embattled with himself; knowing he could not stay in his current withered form and return to a normal life, nor did he wish to risk his life after having struggled to come this far. To turn back now seemed an impossible task, yet it lingered upon his mind. He had caused the death of so many innocent people and destroyed the life of one who had only shown him kindness and hospitality, but here he was putting her life at risk to pursue his own selfish desires. He had obtained powers no mortal man should possess, yet here he felt helpless.

"We can't turn back now," Asra struggled with his conscious while the elixir was within his reach.

"What's done is done," the Djinn responded, "though salvation is but a wish away. I could obtain it for you if you so command."

Asra's eyes turned towards the demon, wondering if the risk was worth the reward. He could cure himself of the blight from the transference of jinn energies, but the demon would likely leave them deserted here in this place should he be unable to find a way out on their own. If he tried to combine both desires into one command, would the Djinn not try to trick his way out of it and leave them both stranded in some far forgotten realm? There would be no world left for him or homeland for Tasha to return too if this malicious demon was released from its contract.

Asra stared into the swirling mass of the abyss as he held the golden lamp within his hands; considering what little effort it would take to toss the lantern into the void and be rid of the demon forever. The Djinn had revealed that its powers were negated in the presence of the consuming darkness which swallows everything within its grasp. He didn't want to end his days here, wandering among these broken ruins hearing the groans the undead and cursing Tasha to such an existence. Turning to see her worried eyes behind the visor of the enchanted helm, he knew what he must do.

Asra carefully set the magic lamp atop a broken column across from the empty hollows where the floor had given way. He then turned to gaze up at the jinn who had a hue of apprehension chiseled upon his angry face while he looked down upon his mortal master. Once he had set the stage for the task, Asra chose to make a final command that would put an end to their contention.

"I have to admit you are right, Jinn; instead of taking the risk to gather the elixir myself I want you to collect it for me, and to return us safely to the forests of Fernwood, as my final wish," Asra commanded.

A quant smile slowly grew upon the genie's fanged lips as he knew his freedom was merely moments away. Once he had fulfilled his sacred vow, the jinn could return to the planes of chaos to regain his former strength. After such a respite, the demon could then enact his vengeance against all mortal men for the internment he had suffered. As the old gods were dead, there would be little resistance from him fulfilling his act of retribution.

"If that is your desire, my Master?" The jinn stated with a mindful tone, knowing he would hear the words that would finally break the binding pact between him and this insolent mortal.

"It is," Asra granted.

The jinn strengthened its form which was securely tethered to the vessel anchored upon the stone column and carefully drifted across the pitfalls open to the void below. The powers of the jinn were also severely restricted this close to the circulating rift which served as a barrier between realms. Without the use of his magics, the demon sought to secure the crystal case with his own hands and carry it across the rift. It was the only way to commit this task while protected his mortal master from any risk of harm before their contract was concluded.

The jinn paused as it wove along the path where the floor was still intact, though flecks of the mist which composed the demon were being leeched away by the vortex below. Reaching the crystal container, the jinn held it securely in its powerful arms and transported it back across the maze to where Asra stood. Setting it before him upon the giant table the jinn appeared to struggle with the strength of his tether to the lamp, having been weakened by the effort of crossing the void. The demon then took a single talon and pierced the outer casing, cracking open its crystal sheath.

The vial was a beautiful work of art. Its translucent bubbled glass was filled with decorative swirls upon a double teardrop shape. Upon each end where several intertwined horns gilded with gold, serving as a rest for the oddly shaped container. Deep within the thick glaze sat a liquid that almost seemed to pulse with a light of its own. Looking back at the counter from which it had been retrieved, there were also several smaller vials; most of which had been toppled or destroyed.

"Are you sure this is the correct potion?" Asra inquired, seemingly skeptical as he questioned the demon.

"I assure you that this is the antidote which you see," the jinn answered respectively, "and now for the second portion of your wish and my services will be complete."

"Hold on," Asra responded, "there are several other vials strewn amongst the rubble, so I need to make sure that this elixir works as you have claimed before we leave this place."

"The divine race who once ruled this realm were one with the spirits that were scattered among the realms long ago; their works are known to all the elementals," the jinn answered with a smug tone, "test it if you will, but be mindful to only take one drop for your mortal body would be strained by its affects if you drew more," the demon warned.

Asra held up the large vial in both hands and fiddled with the horns on one end to see if he could open the bottle. With great effort, he pulled and tugged at the golden antlers until the oversized vessel slipped free from his grasp and tipped upon a broken stone. Cracking open upon the rock, the contents spilled forth as Tasha and the jinn lurched back in shock. The capsule rolled away on its side, spilling the elixir along the way as toppled over the broken tiles and began to fall into the rift.

The demon, seeing that his unfulfilled commission was slipping away from the hands of the fumbling idiot dashed over to save the vial from falling into the bottomless rift. The jinn grasped the broken container as flecks of his essence were being stripped away by the vacuum of the fissure. It was at that moment that Asra stepped over to where the golden lamp rested and forcefully knocked the magic lantern into the open pit below the column. The glowing lamp tumbled into the abyss as the demon flashed an angry glare towards Asra who stood transfixed.

"How dare you trick the Jinn!" The demon roared as it abandoned the broken vial and reached out to grasp Asra in his dusty pale robes whose eyes were open in fear.

With a violent tug, the demon lurched back and tried to secure itself from the ethereal forces tugging at its misty form while anchored to the spinning lamp caught in the vortex below. The jinn fought against the fury of the cosmic forces of the rift, hungry to consume all who enter within its grasp. Seeing that he was losing the fight as his strength was being sapped away, the demon held forth a hand and cursed the mortal who had deceived him. There was a flash of angry flames from the demon's hand which shot towards Asra until Tasha stepped forward to push him out of harm's way.

Asra fell aside as the mystic fire engulfed her. Tasha screamed in pain as she crumbled to the ground, her resounding shriek causing the stones to crumble around them. The blocks of tile the jinn had used to secure itself began to dislodge from their fragile state of decay and came loose beneath him. With a furious rage, the beast roared as it was pulled below among the collapsing debris. The demon's wail echoed through the sullied air for what seemed like an eternity until its voice subsided to become one with the rumble of the void and the ancient Djinn was gone.

Asra gathered himself and rushed to Tasha's side as the mystical flame dancing around her still body flickered and dissipated. He turned her over to see if she was alive and was thankful that she still breathed. The enchanted armor of the Nocturnal had saved her but it was now fused with her flesh. Tasha's huddled form now resembled a corpse covered with a skin of silver; for in a violent flash of mystic fire her metal armor had now become her cage.

"Can you hear me, are you alive?" Asra pleaded with the girl branded in metal, "Don't die on me, Tasha."

"I ...I don't feel well," she managed to whisper with effort, "you lost your chance to cure yourself," she added with a sigh.

"Maybe not," Asra answered.

He stood up and stepped over to the shattered stones where the vial had burst open, finding a small pool of the elixir resting between the cups and cracks. He dipped his hand into what was left of the mystic liquid and gently brought the single drop of the potion wavering upon his finger to his lips. His body suddenly felt like it was covered in ice for a second as an itching rash ran through his veins. Looking down upon his hands, Asra gazed in awe as his withered skin faded and returned to its normal hue along with his former vitality.

Feeling no ill effects, he then carefully brought over another drop in his cupped hand for Tasha to consume. She looked at him with hurtful eyes as he pleaded with her to open her mouth to take the potion. She coughed and gagged in seizures as he tried to hold her still, but within moments her struggles subsided as her charred blisters were mended. However, Asra was confused to find that her armor would not come off. Although her obvious burns had been healed, the set of etched armor had somehow merged with her skin as though it were now welded to her body.

"Can you hear me?" Asra asked as he held her in his arms, trying to revive her.

Tasha rolled her eyes as she tried to regain her strength to speak. She held up her hand in front of her in a weak attempt to try to remove the molded bracer upon her arm. Failing to do so, she then tried to remove the helmet in vain; only to find that it would not budge.

"Something feels wrong," Tasha acknowledged as she became frantic trying to remove the armor from her body; but the fasteners had been burned away. There was nothing for her to unlatch or grip onto except the lip of the molded plating.

"Stop struggling," Asra advised as Tasha began to panic.

"Get it off ...I can't get it off!" She began to cry while wildly ripping at the armor as tears fell from her eyes.

"I can't," Asra tried to console her, "not at this moment. Settle down, Tasha, and try to be calm."

It took several minutes for the girl to stop struggling and realize her efforts were futile. The elixir had cured her wounds and saved her life, but had also melded her to the enchanted armor in doing so. Asra dared not attempt to use his weakened powers to tend to her strange wounds; if that is what they could be called. He found it ironic that at the very moment he had achieved a cure for his condition that one of equal detriment would be cursed upon his companion.

The building around them continued to crumble while the foundations further weakened by the struggle of the jinn which had pulled loose several supports. Debris crashed around them as more walls and pillars toppled into the swirling rift. Helping Tasha to her feet, they retreated to the street as the outer walls and frontal facade of the structure disintegrated before them. In moments, there was nothing left but the steps to the great citadel which had stood for untold millennia. The realm of the Necropolis was cruel and unkind, and it would take an effort of will to find their way back through the vast maze of the city to the bridge of silence from whence they had arrived.

Many long hours passed as they wandered the empty streets, trying to find a passage back to the way they had come. The only landmark of use was the giant obelisk which stood at the center of the city, but it appeared the same from every direction. They were hopelessly lost; and worse yet, they had brought a plague of butcher bats into the city. Asra had sacrificed the magic lamp and was now left to his own devices to find a way back to their mortal domain.

"I wonder why the dead roam the streets and linger near the central tower for the small chance to commit their flesh into the sanctified flames, when they could have merely wandered to the edge of the rift and cast themselves in to escape this torment," Asra suggested with a hint of curiosity as he helped Tasha walk along their path.

"The un-living are hexed from approaching the outer boundaries of the Necropolis, and the rift itself would only absorb their souls into its weave," Tasha spouted in response.

"Uh ...well, okay, you seem pretty sure of yourself," Asra grimaced with a raised brow, "how would you possibly know that?"

"I, I don't really know, the order of the Necropolis just came to my mind without trying," Tasha answered with equal confusion.

"Hmm, maybe that is an effect of the enchanted armor of the Nocturnal when you became one with it," Asra suggested, "I might be able to decipher the magical bindings upon your bonded suit once we reach the waterfalls across the bridge."

Asra was hoping he wouldn't regret having disposed of
their only way to escape this realm by destroying the
ancient Djinn. Now that Tasha was married to the armor
physically, her life would be forever altered. Asra
promised that he would do whatever it took to help rid
her of the mail once they escaped this realm, though the
reason he had claimed the powers of the jinn was so that
he could utilize such arcane magics at will. It was his
way of outsmarting the demon at his own game.

"We may have to travel to the lighthouse again to find
the right direction back," Asra warned, "can you walk on
your own?"

"Yes, I think so," Tasha answered, "I just feel strange
and a bit dizzy. It's as if I hear voices whenever I think
too hard on where I am."

Asra was certain it was the molding of the enchanted
armor with her body that was affecting her mind, much
like the powers of the jinn which had affected himself
physically. It was a dangerous thing to play with such
powers, for they could be so easily abused and twist the
minds of those who bore them. Asra wondered if he had
been a wicked person in his previous life which he had
mercifully forgotten; for the thought of it made him
nauseous that he could have been a willing servant to the
Dark Mistress as she had so claimed.

They had been left so far off track from the mausoleum
that they were forced to weave their way towards the
beacon at the center of the city so that they could retrace
the way they had entered the Necropolis. Eventually,
they stumbled upon a scattering of the undead wandering
through the avenues, but it wasn't until they approached
closer that the walking corpses stopped in their tracks to
turn their attention towards them. Gasps of hunger and

irritation issued from their putrid lips as desperate eyes gazed back at the pair of misfits when they drew near. Asra realized too late, that though Tasha was veiled from the undead that once he had been cured of his withered condition that he no longer appeared as one of them.

"I, I think they sense you!" Tasha noted as she slowly turned towards Asra.

He looked down at his cured hands and realized he have overlooked that one problem before he had so recklessly tossed the magic lamp into the void. Asra had gone through all that trouble to get the enchanted armor for Tasha, but neglected to consider how he would make his way back through the undead once he was restored. The undead closest to them turned and cried with horrible screams as they quickened their pace towards the pair. Asra concentrated on his magics and in an instant, a flaming blade of blue flame appeared in his hand.

"Get behind me," Tasha ordered towards him as she stepped forward between him and the advancing mob of shambling dead. Taking a stance, Tasha closed her eyes and concentrated on the strange words streaming through her head. Her lids flashed open, now white as ivory; her pupils void from her eyes, "Begone and make way, your hunger for the souls of the living will not be sated this day," she shouted in a strange voice not of her own.

The undead suddenly halted their advance and their agitated expressions turned to ones of grief and fear. They stalled, then slowly backed away, dreading the wrath of the Nocturnal. The armor itself was a sacred mantle created eons ago to rule the wayward souls of the underworld. The bearer of the armor was considered nobility among the unworthy rabble which roamed the Necropolis, of which the dead were compelled to obey.

"Well, that saved our sorry hides," Asra spouted with a sigh of relief.

"Stick close to me as we make our way into the city; I'm not sure if I can control a larger crowd," Tasha warned.

The odd pair made their way deeper into the metropolis until they found familiar streets that skirted the main tower. Tasha fended off the resentful dead as they fought their way through the labyrinth until they reached the small bridge where they had first encountered the wraith. Hungry and exhausted, but knowing they were close to escaping this cursed place, they hastened their pace to the bridge of silence. Once the pair had arrived at the long road to the cascading falls they came to a halt when Asra found their path blocked by a familiar adversary.

"You think you could simply depart my realm and desert your Dark Mistress without consequence?" The oracle hissed as she stood between them and their escape.

"I do not serve you!" Asra shouted as he stepped forward with his flaming blade while Tasha turned to him with wonder at his choice of words. There were things he had not told her about his previous encounter with the Oracle in the temple.

"But you do, my child, and always will," she smiled beneath her eyeless mask as she turned towards Tasha, "oh, and don't you look elegant in my ensemble, little one. Remove my armor where you stand, and in return, I promise your death will be quick," she snapped in a vicious tone.

"You will have to deal with me first," Asra flashed back to draw her attention back towards him, "I let you live before, but I won't make that mistake twice!"

"Hah, you do realize that I am called an *Oracle* for a reason?" The dark mistress cackled, "I already know the outcome of this little confrontation and what will happen if you refuse to bow to my will."

"Are you so sure about that?" Tasha spat back without hesitation.

"Sure about what, little girl?" The oracle answered, "That you will be betrayed and die slowly at the hands of this one you call your friend?"

Tasha swiped a skeptical glance towards Asra, as she wondered what he had failed to tell her. Asra had murdered her troupe and the people of an entire city and deceived a powerful demon from the planes of chaos, and had also stolen a set of armor from the ruler of the Necropolis like a thief in the night. Could he actually be trusted? Her discomfort was shown as she steadied her footing as she turned her gaze back towards the Oracle standing before them.

"You lie!" Tasha shot back with anger in her face.

"Oh, I like this one, full of spirit!" The dark mistress smiled with a malicious grin as she turned her face towards Asra and back to the girl, "Tell you what, if you return my armor to me, I will keep you as one of my pets instead of killing you."

"And what about me?" Asra drew the Oracle's attention once again, "What makes you think I would serve a vile tramp like you?"

"Oh, saucy now are we?" The oracle responded, "Has your new plaything here been such a bad influence on your principles that you've forgotten your place?" The oracle snapped back at Asra with a sarcastic pout as she motioned towards Tasha.

"Get out of our way, or die where you stand," Asra demanded coldly as he tightened the grip on his conjured sword and took a stance.

"Maybe I should help remind you who you speak too, and gut this little harlot in front of you while I keep her as an undead toy for all eternity," the oracle hissed back in a bitter tone.

As Asra stepped forward, Tasha felt a presence behind them through the perception of her enchanted armor. An expression of surprise fell across the Oracle's blind face as Asra turned to look over his shoulder to see what had drawn her attention. From the rubble, several phantoms appeared as they slipped from the shadows and gathered behind the couple. The Oracle took a wary step back towards the bridge upon seeing the wraiths as they grouped behind her foes.

The shade which they had aided before had mentioned there were others like him wandering this realm, many whom held a deep grudge against the queen of the underworld. For untold millennia they had suffered by the hand of this fiend who had laughed at their anguish and abused the tortured souls of her domain. But now she stood before them, naked of her armor; unable to command their obedience or repel their advance. Asra wondered what possible harm an immaterial shadow of a soul could do, for they could pose no physical threat.

He found the answer to his question as Tasha pointed towards the vile witch and commanded the wraiths to move her out of their way. The phantoms loomed around the pair of mortals as they pressed towards the Oracle standing at the landing of the bridge. The shadows quickly began their assault by rushing the dark mistress as she retreated into the cloud of silence, stumbling until her heavy headdress fell to the ground, revealing the horror of her sightless eyes. With her mask now gone, the specters shot forward into her skull through the black pits of her eye sockets, becoming one with the darkness lingering there as her silent screams where muffled by the enchantment upon the bridge.

It was a horrible sight to behold as they watched the specters swarm into the face of the Oracle as her mind filled with their blighted apparitions. Now tethered to her body and the darkness that resided there, the afflicted shadows were free from their own remains left wasting within the dark crevices of this cursed city. Driven mad by the whispering voices sealed within her head, the Dark Mistress of the Necropolis stumbled blindly over the edge of the bridge and toppled into the fissure below. The tormented souls had found their means of passage to blessed oblivion and brought an unwilling passenger with them to meet their final peace.

Chapter XIV
Gate of Shadows

Asra and Tasha hastened their way across the bridge, pausing only to peer over the edge where the Oracle had fallen. Here the reservoirs of the sap from the Tree of Life congealed in large pits scattered around them, but they saw no means of an exit through the maze of twisting roots adorning the walls which climbed their way into the murky darkness above in a massive tangle. There appeared to be no direct means of escape unless Asra was able to open another gate.

The first time he had done so, Asra had used a crystal shard he had salvaged from the transference and utilized the chalice upon sanctified temple grounds. Doing so had also absorbed the souls of the dead to keep the gate open as they passed through. They had no such arcane devices to concentrate such energies within this realm, which was like being stuck at a locked door without a key. They began to worry about their chances of ever returning to the world of the living.

The waterfall they had passed through at the mouth of the bridge had washed away ages of grime and oxidation from the enchanted armor which now shined brightly as polished silver. With his jinn powers, Asra could now see the true nature of the ancient armor as it radiated an aura he had not noticed before. The set of plate mail not only allowed the wearer to mask their living force from the undead and control their obedience, but also identify the places and ruling laws of this realm. It was a tool which inherited the knowledge of the Necropolis and could be used to their advantage if they only knew how.

"The armor you're wearing has a strange glow about it," Asra mentioned towards his companion.

"Really?" Tasha responded as she held up her arm, though seeing nothing unusual, "I don't notice anything different."

"The waterfall..." Asra pointed back to the cascading falls, "it purifies anything it touches and cleansed away a tarnish that buffered its enchantments from being seen. I think you should try to use this souvenir of yours to see if it can help us."

"I don't think it would be of any help at this point to commune with the dead," Tasha answered, "I can't control this thing the way you seem to govern your magics," she stated with resignation in her tone.

"Perhaps it reacts differently, rather than wielded like a weapon it provides protection like a shield," Asra responded with logic in his analogy.

This left Tasha to wonder if she concentrated enough on a specific item or subject in the Necropolis, that the knowledge imbued within the armor would be revealed. Standing among the piles of sticky sap she attempted to try out this crazy idea of Asra's to see if it would work. Staring at the walls and the tarry goop that filtered in from the overhanging roots far above, Tasha began to mince her words when a flood of thoughts started to flow into her head.

"This strange land was once called Medina," she began suddenly to Asra's surprise, "a city of the ancients who constructed the realms of the world with the aid of the elementals," she blurted.

"Well, go on ...whatever you're doing seems to be working," Asra noted, "now think about how we can get out of here to our own domain or perhaps somewhere close by."

"Ah, okay, I'll try," Tasha responded with a lick of her lips as she began to ask herself specific questions about this cursed realm, "...the city was once bathed in light until the day the seed to the world tree had sprouted. However, as it grew it began to stretch its limbs and its roots dug in and grasped many domains beyond its own as life proliferated between the realms."

"That doesn't seem entirely useful, try thinking of something else besides a history lesson," Asra suggested.

"Right," Tasha shot back as she tried to focus, "this sap from the heartwood of the tree was used to create several concoctions and remedies which granted a multitude of powers in everything from potions to forging spells and mystical weapons and armor."

"Ah, now we're getting somewhere," Asra responded with a gleam of hope, "go on!"

"Once imbued with such arcane powers, the sap itself could be used to enhance its magics," Tasha exclaimed.

"But that doesn't do us much good," Asra noted with a grimace, "think about finding us a doorway out of this realm, there must be something in the archives of this place which mentions that."

With a sigh of exhaustion, Tasha stepped over to another pool and looked out upon the Necropolis and its high tower which was barely visible at the great distance from where they stood. Concentrating on the city and its inhabitants, the armor spoke to her with words of knowledge that could help her find the answers she was looking for.

"One may find your answers within the Temple of the Nocturnal, where all shall be known," she spouted aloud, though not thoroughly understanding the meaning.

"Ah," Asra sighed, "you've got to be kidding me; that is the last place I want to return. There has to be another way!" He demanded.

"*The gate of shadows lies within*," was all Tasha stated in a spooky voice, leaving her to gaze back at him with a shrug of her shoulders, "apparently there is a doorway there that leads the way out of this place."

Asra tried to disagree with the augur she received from the enchanted armor, but it was clear that they would have no other choice but to return to the unholy Temple of the Nocturnal to find the exit from the underworld. The name she had given the gateway sounded ominous enough, though it fit the atmosphere of the dark realm of the dead. Once they found it, the question was; where would it lead? Tasha had another answer for that also.

"From what I can tell, the armor says the gate leads to the paths of many realms, we only have to choose one," Tasha replied to her companion's query.

Going back into the city was the last thing he wanted to do, despite it being the only avenue to escape this place. Asra led the way having been to the temple before, but Tasha's talent of using the magic armor came in handy for finding shortcuts to their route. Apparently, the armor gave her knowledge of where the portal could be found within the temple walls but getting there would still be a challenge if they had to fend off the guards posted upon the outer steps if any of them attempted to attack Asra. She would have to be vigilant to keep him protected from the undead sentries guarding the great shrine.

As the Oracle had been a living person, she had used the great temple as a sanctuary to escape the dead. The outer ramparts were scattered with armed sentries and

worshippers of those whom still honored the Dark
Mistress and her oversight of this realm. Besides the few
traps within which conjuring the undead, the Oracle
refrained from mingling with the rotting corpses which
she found detestable. Perhaps that is why she had been
alone when she confronted them upon the bridge outside
of the city, for the dead she ruled over disgusted the
priestess of darkness.

After crossing through the rubble and weaving between
several side avenues, they finally came upon the steps to
the great Temple. Strangely though, they found no
wandering dead or sentries standing guard, in their place
were several corpses lying motionless among the temple
grounds. They were perplexed to what had happened
here since the dead were cursed to wander for all eternity
in this place. Picking their footing through the carnage
they were left baffled why the undead would suddenly
fall silent.

"Do you think that the death of the Oracle caused them
to die also?" Asra wondered.

"The rules that bind this realm are bound to the ruler of
the Necropolis, but the spirit of the Dark Mistress was
replaced by the one who dons the armor of the
Nocturnal," Tasha explained as she repeated the words
which formed in her head. When she finished speaking,
Tasha seemed equally shocked at her own words.

"Looks like you're the new Queen of the Dead," Asra
started to joke, but realized the gravity of his words fell
like a lead weight.

There was no way that Tasha could simply purge herself
of her metal suit and be rid of it, and she certainly had no
desire to remain here as the Mistress to the undead.
However, Asra reminded her that the Oracle had

appeared at Ubar for the festival, as she had been present in the mortal world without her set of armor. Clearly, the individual crowned as the heir and titled ruler of the Necropolis was allowed free passage between the realms; so obviously, there must be a way for them to return.

Hundreds of bodies lay crumbled among the ruins that led up the Temple steps. The armored guards left minute evidence as though they had put up some sort of fight, but even more distressing was that almost every single corpse appeared to have a silent scream chiseled upon their frozen faces. It was an eerie sight to behold so many cadavers locked in a moment of terror. As they ascended the long flight of steps to the Temple entrance, in their wake the corpses began to rouse as the orbs of their eyes burned with an unearthly glow.

When the two companions reached the top of the staircase a rustle caught their attention. They both turned to see the littered corpses slowly rising once again, but this time with a cold fire radiating in the eyes of the undead. It was an unsettling sight to watch hundreds of ghouls lumber to their feet as the groaning horde began to creep towards them. Tasha stepped forward to control them, knowing that the armor of the Nocturnal held a greater level of influence over them within the confines of the temple grounds.

"Stay where you are!" She ordered, using the enchanted armor to make the undead obey her will; however, the shambling corpses did not stall.

"I don't understand," Tasha stood back with confusion as she flashed a worried glance towards Asra, "the armor says it should be working against the undead, but it's as if they do not hear me."

"Their eyes have never glowed like that before, and the

way they move is strange..." Asra mentioned as he examined the shambling mass.

A sound of flapping in the air above their heads drew their attention away as a dark object dived towards his head. Within an instant, a flaming blade appeared in his hand and slashed the creature before it reached him. A severed leathery wing fell to the ground at his feet adjacent to a squirming body with sharp talons. The foul creature screeched as was pierced by Asra's blade, setting the vile beast aflame.

"Butcher bats!" He spat as their eyes turned towards the darkened sky above for sign of any more of them.

"I think I know where the rest of the swarm disappeared too," Tasha noted as she gazed upon the horde scuffling towards them up the stairway.

The corpses of the dead had been taken over by the vile creatures who sought to consume them. The bewitched armor plate welded to Tasha's form no longer had any effect on these monstrosities. They would have to fend for themselves without the help of its mystic enchantments. The two of them turned to make their way over the lip of the terrace and across the central bridge as they retreated into the heart of the temple.

"There will be no deterring them if they corner us inside the shrine," Asra cautioned his companion, "We must stop them here."

"But how?" Tasha exclaimed as the first few ghouls clambered over the plateau of pillars to make their way down towards the crossings.

"We have to take out these bridges," Asra stated.

Doing so would be no easy task, as the stone catwalks that spanned the fissure were built with heavy marble and thick supporting anchors to either side. Asra gazed across to the single collapsed bridge to see if might offer a clue as to how it had failed. The break which snapped from the foundation at either side suggested that it was unable to sustain a great weight or that there might have been a fatal flaw in the grain of the marble. Asra began to think about how he could cause a fault to be exploited.

"Try heating the stone with those flames of yours," Tasha suggested.

It was worth giving a try. Asra rolled back his sleeves and set his hands upon the stone bridge, spreading his energies across the surface. The blue flames flickered as they melted into the rock, finding every crack and crevice as it seeped deep into the stone. As the heat intensified a belt of thermal shock cracked the stone.

Tasha jumped back when a fault appeared in the rock and with a sudden boom it gave way. An irregular section shifted and broke free from the central bridge, blocking the path of the horde from passing. All that was left was the bridge that once held the thorny vines which had impeded his path before. Asra moved over to the last bridge as the mob of ghouls closed in.

Placing his hands upon the marble tile as he had done before, Asra felt suddenly weak and out of breath. Though the elixir of the ancient gods had healed his withered condition, it had also returned the inherent weakness of the flesh. The jinn had warned that using magic would drain his stamina and now he was beginning to feel its effects. Using what little energy he had left, Asra pushed himself to buckle the stone.

A series of great cracks raced from one end to the other, but the bridge still held, leaving them worried if it would continue to hold. The horde of groaning ghouls with their eerily glowing eyes funneled upon the pair of broken bridges to cross as though their sight was diminished and could not detect the breaks in the path until they were nearly standing upon them. A mass of them which had crossed over the top the terrace started to make their way over the final bridge. There was little they could do to stall their advance.

"Quickly, back into the temple, there is nothing more we can do here," Asra exclaimed wearily as he motioned for Tasha to retreat within.

The shambling dead inched their way across the bridge and through the debris of broken vines and giant thorns scattered across the surface. Asra led Tasha inside to the area where he had faced the Oracle during the trial of the Tali-ma. He had wondered as to the purpose of the ritual she had placed upon him to face her fiery corpses, where Asra had eventually cheated death by using their ashes to build a bridge to escape the arena. Once they had arrived back at the spherical room he found that the bed of coals which surrounded the central platform had gone cold.

"What now?" Tasha asked as she saw there was no way to reach the upper dais.

The ash from the dead had been cleansed from the stage since he had been here last; so he searched the coals lying within the pit which encircled the platform. Within they found a dreadful sight as the stage was packed by several large jars containing corpses huddled within. Their hands were bound around their throats with chains in a pose of eternal misery. The jars themselves were etched with glyphs of binding making the occupants slaves to the will of the dark mistress.

"Those are bound souls," Tasha whispered with a stolen breath, "they serve the city of the dead and the one who is crowned the Nocturnal."

"The armor told you this?" Asra asked.

"They are, or were, unholy priests of the temple, sworn to serve the Dark Mistress in the afterlife. They are forever a part of this place," Tasha explained as she deciphered the knowledge of the enchanted plate mail encasing her body.

"Is there a way you can use them to our advantage and get us up there?" Asra inquired as he motioned to the upper terrace beyond their reach.

Outside the entrance of the temple, several dozen ghouls had made their way across the bridge before the weight of the masses crossing the weakened bridge caused it to fail. The stone foundations shattered by the resonance and weight of the increased amount of bodies funneled across the last remaining walkway. It broke and crumbled, bringing the undead upon it tumbling into the dark fissure below. The remaining cadavers controlled by the butcher bats filtered into the temple only moments behind them.

Tasha had never tried to use the enchanted armor for anything other than keeping the dead at bay, but she had to try something to assist them in their current dilemma. The unclean priests could only be utilized within this particular temple chamber. By the influence of the priests, a great many rituals could be performed which were used manage the unruly dead of the city, but in this instance, a single service would suffice. Tasha felt the power of the armor running through her as she envisioned what she needed to be done.

Asra jumped back when the large funeral jars began to shake and rattle and the corpses of the bound priests started to rise from the pit. They twitched in unnatural ways until the mystic bindings around their withered necks faded and they were unchained to do the will of the one who bore the ensorcelled armor. Climbing upon one another's backs and shoulders, Asra watched in morbid astonishment as the priests used their bodies to create a bone ladder for them to ascend to the terrace above.

With great loathing, they climbed the lattice of flesh and bone upon the bodies of the silent priests. They reached balcony just as the first of the ghouls entered the chamber and encircled the ringed platform. The undead priests quickly disassembled their construct and began to defend the temple from the trespassers using rusted weapons left littered among the giant vats below. Asra sought to use his jinn powers to aid their outnumbered minions but remembered what had happened the last time his magics became infused with the taint of necromancy.

"Even if they defeat the priests of the temple, I don't think they can get up here," Asra stated.

"Unless they use the same method the bound servants did to let us climb up here..." Tasha responded to his comment; which caused Asra to shrug at his own miscalculation of judgment.

"Can that armor you're wearing tell us where this gate of shadows is located?" Asra inquired as he looked around the upper chamber.

The stone altar covered with golden silk and pillows still sat at its edge along with a room littered with bloodied bones as though evidence that the dark mistress herself was some sort of cannibal. Asra wondered if that was why the Oracle had left this realm so that she could bring back fresh meat to sate her appetite for human flesh. Tasha circled the inner chamber with her arms outstretched as though attempting use of divination to locate the hidden portal they sought. After several tense moments of exploring the chamber, Tasha motioned Asra over towards a pure white marble idol of a female figure.

The face upon the statue where the eyes would have been was polished smooth. The figurine stood in a strange pose that might suggest it was frozen in a state of dance. Tasha tried to locate an opening behind the carving or perhaps a handle to a secret door, but found nothing there. With aggravation clouding her face, she turned back towards her companion.

"The only feeling I get is that the gate is located here, but I can't find anything," Tasha withdrew in surrender.

Looking at the marble idol, Asra could see that there was an aura of enchantment about it which stretched out into the wall to the rear of where it stood. The longer he stared with the jinn-induced eyes of his the more magics it revealed. Soon the entire section of the wall was laced with rings and archaic symbols and wards etched within; all of which were invisible to Tasha. Staring back at the artistic idol, Asra had only one proposition.

"Stand here before the statue and try to mirror its pose," he suggested.

With an awkward glance towards him, Tasha stepped past Asra and stood as he stated as she struggled to mimic the statue's posture. It took a few aching moments for her to get it correct until there was a flash of green light like a ripped seam before her and the small statue moved as though parting a curtain before it. As it did so, the streak of light also widened like a veil opened before them as a strange gate was revealed within its folds. She turned to Asra with a smile of satisfaction as he stepped forward to stand by her side while they peered within its illuminating glow.

"Where does it lead?" She asked, hoping Asra could tell

with his enhanced powers.

"I was hoping you would know," he responded with a raised brow.

"Well, anyplace is better than here," Tasha replied as the noise of combat between the undead resounded from the chamber below.

"I would assume that the bearer of the armor would have control of its destination," Asra answered, "so try to think of your home village and we can hope for the best," he suggested.

Tasha attempted to communicate with the armor as to what her wishes were in her desire to control the path of the gate beyond. Closing her eyes she could see that it led to many intersecting roads looping upon a path which stretched out into infinity. She tried to recall memories of her past, for it had been many years since she had seen the green woodlands and rich jungles of Fernwood, where the mountain valleys would sing with warm winds and autumn showers. She remembered her youth living amongst the tribes who strived to live as one with nature in an alternate world blooming with life; it was a place far from the cold and decaying crypt of the Necropolis.

With a nod of her head, Tasha motioned towards Asra she was confident their path had been grounded. In response, he stepped forward and pushed his arm through the portal, feeling a trickle of energy return to him.

"I'll go through first to see if it's safe since my altered vision should allow me to identify the path we seek," Asra offered.

Tasha agreed to this precaution as Asra stepped through the veil, piercing the wall of the gate. Once beyond the breach, a fierce wind bit at Asra's skin and tugged at his cloak. Around him was a vast curling cloud, not unlike

Michel Savage

the angry mists that surrounded the edge of the city. At his feet was a small path of broken tiles, held in thin air by nothingness.

The trail from the gate intersected with several others which weaved through the void beyond. Navigating such a passage would be impossible if not for a single trace of darkness which drifted along the route, as though someone's shadow had been captured in time and bound for eternity to repeat its trek. He turned back towards Tasha at the other side of the gate and motioned for her to join him. She saw him through the windy gale and stepped through the curtain of light to follow.

Tasha was met with an unpleasant surprise as a look of shock fell across her face beneath the armored helm, finding herself blocked from crossing through. The tips of her fingers slipped through the gate to touch Asra's who tried to help her, but the armor fused with her body was also bound to the realm in which it was formed. No matter how much she struggled, the portal would not let her pass. Asra stood beyond the gate in the howling squall, unable to hear her from his side of the gate; watching helplessly while the rift began to close upon them as the curtains of light folded, and Tasha's fearful eyes and muted screams were silenced forever.

Chapter XV
The Betrayer

Asra stood outside the gate in the void, waiting for Tasha to reopen the portal so that he could pass through back into the temple chamber; but that moment never came to pass. The Necropolis was a prison for the cursed undead as was the armor melded to Tasha's body. She had survived the attack of the Djinn only to become a casualty of the wards that held the realm of the dead intact. With overbearing grief, Asra finally pulled away from where he had waited in vain and turned to follow the path of shadows towards Tasha's homeland.

Asra could see the arcane powers flowing through this strange rift as a realm between worlds connected to every domain. It was a curious place where entities passed one another beyond reach as they traveled to destinations unknown. The winds themselves were alive as though the elements were fighting for balance in a place of chaos where reason itself was nothing more than a fabrication of the mind. Here magic was both a traveler and the cord which laced the trails from beginning to end, creating the passage which cheated the rules of fate and consequence.

After a long and treacherous journey that seemed to have no end, Asra followed the path to a single door that welcomed him as he approached by slitting a single tear in space which allowed him to step through. He found himself at the stoop of a great carving upon a cliff wall where a single doorway had been chiseled a foot deep into the living rock. After he had passed through the portal, the ethereal rift sealed behind him and there was now nothing more than a stone wall left in its place. Surrounding the false door were several decorative pillars, also etched from the rock, set in the middle of a lush forest at the edge of a mountain valley.

Trees soaked in rich moss and giant ferns led to the naming of Tasha's valley. The site where he was spat out of the rift appeared to be a sacred site, though the present overgrowth proved it had not been visited in many decades. Asra set out to find Tasha's tribe and get a bearing where he was upon the world around him. He stood resolved; vowing that if he could somehow find his way back to the city of the dead he would do whatever it took to free her from that unholy crypt.

The air here was wet and thick, smelling of rich earth and wet wood. It was a pleasant change from the stench of the Necropolis which coated the senses like a putrid fog. The sky above was mottled with tall clouds and gray mists of falling rain. Asra found a faint trail from the sacred circle of the portal gate and made his way through the thick brush and hanging moss painting his path in lush emerald hues.

Hidden within the foliage, Asra stumbled upon giant carvings of staunch faces etched upon polished stone; be they forgotten kings or gods he knew not which. The sculptures were buried in the overgrowth, remnants of a time long past. He wondered what her clan was like since she had never spoken about them in-depth in the time he had known her. Asra held many questions which had gone unanswered and his short time with the Oracle and her revelations had left him even more perplexed.

The call of exotic birds and sound of waterfalls pounding rock soothed his troubled mind and eased his anguish for leaving Tasha behind in that dark cursed place. He hoped that the enchanted armor would sustain and protect her if she found a way to fight off the rabid ghouls which had infested the Necropolis. Now that he was back in the world of men, Asra was whole again and felt his jinn powers return in strength. Looking down upon his healed palm, Asra considered he was free from the Djinn, and could now pursue a destiny of his own.

Though he felt the power of the jinn flowing through him, Asra couldn't help but feel exhausted from his recent venture and the hardships endured. He wanted nothing more than to have a warm meal and find a safe place to sleep away his woes. The path he followed snaked its way into the lower valley between the tall jagged mountains which soared like pillars that held up the sky. Atop each crest lay an island of greenery isolated from the world below.

As the evening began to fall across the forest, the cry of the night birds changed to one of warning. Strange unseen things moved amongst the trees, their presence camouflaged among the foliage and scattered shadows. Asra felt eyes upon him but could not detect the mundane as any residual magics appeared to well up from the roots of the earth itself. He was lost and knew not what he should do as the sun began to set across the narrow valley.

Upon the path, a small child appeared before him, ragged and soiled dirt upon its face. Wearing a necklace of colorful beads and bright feathers in her hair, the youth stood like a statue gazing towards him. Asra was startled at first, for all his powers bestowed upon him gave no warning of the youngster's sudden appearance. Stepping forward with caution, Asra called out to her.

"Hello there ...can you understand me?" Asra added as

an afterthought; not knowing if the child spoke his language.

The child continued to stand poised upon the path, silent as stone. Asra suddenly stopped, realizing this must be a trap as he slowly turned to gaze around him. One by one he began to see pairs of eyes appear from the forest which had once melded with the surrounding bark of the trees and the leaves of the bushes. They were the forest people of the Ouswan; Tasha's people.

"We speak," a cold voice range from the jungle; though Asra could not pinpoint from whence the words came, "who are you to be here in this place?"

"I am Asra, a friend of Tasha-nell LeAir Ouswan," he answered, hoping there were people here who knew her.

"LeAir?" The voice echoed as hushed whispers among the tribe filled the forest air, "Nell LeAir," it repeated, "a lineage of our valley, it means 'Song of the Wind,' who is Tasha to you, stranger?"

"A friend of mine," Asra exaggerated, as Tasha could have been considered more of a casualty of his reckless behavior, "she told me this was her homeland and that I could find many here who could help me."

Another round of dull whispers echoed through the trees as the villagers spoke among themselves while Asra awaited their response. An elder stepped out from the foliage behind him where she had stood poised and undetected. She was an old woman with braids and tassels tied into her hair. Her skin was covered with exotic tattoos of spirals and flowing shapes, while upon her neck she wore several pendants similar to the talisman Asra had around his neck.

Seeing this, he pulled out the pendant from underneath his soiled robes to examine it once more as the elder herself and other members of the tribe saw it was the same. Asra was understandably confused, for Tasha had said that she had found the talisman hung around his neck when she had found him stumbling out of the desert and tended to his care; but it appears that she had, in fact, placed the arcane pendant upon him and told him a falsehood so that he would retain it as a keepsake. The question was why she would do such a thing? Asra's eyes met that of the tribal elder as he held up the pendant between them.

"You have been bestowed a gift of the wind, and thus you are welcome among us, Asra, friend of Tasha," the elder granted with nod and tap of her belled staff.

Dozens of other members stood out from the forest draped in their colorful adornments, causing Asra to wonder how they had cloaked themselves so thoroughly with the foliage around them. A pair of children took Asra by either hand and led him in the direction of their hidden village. At the edge of a river, they entered a pebbled path along a small stream which led into a concealed entrance behind a great pile of mossy stone. Only just before he entered did Asra look up to see the hidden dwellings nestled into the cliffs above him, masked as though they were one with the mountain.

The small gauntlet that led into the upper dwellings was well protected from intrusion as the entrance held many traps and barriers that could be armed at a moments notice. Once inside, the vaults spanned out into a series of stairways and ladders, including ingenious pulley systems that allowed them to haul large amounts of cargo up in woven baskets to the upper terraces. There was a feeling of primal energy and creative design which melded well together in this strange abode. The people themselves were a wild mix of personas which all shared a common design of being one with the land.

Asra was led to an upper balcony which had a view of the valley from high above the cliff. The elder he had first met joined him with two other women of varied ages. A pair of young tribesmen came in and took his soiled robes and left him with a replacement set of native clothing rich in color and design. Eventually, he was directed to sit upon the matted floor between them at the edge of a short circular table.

"What is the fate of the daughter of the Ouswan?" The youngest of the elders asked as Asra tried not to cringe with emotion upon hearing the question.

"Tasha sent me here to ask for your help," Asra lied, for he feared he might offend her tribe or facing retribution for having to explain how she became trapped in the City of the Dead. He wasn't sure if anyone in these far lands would even believe such wild superstitions if he should reveal his tale in full, nor did he wish for them to think that he associated with the likes of demons.

"But what has become of her, was the question," the middle-aged elder asked as she continued the inquiry of the youngest elder.

"She was granted powers of a queen over an ancient kingdom, but her duties trap her within its service," Asra embellished his lie with a half-truth, woven to protect himself from reprisal.

"So, you are saying she is a captive?" The most senior of the three asked as their blank stares fell upon him.

"In a manner of speaking" Asra answered, "...as I was able to travel from their domain I came here to beg for your assistance if you could aid me in freeing her from her bound service?"

The three elders glanced at one another with looks of concern, though they did not utter a word between them. After an uncomfortable moment, one of them raised a hand and an attendant brought in a platter with three lit candles of varied height and placed it upon the table between them. They were then all brought four cups of baked clay; each filled with water. Asra waited and proceeded to drink only when he saw one of them take a sip from her earthen goblet.

"We are the elders of the Fernwood tribe, representing each generation; those of youth and vigor, another of ambition and experience, and the other of wisdom and knowledge," the second elder stated as she motioned between the younger and eldest beside her, "you sit here at this circle to choose which may represent your endeavor with the blessing of the elements."

With that said, the youngest elder drank from her cup and placed it face down upon the table, she then gave a motion of her hand with a snap of her wrist and the tallest of the candles snuffed out. The elder next to her picked up her cup and gave the contents a light swirl, and with one hand she dipped her fingers into the cup and flicked them at the candelabra, and the droplets of water extinguished the second candle. The eldest also drank from her cup and spun the empty vessel upon the table, and with a flick of her hand, it flipped atop the last candle to asphyxiate the flame. They had performed all of these slights of hand by use of skill alone, as Asra saw no magic in use with the jinn powers he had inherited.

He recognized the first woman had used the element of wind to blow out her candle by throwing the air with practiced precision; as he had seen such tricks executed by street magicians at the carnival in Ubar. The second had used water and a practiced aim to drown the wick; while the third woman had used an element of the earth to choke out the flame. They had touched upon the points that their tribe followed the teachings of the elements in their daily lives. Looking around the small chamber he could now perceive the design of earth, water and wind within the carvings upon the walls and decorations in the patterns in their clothing and tattoos, even down to the fashioning of their jewelry.

Asra removed the strange talisman which hung around his neck and looked at it with new eyes, now seeing the symbols Tasha had mentioned to him before when she had read his rune stones the night before the city fell. The other strange artifacts etched within his pendant were also present here in this room upon the painted emblems on the walls and carvings within the wood. Though the deities of the elementals had long been forgotten across the world, they were still revered in this ancient place among these primitive people. The flame that lit the candles was a representation of the last element, which the other three had suppressed by their symbolic ritual.

Asra remembered the story Tasha told from her youth about the old world in its days of birth. The ancient Djinn from the planes of chaos were masters of fire. Thus, it was why Asra's powers centered upon the power of the flame in nearly every aspect. With that image in mind, Asra flicked his hand at the platter of candles and their wicks burst into flame once again.

The trio of elders was visibly stunned by this trick, for such forms of chaotic magic were unknown. The generations of their descendants who had passed through this lost valley had become one with nature, which was an integral part of their daily lives. Fire was not an element mankind could directly connect with, but only utilized at a respectable distance because of its volatile nature. Fire could provide warmth and light, to cook or used to forge elements of the earth; however, it could not be held in one's hand without suffering the consequences.

Fire was not an element natural to the race of men, but one which had been stolen from the ancient demons known as the Jinn. This was a time-worn tale passed through countless generations of their people. The tribal elders' eyes were wide with shock as they flinched, for Asra had proven himself to be a sorcerer. Such magics had been nothing more than tales and legends to them until this moment.

"You control the powers of the forgotten ones," the youngest elder finally dared to speak as they tried to collect their composure.

"I merely bear a gift from the ancients," Asra answered as he noticed a new glint of respect in their posture towards him.

A moment of awkward silence followed as the three elders spoke with one another without words. They then stood in unison side by side to address Asra with a respectful bow; for they honored masters of the elements. Several attendees entered the chamber with a dignified demeanor at the instruction of their tribal elders as they removed the items from the table and cleared the room. An old withered man then appeared at the entrance and approached Asra where he sat.

"This man is the last direct relative of the Ouswan family, Tasha-nell's great family elder," one of the women announced, "It is he who needs to know the circumstance of his daughter's plight."

Asra looked upon the old man whose eyes were nearly blind, his hair now but wisps upon a barren head tiled with blemished spots of age. He had a strange calm and strength about him, the type one might find standing near an ancient oak tree. Asra stood patiently, waiting for the man to have his say, but he only placed his frail hand into his and bowed his head in sorrow. Tears came to his eyes as he heard the old man's pleas.

"Save my Tasha, great Shaman," he beseeched, "and the strength of our tribe is yours to command."

Asra couldn't bring himself to telling them the entire truth as to what had happened for fear they would persecute him. He had indirectly been the cause of murdering several thousand people and the destruction of an entire city, including the mutilation of the old man's relative through the infusion of the mystic armor which entrapped Tasha in a realm of the dead. Telling them the whole story at once might invoke the tribe's retribution instead. For his own sake, Asra decided it would be best to release the facts surrounding Tasha's dilemma at a measured pace.

Over the next several days, Asra took the time to recoup from his ordeal and gather his senses. He discovered this tribe was nestled in a branch of high mountain cliffs which rested among lush valleys north of a string of high peaks known as the Silver Mountains. Their valley was fed by a holy river revered for its beauty and purity. There was little they feared in these lands for the thick vegetation was impassible and their cliffside fortresses were impenetrable to attack from outside forces.

No foreign army in their right mind would partake upon an incursion in such a difficult terrain as these forest valleys. They had lived within these canyons in relative peace for centuries, and from what Asra had witnessed, it was a paradise in itself. It made him wonder why Tasha would leave her homeland only to wander the open desert among the southern lands of the Oman Empire with a troupe of gypsies. It was a story he desired to ask her elder father, but could not find the courage do so for fear of adding to his grief.

In the days that followed, Asra found himself at the center of attention as he had been lifted into an honored position as a talented shaman among the Fernwood tribe, though he only tried to fit into the post because of the perks which came with the title. Sorcerers of real magic were the stuff of legends and many looked upon him as though he possessed the power of a god. Asra would frequently find himself performing parlor tricks for the locals and children, but it felt as though he did so only to keep them mesmerized and confident in his abilities. Even Asra, himself, did not know the full extent of his own powers, for true to the Djinn's cautioning, every use of his magics drained him physically.

The people of Fernwood were not the followers of war, for they lived in rapport with the forest. Their sense of magic was restricted to the mundane, and no one else understood the changes Asra was going through. Such powers affected one's sense of self and balance of mind, and as time passed the farther he fell into a well of isolation and solitude. Asra realized that he needed to build an army for any chance to rescue Tasha from the Necropolis, which seemed like an impossible task the longer he waited.

One early morning, Tasha's family elder came to visit Asra in his shaman's tower to ask when he would begin his quest to rescue his lost granddaughter. It was a confrontation that did not go well for Asra, as he had been playing for time to create a viable plan. He had no idea where the Isle of Limbo lay upon a map, nor how to reach it without the aid of the Djinn. After much effort, Asra discovered he was only able to open rifts from such sacred sites which held the utilities to focus his magic, and the gate he arrived from would not respond to him.

"Great Shaman, I have come to ask when you will begin your quest to retrieve my Tasha," the old man inquired in a voice weak with age.

"Soon, father of the Ouswan," Asra answered, "I have devised a plan that I will share with the elders shortly."

"My Shaman, with no disrespect, we have waited patiently for many moons and you have not given details as to what happened to her," the old man replied, "we do not question the powers you possess, only the integrity of your ability to take decisive action."

The old man's words cut deeply into his pride, for it was a slap to Asra's dignity which was already tender at this stage. Since he had first met Tasha and her troupe, Asra had no background to depend upon to who he actually was or what source molded his personal values. He had caused a great deal of grief and harm to others and bore the burden of that guilt. He had every intention of retrieving Tasha from the Necropolis, but no viable means to do so; and for all his arcane powers, he still felt powerless in that endeavor.

"If you would please sit, I will try to explain what happened to settle your restless soul," Asra offered in a change of heart to grant a measure of honesty, "...all I would ask is for your confidentiality in this matter."

The old man agreed and joined Asra in his tower as he sat among the lavish furnishings gifted to their honored shaman. Asra felt as if he owed the elderly man an explanation since his venerable age did not leave him many years of patience before he would be swept from the world of the living, leaving his worries for his only living granddaughter left unfulfilled. With a deep breath, Asra began his long tale, only omitting certain details as to his questionable past and accusing words laid upon him by the Dark Mistress of the underworld. It was a tale that no one would believe unless they had absorbed the experience and wisdom of many generations.

"...and that is how I came to be here, upon the path to your valley," Asra finished his lengthy narrative as he gazed out the window to notice the day had passed fairly quickly and the sun was soon to set.

Tasha's great relative sat silent for many moments absorbing in the tall tale Asra had claimed, but giving credence to many parts though he was unfamiliar with history and tales of the isle of limbo and the underworld along with their realms. The frail man stood up to stare out the open window of the tower which looked out upon the rolling forest canopy and colors of the setting sun as he contemplated the allegations of the shaman's saga. It was difficult for Asra to read the man's wrinkled face to understand his mysterious reaction; for the man nearly nodded and departed Asra's chambers and left him alone to wonder if the old man had thought him insane. Considering it was a lot of information to take in and that his granddaughter was a trapped queen of the Necropolis was a bit much to handle, Asra took to his bed with the relief that he had finally unburdened the truth from his shoulders and felt at peace for the first time in months.

While the night birds were singing with the crickets and creatures of the night under a moonlit sky, a commotion was heard beyond the halls of the tower. His chamber door burst open as several strong-armed members of the tribe poured in and rustled Asra from his bed. His hands were quickly tied and his mouth gagged from speaking any words of magic he may use, and he was swiftly ushered from the room. He was dragged through the halls and out into the open forest by a company of angry villagers on the long journey to the ruins of the gates from whence he had arrived.

There he found a circular pyre had been set and he was bound to the central post placed within. His muffled screams went ignored the entire way until Asra was exhausted from the ordeal as fear filled his eyes upon seeing the fate they had intended for him. Before him stood the three women elders of the tribe, now dressed in familiar bleached attire of the worshippers of Allat. His eyes turned upwards to the full moon above as the lunar goddess they served.

"Asra, the betrayer and false shaman, your secrets have been revealed this day. Under the light of the moon you will be judged and cleansed by sacred fire," the middle elder announced as the trinity held flaming torches before him, "you are ordered to open the gates of the enshrined to the City of the Dead so that we may return the lost daughter of the forest, or you will perish here and now."

Chapter XVI
Rise of a Tyrant

When the tribal elders claimed he had betrayed them the label they had chosen rung like a bell and Asra understood how the title bestowed onto him by the Oracle had come full circle. The people of the forest had felt misled by Asra's small tricks of magic, for the tale retold by the grandfather of Tasha-nell LeAir to their elders was one filled with treachery and deception, and Asra was incriminated as a tyrant who had slain an entire city by his hand. The people of Fernwood did not wish to be casualties of such a madman, and their false shaman would be given only once chance to prove the fable he wove had any truth to it or be executed as an imposter, for the grandfather now believed that Asra had murdered Tasha and stolen her talisman. Asra had previously spent many days at this sacred site attempting to open the gate of shadows so that he may find his way back to the Necropolis but realized such a task was impossible to complete without the proper artifacts to focus his power.

"The accused claims to have consorted with demons and destroyed Iram of the Pillars, the desert post of Ubar, and all its inhabitants; defiled the Tree of Life and entombed a daughter of the Ouswan within the City of the Dead," the youngest elder called to her people who surrounded the pyre, "it is our belief that he has woven these tales to deceive us, as an insult our kindness, our hospitality, and our trust."

"Under the eyes of the moon goddess, you will be given

one chance to redeem yourself," the senior elder declared towards Asra as he stood bound to the stake, "you will open the doorway to the netherworld so that we can bring Tasha back from the realm of death where you had so cruelly abandoned her, or you will be considered a thief and a murderer of a child of the forest tribe and your sinful spirit will be removed from this world."

Asra's hands were untied from the post and each arm placed in shackles to either side where they were held by a pair of clansmen while he was turned to face the stone gate of the ancient shrine. His gag was then removed as another tribesman held a sharpened spear at his back, ready to run him through should he attempt to use his mystic powers against them. Thus far, the forest people had not seen the depths of the jinn powers which Asra possessed, and knew not what danger they faced. They had, however, taken rational precautions to retrain his incantations should he try anything suspicious besides opening the portal.

There was little Asra could do to persuade his hosts to the folly of their request, for he had been guilty of their numerous allegations against him.   Even if he had managed to open a rift, there was no known way to peel the enchanted armor of the Nocturnal from Tasha's body without killing her. He was responsible for the deaths of many countless men, women, and children by his reckless actions. In the end, it appeared that the Oracle had been flawed in her predictions of his destiny for he had done nothing but caused harm to others.

Another crack in Asra's soul snapped his mind and spirit, and he saw little worth in himself or continuing to live like a pawn in such a cruel and unfair world. He wondered if his own soul would end up rotting in the

Necropolis; only to spend eternity witnessing his once-friend, now the Dark Mistress of the underworld, suffer herself. It was not a kind fate he foresaw. There was nothing left now to do but face his destiny to become a lost spirit left wandering through the cursed realms who would never know peace.

A painful jab of a spear to his back prompted him to do as he was instructed by the elders, but they would soon see that their request was mere folly. Asra was resigned to play his part in this charade and grant them the justice they sought, for it was the least he could do. Despite the futility of it, Asra began to concentrate on his powers, even if this was his last act considering he was going to die in the moments to follow. He had no wish to harm these people in a vain attempt to save himself, so he went through the paces he had committed before to crack open the rift.

Hushed whispers of astonishment rolled from the tongues of the tribesmen as stems of light streamed from Asra's fingers while they encompassed the image of the doorway carved into the stone. Asra had little progress from this point, as the grounds of this ancient site lacked any artifacts of focus required to breach the barriers between the realms. He struggled to remember the road back to the Necropolis; backtracking the path in his mind. The trail was too long and the maze too intricate for his vision to pierce, and Asra knew that his moment of failure had come as the doorway failed to open.

"You have proven yourself to be an imposter, though you had claimed to possess a gift from the gods, which have shown to be nothing more than the dark magics bestowed by demons," The senior elder announced as the strings of energy from Asra's hands dissipated.

The youngest elder raised her hand to direct the sentries which tethered his arms to shackle him back upon the post. Without further ceremony, in unison, the elders touched their torches to the pyre. The fire flared and encircled the pillar to which he was bound, and Asra struggled as he felt the heat of the roaring flames. Suddenly the three elders in white turned their attention towards the stone gate as a clap of thunder shook the ground. A dark aura outlined the doorway, sucking in the light of the burning pyre set before it.

Asra had already been bound and knew that it was not his magics which were now at play. Hope danced in his mind; had Tasha somehow found a way to escape the Necropolis on her own? Asra continued to speculate as the tribesmen surrounding the pyre leaped back when a darkened mist of ash poured from the breach of the rift. An angry cloud gushed from the void which quickly snuffed the flames of the wooden pyre, only to be replaced by violent sapphire flames.

With his gifted vision, Asra saw familiar magics seething through the raging fog which swept around them. From its billowing mass the ghost of a great demon formed with its wings cast so wide that it surrounded the entire assembly. Many of the men and women present shuddered and screamed, having never known such beast of terror could exist. Many cowered and chanted prayers while others fled for their lives. The unfortunate few who were frozen spellbound with fear stood to hear the words of the fiend which growled in a voice with the depth of a mountain storm.

"It is not Gods, nor Demons, who bring grief to the world, but the deeds of men by their own hand," the phantom Djinn roared.

Asra saw now that the jinn he had tricked and cast into the consuming void had not been annihilated, but only drained of its ethereal forms and reduced to its primal energy. In a sense, the Djinn still lived but did so within an abscess of darkness. As one of the primordial elementals, it could not be destroyed by such a means. From the void, the demon had felt Asra's presence and returned to fulfill its binding oath.

"How is it that you are you here?" Asra muttered in disbelief towards the towering brute as its angry gaze turned down upon him.

"I am bound and you are owed," the gray Djinn answered in a tone that caused the ground to rumble, "...the oath of an eternal is unbreakable."

Even in the Djinn's diminished state, he was still constrained by the laws of the Trinity he had agreed too fulfill. A plume of smoke snaked its way up the pyre and crushed Asra's shackles, setting him free. He knew the demon was not acting out of loyalty to the master who had deceived him, but by the honor of the vow he had made; and was thus forced to protect Asra until his pledge was fulfilled. Asra feared that in the end, this immortal demon would have its revenge upon him a hundredfold.

In an act of rebellion, the parlor tricks of the elders attempted to fend off the jinn was their undoing. Their defiance granted them a jet of blue flames from the crackling pyre which ignited their ceremonial robes. The screams of the women added to the nightmarish scene as their hair burned and faces melted with bubbling blisters from the wrath of the mystic fire. Asra watched helplessly as strings of blue flame indiscriminately lashed out to incinerate anyone within reach as the villagers fled in terror.

The demon itself was now tethered to the forces of oblivion beyond the gate of shadows and could not venture from its source. When the screams ceased and the groans of the dead fell silent, the demon turned its attention towards Asra where he had retreated to find refuge against the cliff wall. Asra's nose was filled with the stench of burning flesh and hair as he stood amongst several burnt corpses littering this once tranquil grotto. There was little left of the three elders, whose baked bones sat in piles of whitened ash among which lay several talismans.

The ghostly jinn formed of soot and cinder motioned for Asra to retrieve the sacred pendants. With hesitation, Asra stepped through the field of flickering flames and tendrils of smoke to the remnants of the elders and retrieved the strange talismans. Asra was still confused as to what they were for or what value they had, for he still recalled the odd and fearful reaction of the old man back in the city of Ubar upon the steps of the Celestial Temple. He looked down upon them as they sat in his palms and began to recognize separate symbols of the elements stamped within each ornament; though still perplexed as to what it might mean.

"Those are not mere trinkets, but artifacts of power cast from a time before time," the jinn noted as Asra found that the metal from which the pendants were cast was still cool nor was it blemished from the enchanted flames, "with these five tools you will be able to focus your powers and return me to my rightful place in the planes of chaos," the demon stated.

"Five elements?" Asra asked confused, for having only known of four.

"Five talismans, but six elements in total, to include the one you wear upon your neck," the Djinn answered, "Earth, Water, Fire, Air, and the Void," the demon gestured towards the open gate to oblivion, "the final is life itself, which is essential to bind them."

"Me ...I am this binding element?" Asra mumbled to himself, trying to fathom the words of the ancient Djinn.

"Yes," the demon replied, "as long as you breathe and have life flowing in your veins."

He held the strange pendants in his hand and noticed that they fit together in a certain order, becoming one. Asra pulled a loose cord from his own pendant and laced it through the loop and set the united talisman about his neck. A jolt of electricity shot through his body as Asra held up his hands to see arcs of lightning spark between his open fingers but within moments the strange effect faded away. He felt an odd but familiar sensation, similar to the feeling he experience when the jinn had transferred a portion of his powers to him upon the salt flats beyond the isle of limbo.

"What am I to do now?" Asra asked himself aloud as he glanced across the glade of dead bodies and charred remains. He had made an enemy of the people who had welcomed him into their folds and materialized into the murderer they had accused him to be.

"With such a talisman, you are now all-powerful in this mortal plane," the Djinn replied, though the question Asra asked was rhetorical, "you can conquer lands and bend anyone to your will, should you so desire. However, you must make your final wish so that I may be released from our bond!" The demon of ash and smoke demanded as he saw Asra beginning to walk away; for without a body the weakened genie was now anchored to the swirling void that was the barrier between domains. The dreadful demon could no longer accompany him beyond the reach of the mystic gate.

"I will do so," Asra answered, "when we have freed Tasha from the Necropolis," he finished with an accusing glare, for it was the attack of the jinn which had nearly killed her, "only then will you be free to return to the realm of chaos as reward for your service; but I must prepare myself for this task, my servant."

The giant jinn only glared down at him with a sneer forming upon his cloudy lips for the belittling insult bestowed by Asra's remark. With a grunt of contempt, the Djinn collapsed into a turbulent cloud and withdrew back into the rift whereupon the doorway promptly collapsed. In that instant the blue flames scattered among the pyre and the smoking corpses snuffed out, leaving Asra standing among the silence of a smoldering graveyard.

Asra, the false shaman and sorcerer of dark magics, marched his way back towards the cliffside fortress to return to his tower. Those remaining villagers who fled his path were spared, while others who gave armed resistance were not. With a flick of his wrist, mystic fire shot forth to consume them while their kindred abandoned their weapons and begged him for mercy. Asra had seen too much death to care anymore and refused to be a victim, and would no longer tolerate being opposed.

He had grown tired of feeling shame and regret for all the unfortunate circumstance and hardship he had endured in his life, and instead sought to forge his own destiny using the unique gifts he had been bestowed. He would no longer allow himself to be pushed around or persecuted for circumstance beyond his control. This moment would be his new beginning. Asra may have forgotten who he had once been, but nothing would stop him from creating a new destiny.

While Asra stood alone in his tower the sounds of commotion echoed from below as the people fled from the fortress; and bitter spite began to grow in Asra's heart. Questions still remained, but he was ready to embrace the title of a betrayer if it bore respect as compensation. Asra felt the conflict within himself, knowing he wasn't a bad person, but there were times when others refused to open their eyes to the suffering of another and would judge them by results of circumstance rather than by their intent. He was determined to use his magic for the sake of conceiving a new life for himself and to refashion his mistakes so they would no longer haunt his dreams.

Asra sat contemplating for many days until a timid knock came upon his door. After the event when their Elders had been brutally executed, several of the terrified members of the tribe of had returned to the fortress, for they were now without traditional leaders to guide their clan. Asra had considered the situation and that he would need able bodies to aid him in his quest to remake their cliffside citadel into a stronghold. Weeding through the residents available, Asra assigned a slew of vassals for his court to serve under his new rule.

In this mortal domain, Asra would be considered a mighty sorcerer with the powers of a god and could persuade others to do his bidding. Through threat and intimidation, he could sway allegiance with promises of security and prosperity. It was a new concept for the peaceful people of Fernwood to accept, for they had lived for countless generations in perfect tranquility with the forest, far from the conflicts of the outside world. There were several tribesmen who fell under Asra's wing that found the idea of such conquest alluring.

There was an entire world out there waiting to be conquered and bent to his will, and little in the way to stop him. Everything from the Silver Mountains to the far shores of the Oman Empire and beyond could be his to rule. He could be the sheik of the sands, the sultan of the jungles and the caliph of the surrounding empires once they were subdued.

Building an army would take time, but it was his own servants who suggested a system of worship towards their new lord. They proposed the building of a temple to him as a living deity among men. However, Asra rejected such a notion, for the things he had seen of such creatures from the realms beyond had left him with vile disgust in his heart. He would not become an effigy to be falsely praised or have his name twisted into a curse.

"Men build temples to their gods, which in truth, are nothing more than monument to their egos," Asra stated to his vizier, "and when their deities are forgotten such pillars of tribute become nothing more than towers of solitude," he exclaimed, having held a bitter place in his heart for the sealed temple whence he had stumbled upon the trapped jinn which had led his path astray.

The elemental spirits had abandoned the world of men long ago, leaving behind a wayward demon forgotten in its dark tomb. The followers of the Temple of A'ra who had entrapped the chaotic spirit had forfeited their ability to properly contain the beast when they lost favor in the world of men. New deities from distant lands sprouted up in their place as the memories the old gods were all but erased. Asra chose to live for the here and now and not as some bygone effigy when his time was done.

The customs of the forest tribesmen were systematically reshaped from the serenity of nature into the silence of obedience. They had elevated their new lord to a place above the trinity of their previous elders. A people who once existed by their values of honor and common respect had their code of ethics traded for a sense of order and duty. It was a lesson as to how easily morals of a society could be molded by the narrow sights of a cruel and heartless tyrant.

Asra kept one goal in mind ahead of all else; that he would find his way back to the Necropolis and recover the woman he left trapped there. In his mind, saving Tasha was his personal redemption; the one act that would forgive all the evil things that he had done as atonement. There finally came a day when he moved his forces from the valley forests and across the sacred river and through the steep pass between the Silver Mountains. City after city fell under his arcane magics as new recruits added to their ranks, for people both feared and worshiped him as a dark sorcerer.

Traveling south back to the southern coasts, Asra's advisors enlightened him of a holy city were wealth and riches could be found. Asra, however, had higher prospects that such a sacred place as the city of Petra would contain ancient relics and portal gates where he could once again contact the Djinn to enable him to pry open a rift and find his way back to the Necropolis. Asra felt anxious to arrive at this site and ravage its stored artifacts for anything that might help his cause. Once his troops arrived at the outskirts of their holy shrines, Asra rode in alone on a black stallion while he left his army to wait beyond its tall gates.

He did not wish to commit sacrilege upon the priests who ruled this holy city carved from stone, for they could be of far more use alive than as casualties of his conquest. His dark mount trotted in upon the dusty path toward seven priests who stood awaiting his arrival. By the number of armed sentries lining the streets, Asra could tell they had been prepared for war. Daring to approach alone, Asra had sent a message that he was both willing to negotiate terms and that he feared no man.

Word travels fast across the desert plains, for the citizens of Petra had heard of this dark sorcerer, the destroyer of cities who could burn a person to ash with his glare. Many tall tales and fanciful stories about him had crossed to the four corners of the territory. Asra was known to be lenient to those who displayed fealty but offered only cold and wicked cruelty to those who did not. These half-score priests were skeptical of the sorcerer's intentions. He had come here either to invade their city or to seek the wisdom of the deities who blessed their hallowed sanctuary.

"Great lord from the North, we humbly bid you welcome to Petra, the city of a thousand voices. What is it that brings you to grace our holy shrines?" Oran, the head cleric, inquired as the line of priests offered a bow of respect before their distinguished guest.

"You've no doubt noted that I left my horde beyond your city gates, priest," Asra answered as he dismounted his steed to approach them, "but if I allow, they will ravage this city and its inhabitants, and I can guarantee you there will be many fewer voices to be heard here when they are done."

His harsh comment made the surrounding priests uneasy as they exchanged worried glances. Oran stepped forward, being the most level-headed of the lot, and attempted to placate Asra with assuring words.

"There must be some service we could provide to you for your mercy, great lord," Oran asked with a generous measure of humility.

"I wish to inspect your shrines and will take what I find of use," Asra replied with an air of indifference, "you will also provide food and drink to my forces, which will remain outside your gates if your priests conform to my wishes," he finished with a gesture towards the shuddering clerics standing behind their head priest.

"Your will shall be done, great lord," Oran answered, and with a tap of his staff, Oran sent off several servants to gather food and wine along with water and grain for their mounts, "and I can offer you a tour of our seven holy shrines myself."

There was no exterior construction within Petra, but rather the buildings were carved from the rose-colored cliffs that lifted from the desert floor. The craftsmanship of their sculptors was exquisite, yet simple in design as they had etched each facade from the living rock, where tall pillars were accented with crowned arches adorned with strange and fearsome beasts. Running through each of its narrow corridors where sealed channels engineered to capture rainwater which was funneled to the open orchards and lush gardens that graced the inner city.

Asra was impressed by how these people had attained such a rich existence in their struggle against the desert. From the cliff walls around him there were throngs of onlookers who stood in lavish villas carved into the cliffs, each filled with colorful murals and adorned in fine silks. Petra had been the central trade route which Asra had followed from the Silver Mountains as he marched his army southward. To secure Petra meant that he could paralyze trade throughout the known territories, and thus, control all commerce throughout the region.

Oran brought Asra to their most predominant temple at the inner walls to the city and bowed as he stood aside to allow the sorcerer within. Once inside, the plain walls were a stark contrast to the elaborate carvings which draped its exterior. Its back wall was gilded with gold leaf while in the central alcove carved within the stone stood a wooden stand with a curious idol upon it. With jinn magic flowing through his veins, Asra could see that the decorated alcove actually hid a rift doorway within.

"This is the oldest temple in all of Petra, my lord," Oran stated, "legends say that the city was built around it over the countless centuries which have passed. For what or whom it was originally created for is unknown, but it now stands as a monument to the dead," he finished with a gentle nod towards the tiled floor.

Walking its length, Asra could see the grand mosaic at his feet illustrated seven doorways that fed the roots of a giant tree, and within its trunk it held the mummified souls of the dead. From this branched a vast city of the underworld depicted as a paradise, where at its center stood a towering obelisk upon which sat a bright burning flame. Asra recognized the central lighthouse of the Necropolis in the illustration, and knew that his journey back to Tasha would begin within these temple walls.

Chapter XVII
The Awakening

Asra was granted a tour of Petra, which was fortified by a series of narrow passages through an intricate maze of tight cliffs. An invading army would find it difficult to advance into such complicated geography, regardless of the countless blind corners and cramped corridors which were vulnerable to ambush. However, having a powerful sorcerer at the lead would likely be able to bypass these obstacles with ease, and Asra's proceeding reputation could destroy the moral of any defending forces. Until recently, such dark magics Asra possessed were only observed in the ancient myths from a time long forgotten; stories which struck fear in the hearts of mortal men.

Petra held an impressive amount of orchards and fields in their protected valley which was lush and green with life. Livestock and crops were also ample as were exotic oils and spices which were brought in by the convoy of trading caravans year round. The people who resided here were well off; as such a rich oasis provided most of their needs as long as the routes of trade through their valley continued. The residents had become master craftsmen in stone cutting and utilized the evacuated fill carved from rose quartz cliffs and reformed them into common objects and furniture of everyday use.

Asra sent for his war advisors to join him in the main temple in order to help him set up the rituals he would need to perform to crack open the ancient doorway to the netherworlds. His army had collected many sacred artifacts from the vaults of conquered cities during his regime; ancient relics with unique abilities which Asra knew how to make of use. His plan was to anchor the rift open so that it could not close upon him until he had separated Tasha from the magic armor which bound her to the realm of the undead, or defeat its enchantments altogether and return her back to the world of the living. Asra considered he would likely be able to use the Djinn to accomplish this deed if things went sour during her extraction, but he would only do so as a last resort.

The last time Asra and the genie had met he could tell the winds of oblivion had stripped the demon of all of its material strength, leaving it only its raw elemental essence. The jinn would have to return to its own plane to recover, which might take a thousand-fold lifetimes to replenish its former strength. Only then could it return to the world of men to exact its vengeance upon them; but by then he and the world Asra knew would be long gone. It would be poetic irony if the great demon returned one day to enact retribution only to find that there was nothing left of the world of men but a dusty graveyard full of shattered bones and broken dreams.

Oran had gathered the high priests of Petra to offer Asra what he needed for his endeavor, though they frowned upon relinquishing their main shrine to such a tyrant. Having the dark sorcerer in their midst was threat enough to gain their compliance, let alone the vast army stationed outside the high cliff walls of their city. The priests were familiar with many rituals and rites, but had never heard of what Asra had asked them to prepare for. The spiritual leaders were worried, and justly so, that the reckless sorcerer would be opening a door between the world of men and the domain of the dead; for it was an unnatural deed that shook the foundations of their faith.

Asra had timed his visit to Petra with care, for the phase of the full moon was in the following days to come. Preparations for the rite to open the rift and summon the demon of the void had to be calculated precisely. There was little Asra hadn't foreseen during his long journey here. He had expected to find answers at the ruins of the desert outpost where Ubar had once stood, but Petra was both a viable and convenient alternative after discovering it contained the site of an ancient gate.

"I want everything ready by the eve of the full moon," Asra ordered to the priests of the city as directed by his advisors, "there will be no leniency for delays!"

Asra spent the following days venturing into the winding streets of Petra and experiencing the unique lifestyle they had achieved. After much thought, he found it strange that he hadn't crossed any areas of squalor where the quality of living was far removed from the rest of the residence. Apparently, the people of Petra held an instinctual pride in their levels of common respect and standards which had been imposed by the teachings of the priests of the seven temples. They had found balance and tranquility through education among their people which bred a natural sense of awareness and dignity through their entire culture.

This made him consider the type of world he wanted to mold in place of those he had vanquished. Asra had grown to enjoy the perks of power and the fear cast in the eyes of others who glanced his way and whispered his name. He had become addicted to the tyranny he had fathered and recognition he bled from those around him. It was all due to the jinn magics he had leeched from the demon, for instead of just commanding the elements he now controlled the minds of men.

In the meantime, Asra took his leisure to tour the additional temples within the district, which led him to surveying their unique attributes.

"Ah, the great sorcerer from the north comes to visit our humble shrine," an old woman standing out front of a sanctuary remarked while offering to hand Asra a flower from her basket; a gesture of kindness which he refused to acknowledge, "please, do come in, and I would be happy to offer answers to any questions you may have."

Asra was struck how this disciple of the shrine did not seem to display any measure of fear in his presence. The old woman spoke to him as though they were equals, which is something Asra had not been accustomed too for some time. He explored the interior of the shrine which was similar in its basic dimensions as the others with their high ceilings and open space, but this one had been lined with a many sheepskin rugs upon the floors and large tapestries lining the walls. Immense pots holding palm trees stood indoors, gathering light from several mirrors placed in the sunlight at the inner entrance which helped illuminate the interior. Lavish tents were also set within the temple, filled with pillows and bowls of burning incense which left a delicate scent of honey blossoms lingering in the air.

"This is an interesting set of decor for a holy shrine," Asra mentioned casually as the barefoot woman kept pace beside him.

"The rugs help to muffle the resonance to which this chamber is attuned," the senior woman answered, "for without these barriers to absorb the sounds then the words of the living would pass to the realm of the gods."

"I don't quite follow you," Asra admitted.

"The seven temples of Petra were carved from the living

rock many generations ago in the same design as the great temple which legends say was created before the time of men when ancient gods walked the earth," she replied, "when they are empty and one stands within its center, there are certain words when sung which resonate the entire chamber!"

"Such as a mantra or ritual chants?" Asra inquired.

"So it is said," she agreed, "though I have only heard it performed once when I was but a child. In the other temples such acts of meditation complete these effects and our priests have claimed they can hear the words of the gods and even of the deceased beyond death's door."

Asra found it interesting that the use of sound could create such magics, for he had never considered such a trick could be performed except through incantations. At the rear of the temple there stood but a single stone, quite large and apparently unremarkable from any other he had seen among the valley roads. He saw no residual magic about it, nor any within the temple itself, but this strange artifact bothered him. Why was it here?

"What is the story behind this holy artifact?" He inquired upon his informal guide.

This simple stone was said to have come from mount Jabal, a holy mountain created by followers who brought with them but a single stone upon their pilgrimage to its sacred site," the woman noted by representing a single rock in the palm of her hand, "stone by stone the mountain grew over the years and generations that followed until it towered into the sky. A great path led from the valley floor to its peak where devotees would place a single pebble as a symbol of the burdens they carried in life and leaving them behind."

It was a quaint story which made Asra consider if there

might be any truth to the tale? From what strange sights he had seen when visiting other realms, there likely was. During this spiritual pilgrimage they called a hajj, instead of symbolic pebbles of their faith, some followers chose to carry far larger stones than others as a token of their sins to be forgiven, thus forging a greater sacrifice by those who toiled to reach its summit. What had once been a trek of fealty to leave a small token of their conviction, over the years had transformed into a visage of vivid anguish and despair as pilgrims strained and struggled up winding paths bearing heavy stone blocks from across the world, merely to purge themselves of their spiritual burdens to receive their self-anointed blessing from the mountain of mercy. Asra understood the symbolism more than most, for each follower had measured the troubles which they bore.

Asra touched the stone and wondered from what distant lands it had traveled to end up here? How many hands had it passed through to come to rest in this holy shrine? Most important of all, what sins had this boulder once represented as a memento to a life of guilt and regret. Asra remembered the small rune-stone Tasha had gifted him those untold years ago and realized these two icons where one in the same.

Asra, the Dark Sorcerer of the north, was not used to being so moved. Such a shaking of his thoughts brought a tear to his eye, though he turned away from the woman so she would not see his weakness. It took a moment to regain his posture and return to his air of restraint. Asra promptly left the temple as the old woman followed quietly in his wake until he stopped at the doorway and issued an order towards her.

"Have that stone relic brought to the main temple before

sunset," he snapped before turning to disappear among the narrow streets of Petra.

There was little the priests could do to oppose him, but thus far this ruthless sorcerer had not violated their sanctum with bloodshed. Though their people had readied to defend themselves there was the hope that Asra would find what he was looking for at their sacred sites and choose to leave them in peace. Feeding his vast army was a small price to pay to keep their heads on their shoulders or from being burned alive by mystic fire.

Asra arrived back at the great temple before sundown to make sure all the preparations were in order. The great stone had also been delivered to his satisfaction. The priests of Petra were understandably worried as the dark sorcerer had returned from his camp with a squadron of his strongest warriors. Asra had trained his personal guards in the arcane knowledge of what to expect from beings who occupied the underworld.

When faced with the demonic jinn and undead from the Necropolis, his selected warriors would not tremble in the face of such monstrosities. He had hoped that the acquired tools and artifacts Asra had collected might be able to overcome the binding wards which enveloped the city of the dead and its ties to the armor of the Nocturnal. From times of antiquity there have been tokens of power scattered about the world, and he had obtained every charm and spell he had crossed thus far in his journeys. If all else had failed, Asra promised himself that he would use his final wish to free Tasha from her curse and return her home.

It was this sole dream which had drove him into madness and molded Asra into a person who callously cast aside the lives of anyone he deemed an obstacle to this goal. Scores of thousands had perished by mortal blade and mystic flames as he ravaged cities and settlements in his consuming grief and unbridled rage to make the world respect and honor him, even if he had to drag them to their knees. Though Asra had wronged countless innocent people during his brutal campaigns, he would sacrifice everything to the one person who had helped him in his time of need.

"I hope you will find all is as you requested, great lord," Oran offered as Asra strolled into the ancient temple, "might there be anything else you desire before the ceremony begins?"

"The rite I will be performing will begin at midnight when the full moon is at its peak in the night sky," Asra answered, "you and your priests are welcome to observe the ceremony as long as you do not interfere; though be wary that you are responsible for your own lives if you should choose to stay."

As ominous as his warning was, a few of the priests elected to remain and witness the event. The clerics had spent their lives teaching doctrine about ancient gods and their fantastic tales but had never experienced anything paranormal in all their years. They had weak hopes that the faith in their theologies could be strengthened if they had but a mere glimpse into the afterlife and lived to tell about it. As everything was arranged, the procession began when Asra stood at the temple door and gazed into the night sky, seeing that the moon had reached its apex.

Tasha was a follower of the lunar goddess, Allat, and he would use that affiliation to gain the favor of the deity to help aid him direct its energies to unfurl a gate to the underworld. The walls of the temple had been stripped bare and several large chimes had been set to either side.

The priests gasped as Asra brushed his fingers which produced a blue fire that licked into the air. Touching each of the chimes with the mystic flame he set them ringing at a constant resonance, as the deep tone brought the walls of the temple vibrating until it seemed as though the air itself moved.

His warriors stood firm as Asra stepped aside and motioned for the assistants outside to focus a large silver mirror to reflect the moonlight through the open doorway directly upon the etched gate at the back of the shrine. Moments passed as the tone of the chimes faded while Asra began the chants and prayers he used to control the magics that were weaving within the chamber. Only his acute vision could witness the rings of energy bouncing between the walls of the ancient temple, seemingly trapped within this sacred place. Suddenly the ethereal rings became parallel to one another and settled upon the beam of moonlight streaming through the open door.

As though each ring was a focusing lens, the moonlight pinched into a single small beam which appeared to pierce the stone. Whispers could be heard filling the room, mumbling warnings and premonitions of doom. They were the voices of the dead drifting from the path of oblivion through the fractured rift. Asra became anxious when the tiny rupture began to reseal upon itself, as the magics used to open the doorway were spent.

"No, no, not when I am so close!" he yelled as he flipped a conjured blade into existence and used it to slice the scarred fate line upon his hand; reopening the old wound.

Asra pressed his bloody palm onto the mystic stone from its sister temple, creating a ward which he quickly positioned upon the seam of the closing rift. When

Asra's blood touched the dark fissure a powerful gust pushed through the gap, tearing it asunder. Priests and trained men who thought they were prepared, took a wary step back when a foul cloud of smoke and ash billowed through the fracture as it peeled back to the frame of the doorway. The angry cloud formed itself into the outline of a giant winged Djinn, an ancient elemental from the planes of chaos.

"You have kept me waiting, Master." the demon declared in its horrible voice that shook the temple walls.

At the sight of the great monster, one of the priests fainted while another wetted his robes as he shuddered in fear. A pair of clerics scurried out in terror through the doorway, momentarily cutting off the reflected moonlight streaming in. This caused the gate to choke and spark, to which Asra turned in ire towards the distraction to his delicate ritual. Asra spun back to address the jinn who had been left impatiently waiting these long years.

"Does Tasha still live?" Asra demanded to the smoky demon towering above them.

"She does," the Djinn replied, "and she has been eagerly awaiting your return," he offered with a malicious smile which Asra found odd given his remark.

Asra boldly stepped over the loadstone holding the gate ajar and entered into the gate. His unit of soldiers followed in after, each bearing pendants, shields, and artifacts marked with runes for protection during their trek through the deadly rift as the vaporous demon watched. Howling winds buffeted them as each warrior crossed through the threshold, finding themselves in a dark and terrifying setting woven from nightmares. The passage ahead was precarious as there were sections where the path was suspended above nothingness.

Fear overtook the few who were pressed forward by their comrades as they fell victim to the screaming phantasms in the wind and vertigo their natural senses could not perceive. Though the priests peered through the open gate, they dared not tread into the abyss. The great Djinn sneered at the clerics as they cringed before him, and dissipated back into the rift to follow his master. Asra took the lead with a crystal scepter he had acquired from a royal treasury which offered its bearer guidance, thus enhanced by his own clairvoyant powers.

The passage was long and treacherous, for even his warriors trained in the arcane arts had no defense against the hostility of the void. During the journey a handful of his guards fell, carried away by the violent gales as the cloudy form of the Djinn watched in mild amusement at their untimely demise. The wails of banshees and tormented souls whispered curses into their ears, unsettling their minds. After the long passage back to the Necropolis, the scepter of light had led Asra to a secluded path which came to an abrupt end.

He knew the doorway was here, but was unseen from within the rift itself; however, Asra had not come all this way unprepared. Pulling a small mirror from his vest, he folded the gilded silver artifact taken from the tower of a vain and vindictive queen who had once used it to spy upon her lovers, and turned his back to the empty path.

He gazed into the mystical mirror and saw the doorway as it was placed, which led into the chamber of the dark mistress. As he turned and was closing the mirror, Asra had caught a glimpse of the Djinn in its reflection, and what he saw at that moment caused him to pause. The demon was whole as he had once seen it when it was trapped under the city of Ubar, but it was now streaked with a dark stigma as though a scourge had infected the immortal creature. The moment the smoky demon returned the glance through the mirror, Asra snapped it shut and quickly returned it to the safety of his vest.

Asra gripped tightly onto the elemental pendant around his neck and struck the lighted scepter into the emptiness before him; piercing the hidden gateway. Fine cracks appeared in the pane that separated the realm of the dead from the barrier of the void. Adding his magic to that of the scepter, the ward finally shattered and Asra was able to step through. He quickly ushered his men to follow him past the breached gate and turned back to see the demon poised beyond the portal.

"Why do you not follow?" Asra demanded of the Djinn.

"A ruptured portal is impassable to me in this primal form, my Master," the demon answered, "you will be on your own while within the realm of the Necropolis, as I cannot assist you beyond this shattered gate."

Asra remembered that the jinn was now tethered to the rift itself rather than a physical object like the mystic lamp which had long since been destroyed. As his men filled the upper chamber, Asra noticed it was now far different than he remembered. The golden silks and bloodied bones had been replaced by many hundreds of icons of the lunar moon, a celestial body unseen from this dark tomb. Broken skulls of the dead now lined the entirety of the walls from floor to ceiling, painting a morbid mood among the men.

His elite warriors were not unaffected by the choice of decor. They had seen much death and despair serving the dark sorcerer, but this cursed place had a dreadful air which seemed to sap their very souls. Asra searched the chamber with mild desperation, wanting to call out to

Tasha through the halls of the temple but did not wish to weaken the moral of his guards by appearing desperate. There was little he could do but order his men to spread out through the temple grounds to find her.

The architecture within the unholy temple had changed dramatically, for the pit below the antechamber that was once filled with the bound souls of the undead priests had been renovated with a trimmed staircase. The central arena was now fitted with an enormous iron ring gilded with brass accents. Asra assumed this odd icon also represented the lunar goddess in some form, but its purpose was not clear. The branching hallways which led to the main entrance had been greatly widened and restored with opaque glass containing glowing orbs.

Asra knew that the enchanted armor of the Nocturnal gave its wearer the ability to control the dead; thus, he presumed Tasha had used the walking corpses of the Necropolis as slaves to remodel the city to her desires. How she had survived all this time and on what sustenance was another question altogether; but if what the demon had said was true, then he would be happy just to find her alive. Saving Tasha from this place had consumed his waking moments over the passing years as a means to his personal redemption, and he refused to fail at this moment. Once they had cleared the temple and arrived at the entrance, Asra and his men stumbled upon a disturbing site.

A massive covered bridge constructed of human skeletons had been erected which spanned the entire width of the three collapsed platforms. Dried skin and rotting sinew had been used in place or mortar as human leather bound the supporting braces of the pass together. Asra's warriors came to a halt, wary of crossing such a blighted monument of death. Gazing among the carnage that made the grotesque edifice, the horrid faces of countless dead woven within its structure appeared to stare back upon them with empty blackened eyes.

Asra stepped forward and crossed the bridge alone to stand upon the raised lip of the stairway which led to the main temple while his soldiers lingered behind. From below they could not see what had caused the dark sorcerer to pause as he stood upon the terrace frozen in shock. Ascending up the long stairway to him was Tasha in her ancient armor, trailing a crimson cape which fluttered in the ghostly wind that swept around her feet. Behind her stood a vast army of the undead, armed and ready for battle.

"Tasha..." Asra called to her, though he found himself searching for his words as it was not how he imagined this moment to be, "I have fought my way back here to free you from this place."

Tasha stalled in her ascent to take a breath as though flustered by his naive comment. She raised her hand in a casual gesture and the army of the dead behind her struck their shields and tapped their spears upon the stony ground, thrice. It was a wordless display that she had now become the royal Mistress of the Necropolis by her own hand and was not his damsel in distress. Forced to survive against the odds in such a grim and ghastly realm, Tasha had embraced the teachings of the Nocturnal and proudly adorned its crown.

"You, the murderer of innocent souls, have come to rescue *me*?" She thrust with a dagger of vile contempt in her tone, "You, Asra, thief of magics and betrayer of worlds, thought you would be able to release yourself from the sins you wrought?

Asra was confused by her choice of words, for they struck a deep chord inside him. He fought the mixed feeling suddenly sifting through his mind, for he had not considered this turn of events.

"I have opened the gate for us so you can return to your valley and be rid of this vile place," Asra's usual air of authority had bent into a plea.

"When you left me abandoned here I waited without moving from the portal where you had disappeared. There is no day nor night in this accursed place to count the days or years with no sun nor moon to grace this dreadful sky," Tasha replied as she looked up into the dark swirling void of billowing haze above them, "when I realized you weren't coming back for me I surrendered to the armor of the Dark Mistress and became one with the city of the dead. These poor lost souls found new meaning in serving one who shared their plight, and so I promised to deliver them from this foul eternity!"

"I ...I don't understand, don't you want to return to the world of the living, Tasha? Asra asked with confusion ringing in his word.

"I have faced the trials of the Tali-ma, and one of the gifts of the Nocturnal is the ability to listen to the dead," Tasha replied as she turned to face her army of corpses, "and I have heard of your cruel deeds over these long years, and if you look will find those whose lives you have stolen among my children before you," she granted as the great horde of undead below grunted in contempt, "I know that you invaded my homeland and killed my people, and abused your magics to twist their good hearts to serve as your slaves, Asra the mighty," she added in a spiteful tone, "you ask me to return to the world of the living, when you, yourself, have become dead inside.

Asra stood stunned, not knowing what to say. He had used his powers to protect his own life but fell into a chasm of darkness by pursuing a path of power and greed. He could not say he had lost who he once was, for that person was a mystery to him. However, he had a chance to start anew but had squandered it on selfish pride and retribution; much like the demon he so loathed.

The powers of the jinn had polluted him, just as the Djinn had intended. Such magics were not for the likes of mortal men for they possessed neither the maturity nor wisdom of the eternal elemental spirits which had formed the world. What use were such mystic powers if all he had was bitterness in his heart? He could have done much to change the world around him for the better, but instead chose to seethe in pettiness and revenge; only to become the one thing he despised most, leaving him to wonder in the end what it was he struggled for?

"What is it that you want, Tasha; to stay here among these rotting abominations?" Asra shouted back in spite, for her words had wounded him.

"No, you misunderstand," Tasha, the crowned Mistress of the underworld replied in a calm tone, "I wish to take vengeance upon you, Asra, and my brood will take their wrath upon the living."

Chapter XVIII
Redemption

There was a tense pause after Tasha spoke her words, for Asra realized that she was no longer the woman he had once known. In the irony of it, he saw how power had twisted who she had once been and the kind gypsy girl he once knew had been corrupted by the magics of the mystic armor and cruel influence of this cursed realm. Out of instinct, Asra conjured a flaming scimitar into his hand but had almost forgotten how the Necropolis hindered his magics. It had been a long time since he had felt weakness, and the drain of that one small spell sapped him of strength.

He realized that Tasha had become the embodiment of the Nocturnal, the Dark Mistress of the Necropolis. With a twist of her hand the hordes of undead that filled the streets behind her as far as the eye could see, raised their weapons and began charging up the steps. With but a moment's hesitation, Asra backed away to retreat across the bridge of bones. When Tasha finally breached the landing atop the stairway, she waved a hand towards Asra as he fled.

From the floor of the bridge, withered hands and bony arms reached out to snare Asra in their hungry grasp. The sinew and strips of flesh came alive at the command of their Dark Mistress to apprehend this trespasser. Skulls snapped with their jaws while dismembered ribcages shuttered like traps as several of his warriors were caught unwary. Screams of the living mingled with the shrieks of the dead as the soldiers receded back into the Temple.

Asra hacked with his flaming blade to carve away the writhing appendages clutching upon his boots and tearing at his cloak. Every step was a struggle as a field of grasping arms sprouted before him from the tangle of the bridge. Several of his soldiers stepped forward to lend aid, only to be grappled down and torn to bits as Asra reached the other side. Finally pulled to relative safety of the entrance, they looked back across bridge through the gauntlet of squirming corpses as the army of the undead advanced upon them.

"What is happening?" One of Asra's chiefs shouted in the confusion with fear washed over the soldiers faces as they prepared a defense. They were told this would be a rescue mission, but their target appeared to be colluding with the opposing force.

"There's been a change of plans," Asra stated with conviction as he placed a wall of flame at the doorway to the temple with his magics.

It was a weak barrier considering how taxed his powers were in this place, as the void encircling the city would leech all mystic energies within its perimeter. Bracing for the onslaught, the interior corridors would have been far easier to defend if they had not been widened, which made him wonder at the reason why they had been expanded? Beyond their view from the temple, a great beast coiled upon the spire at the center of the city slithered its way into the maze of streets. Through the twisted alleys it pushed its way between the shambling dead as they advanced upon the unholy temple.

The frightened men wondered why the charging horde beyond the wall of flame suddenly withdrew, falling to either side of the entry. A great rumble could be felt in the ground at their feet as a clamor could be heard rising upon the distant stairway. Marble pillars crumbled and split into shards as a dark figure loomed over the landing and pressed its way through the arched passage. Waves of bodiless arms caressed the hardened scales of the leviathan that slithered across the great bridge.

"Ah, Dahaka!" One of the men yelled as the shadow of the giant beast encompassed the entirety of the gate.

"What does that mean?" Asra spat back to calm his sentry whose face was drawn with dread.

"It is the dialect of the eastern desert, my Sultan," his chief answered, "it means, Great Serpent!"

As the words fell from his lips the head of the enormous cobra pierced through the curtain of flame; smothering it under its mass. Its forked tongue whipped out from between its armored lips as its soulless eyes glared down upon them. Instead of the pinched iris of a cat, this beast eyes were alive with a toxic glow which Asra recognized as the effect of the butcher bats filling its skull. Tasha had managed to make use the great mummified beasts in the mausoleum and bent them to her will.

As the monstrosity burrowed between them, it was clear now why the halls of the temple had been renovated so as to accommodate this ancient dragon of the desert. The men stabbed at the armored skin in vain as the serpent slithered past. They pursued it into the main chamber where it had coiled upon the great ring erected in the center of the arena. The sorcerer's soldiers encircled the beast while others climbed the great steps for a better angle of attack; however, the upper platform only proved to be an inconvenient elevation for those victims who were quickly dispatched between its jaws.

The serpent struck out at the men while blade of both

spear and sword failed to pierce its natural armor. Several men were caught in its jaws while their mangled bodies were dashed against the stone walls. Those few blades that cut into its hide found no trail of blood to weaken it. Such a monstrosity could only be stopped by magic; powers which the Nocturnal possessed in abundance in this domain, but Asra did not.

Asra realized he needed the Djinn to aid him in this battle, but the demon was trapped beyond the other side of the portal gate. The dark sorcerer who had murdered thousands and conquered empires was powerless in this domain against such a foe. Ordering his men to retreat, they fled towards the cracked portal as they were cut down from behind by the advancing horde of undead pouring into the temple. As he slipped through the gate and into the shadow of the void, Asra realized too late that his arrogance would cost him dearly this day.

There was little time to spare, with the clashing of blades spilling blood and bone across the temple grounds. Asra had hoped he could close the rift before the dead pushed through. The artifacts he had collected during his conquests throughout the surrounding empires were merely parlor tricks in the face of raw magics, and even here the void continued to sap him of his energies. The demon, however, was there to greet him.

"What mischief have you gotten yourself into this time?" The cloudy jinn inquired, half in jest, for over the years the demon had watched from the rift as Tasha transformed into the cold succubus she had become.

He had spent his lingering torment in the void anticipating what twists of drama and fate would be sewn between these two mortals when they finally faced each other once again. One had become a tyrannical sorcerer who abused his stolen powers to spread death upon the world of the living, while the other had become a servant of ancient magics who made use of the dead. Tasha had transformed into a puppet of the old gods who had abandoned their utopia and left it forever locked in darkness and ruin. Over the countless years she had tempered her will, showing an impressive strength and resolve with a fair ration of ambition.

"The dead will pass through unless the gate is sealed!" Asra yelled over the howling winds of the void.

"I agree, if that what you so desire, my Master?" The genie replied, seeing opportunity in his desperation.

"It is what has to be done to protect your Master!" Asra snapped back, knowing full well the Djinn was trying to trick him into releasing his final wish to fulfill the task.

The great Djinn merely folding his arms in contempt as a staunch grimace etched deeply upon his face. The demon had suffered much at the hands of this mortal trickster and had been sapped to his rawest form in a struggle to survive within this empty void. The demon was perpetually bled while entrapped here and the torture of it caused the genie the loss of all patience and resolve.

In his vanity, Asra had anticipated that the demon would protect him once again as it had done when he was nearly burned at the stake in the forest valley, but the demon was offering no such mercy. The jinn sought liberation as much as the undead desired to be free of their unbearable torment. The dead pressed their way to the gate as their decayed fingers reached through, finding a means to escape their torment. Asra placed a shield of mystic fire before him, but even here the magic of it was sapped away by the violent gales within the rift.

It would not be long before his powers faltered, and he

shot an angry glace at the insubordinate demon who sat defiant. The dead that pushed through were met by Asra's soldiers; who struck them down and sent them tumbling into the void. Within moments after the assault, a crack of thunder clapped through the rift as the doorway ripped asunder when the giant serpent pierced its way past the shattered gate. The creature slithered through and reared its ugly head towards the few soldiers who were left and continued pressing its attack.

The ghostly whispers of the void turned to violent shrieks as the wailing of souls lost to the void felt the wound from the ruptured portal. As the mortal men fought their way back through the floating paths beyond the rift, the demon played his hand; waiting until the moment his impudent Master would beg for his final wish from the Djinn. The demon taunted the beast while the soldiers retreated, fighting their way as the living and dead became casualties to the howling winds of oblivion. Asra's soldiers, finding no respite, traced the lit pathway left by the mystic scepter the sorcerer had used to mark their trail.

With great loss, Asra's warriors retreated from the onslaught from a fountain of undead flooding in from the broken fissure which seemed to have no end. Only when Asra stood upon the threshold of the gate back to Petra did the demon intervene as the giant serpent fell upon him. As the wurm struck to consume him, Asra cowered before the open jaws of the beast. An arms length from being devoured within its putrid maw, the serpent was snared by the Djinn and denied its mortal prey.

The two leviathans battled as the serpent fought to find a grip upon its new foe, finding only mist and ash to coil upon as the demon reformed itself. Bound in their deadly embrace, the only powers the great elemental had left in its primal form was that of fire and flame. The great serpent had been revived from the husk of its former self left rotting within the vast mausoleum of Necropolis, and despite its tempered hide, fire was its one weakness. The jinn amassed its magics from his core and formed a sphere of mystic flame within its clawed hand, and finding its chance to strike, shoved the burning sphere down the gullet of the beast.

A hot glow erupted from deep within the serpent as it began to convulse; its enormous tail whipping as the ancient dragon destroyed suspended paths and sending debris scattering among the void. The demon kept its stranglehold upon the serpent as it bit down upon its arm until its struggles weakened and the Djinn released the monstrous serpent to be swept away by the violent winds of the rift. Tasha stepped beyond the gate and paused at the entry to the void in her gilded armor, glaring with disdain at the defeat of her great serpent. Waves of the dead swarmed around her as she stood defiant.

"I am coming for you Asra," the dark mistress screamed above the howling winds, "my minions will retake what you have stolen from us, and you will find no place to hide in the world of the living."

Still shaken for having come so close to death, Asra backed out of the rift and into the ancient temple of Petra while his warriors swept past him to escape the void. The priests were caught in a moment of despair, seeing their worst fears had materialized as the fleeing soldiers cried that the dead were coming through. The clerics of Petra withdrew as frightened and wounded warriors of the dark sorcerer swept into the temple from the rift held open by the loadstone. When Asra attempted to remove the artifact, he found that it would not budge.

He had realized too late what he had done, for the old woman's tale about the origin of the stone revealed the impact of his enchantments upon it; for it now held the weight of a mountain.   Hardened soldiers and temple disciples alike fled in terror as the withered cries of the undead echoed through the open gate. The remnants of Asra's original squadron were cut down as the walking corpses poured through, stepping over the stone that kept the doorway to the underworld from closing. The dark sorcerer had brought doom to the people of Petra.

Under a pale moon, the undead flooded into the narrow streets as the people ran for their lives; a wave of rotting bodies and rusted swords cutting deep into flesh as the sand turned red with their blood. The priests retreated to their abodes cut high into the cliffs, where those few who had reached safety struggled to pull up ladders and ropes to fend off the army of the dead. Asra withdrew towards his main force stationed outside the city gate, who had rallied only when the heard the screams of people and the sounds of battle in the night. Having returned to the domain of men, Asra's powers elevated to their full strength where he could attempt to turn the tide against the undead which had overtaken the city.

If he failed now, then everything he had fought to achieve over these long years would be swept away. This scourge would spread like a poison to the outer kingdoms and destroy everything in its path without prejudice. Asra had to contain them here and end this catastrophe by any means necessary.   As his stationed troops abandoned their camps and prepared arms to the front line beside the sorcerer, Asra had called for his siege engineers to unload their cargo. In haste, several massive carts were brought forward to the perimeter before the city gates.

Asra found a strategic place between the two canyon walls as the perfect place to erect a wall of fire, burning cold with mystic flames. The dead, having returned to the world of the living, now sought bloodshed and revenge against the world which judged them for their sins rather than a release through immolation. From the line of readied warriors, the engineers deployed floating lanterns into the sky. Asra had conceived the idea from Tasha's dance during the ceremony of the moon years before, and used this military tactic before on unwary cities and citadels to breach their walls. With the elemental talismans, Asra was able to command the winds to carry the paper lanterns into the narrow canyons that weaved through the city.

The undead had slaughtered many innocent people while the survivors had sought shelter in high terraces, unreachable by the rotting corpses mulling below. The horror and screams in the night were replaced by an incandescent cloud that drifted silently in the night sky which drew the attention of the living and the dead alike. They stood as though transfixed, staring upwards with their hollow eyes, having forgotten the beauty of the stars and the bright lights sailing above them like a swarm of fireflies. Even the people of Petra paused in their panic to step to their balconies to view the majestic sight.

For a moment an eerie peace had swept through the city as the floating torches drifted through the streets; for it was a breathtaking sight of grace and wonder as thousands of paper lanterns migrated into the canyons, turning them into rivers of light. Asra's lanterns were designed with candles molded with bases of sulfur and tar. Their pointed bottoms were devilishly crafted to tip over once they touch any surface. These worked well in cities constructed of wooden roofs and open fields that would instantly ignite into raging flames.

The foremost lantern to settle was caught by a single curious soldier, whose withered dead hand reached out to grasp this strange lamp; only to have it burst into flame as his body was engulfed within the sphere of its blistering heat. The rain of fire fell like a hail of vengeance upon the city, lighting anything the lanterns touched into a pool of roaring flames. The army of the dead was trapped within the narrow streets and knew no fear for their own preservation when following the commands of their Dark Mistress. Fire was an enemy they could neither cut down nor bleed but one which readily consumed their wilted flesh.

In their own way, the residence of the Necropolis had found their eternal release with their last visit back to the world of the living. The undead staggered and stumbled through the twisting sandstone corridors as their bodies were set aflame. Those who had escaped the initial bombardment were set ablaze by their comrades who wandered into them. When the rotted kindling became exhausted and flames began to settled, a solitary figure stepped from the central temple.

Tasha strode through the charred streets, stepping over smoking corpses of flesh and rotting bone. The barrier of mystic flame extinguished as Asra strode forward to meet her upon the barren meadow outside of the temple grounds. She looked unsettled; angry yet resolved. Asra had kept his promise to release her from the city of the dead, only to be received into another.

They stood apart, him in his sultan's robes stained

scarlet by the blood and splatter of battle, and she in her armor with her crimson cape wrapped around her form like a death shroud. Behind her, the smoldering city of Petra had been transformed into a scorched catacomb filled with the remnants of the dead. The once colorful temples and lavish villas were now but burning crypts. The dark mistress of the underworld held no weapon but her long dark nails which had grown like talons that she flicked open in defiance of him.

"It doesn't have to be like this, Tasha!" Asra shouted, "You are free now," he pleaded with her to stop her unyielding assault.

"That is a name I no longer recognize," she hissed, taking on the familiar dialect of the Oracle who had worn the armor of the Nocturnal before her, and for a moment her head turned to either side of the hidden valley as though she saw something that Asra could not and began to cackle aloud, a sound which ran cold the blood of the soldiers who stood beyond them, "...so you think you have defeated me?"

Asra stood baffled, for he had decimated her army and cleansed them by fire. Their charred bodies would not be returning to haunt them. His attention suddenly drew towards the sound of rattling armor and shuffling boots that echoed from the temple as more undead poured through the open gate to replace those who had fallen. There seemed to be no end to their numbers.

The dark mistress unfurled her cape, revealing the gilded armor beneath as she opened both her clawed hands; a dark magic seething from them. Asra's legion of warriors shuddered and faltered as corpses of Petra's buried dead from countless generations past began to crawl their way from beneath the sands of the valley floor around them. Even the great sorcerer he had become, Asra knew he was outnumbered, for he could not suppress the countless dead rising from their graves. In the years past, he had only added to their numbers, and those defeated would now rise to vanquish him in kind.

A cloud of ash and smoke poured in from the temple, coursing between the feet of the undead who marched untiring. An endless army that needed no food or rest, which could not be bribed nor swayed by power or riches and only sought the destruction of life was not a foe, but a plague. From the smoldering ash that wafted from the temple the ancient demon materialized behind her; drawing Tasha's resentful gaze. Outside the rift and back into the world of men, the powers of the Djinn grew a thousand fold.

The second the Dark Mistress became distracted, Asra leapt forward as a flaming sword stretched from his hand. The mystic blade pierced deep into the chink in her armor; a fault in its design he knew well from helping her adorn it those many years ago in the Necropolis. The blade slipped through her and burned its bitter flame as Tasha's cold eyes returned to their bright blue color as a well of tears fell from her cheek. The possession of the Nocturnal had been extinguished as it retreated into the enchanted armor which slowly began to peel from her skin as she died while he held her within his arms.

"Tasha ...I'm, I'm sorry," Asra muttered gently, knowing no apology could undo the wrong he had done, "I never meant to harm you or your people," he implored, trying to seek forgiveness in her final moments as the demon towered over them. Her gaze turned hard as she glared up and the full moon above and back towards him with a look indifference as the color washed from her face.

"There are many good people in this world, but you are not one of them," Tasha whispered back in a weak voice before her entire body shivered once, and she was gone. Each plate of armor fell from her limp arms, her legs, and chest, and finally, the helmet tumbled to the ground. All that was left was the disfigured body of a once kind and beautiful gypsy girl who danced under the moonlight among the green forests.

A flood of emotions overwhelmed him, for the absolution he had fought so long, and killed so many for, would never be attained. He had twisted the soul of another by his own misdeeds and knew not how to face the burden of his guilt. The sound of groans and marching feet of the undead halted as they appeared to turn and stumble into one another as though confused. One after another the undead crumbled to the ground, their armor and rusted weapons rattling as they fell.

It took several moments for the wave of death to filter back through the narrow streets of Petra and into the temple gate, through the rift itself. After the dust settled, only the piles of rotting bones and armor and their accompanying stench were left behind. The roars and cheers of his army were only stifled by the presence of the smoldering Djinn towering above their heads. A trail of ash and smoke snaking back to the open gate in the temple was tethered to the great demon which loomed over Asra as he gently laid down Tasha's limp body.

"Is this the price of such power?" Asra wondered aloud as the jinn overheard.

"No, mortal," the demon answered, "magic only makes you more of what you already are," he answered, his voice thundering and deep, "if you are kind and generous, such powers allows you to be even more so;

but if you are small, petty and selfish inside, then that is all it will magnify."

Asra understood now what the jinn had warned him about those many years ago. His fear had led him to a path of tyranny and spreading grief because he had chosen for himself rather than others. The magics of the elementals were never meant for mankind because they could not conceive the enormous duty of restraint. He had upset the balance of the Trinity and had paid by casting those he cared for aside like ballast.

"I desire to decree my final charge," Asra spoke through the remorse welling in his throat and the shame he felt gripping his heart, "I wish that our meeting had never come to pass," Asra spoke with shaky breath.

The demon heard his words with elation to fulfill his final duty but his expression quickly turned to a scowl; for what he commanded would only return the Djinn back to his prison. The demon considered for a moment that such a fate would return his former strength which had been stripped from him by the rift, and there was always the chance that some other fool might stumble into the forbidden temple seeking their fortune. What were a few more years of sleep considering the thousands which had passed? This was acceptable to the Djinn, but the oath he swore would need to be amended.

"If that is your desire, my Master? The jinn replied with a grave tone.

"It is," was all that Asra answered.

"Then to undo what has been done, you must speak aloud the spell of binding upon the name of the A'ra, the temple guardian where you found me confined. Only then will we both be released from our sacred pact," the demon answered; and when he looked up the demon was suddenly gone as the moon seemed to swirl in the heavens above.

He suddenly found himself sitting among the barren dunes while the heat of the desert began to wane as the sun slowly fell upon the horizon. If grief had a scent, he now reeked with it. Welling despair could be seen in his weary eyes if only he would raise them from the shifting sand gathering at his feet. The bitter taste of regret was sour upon his tongue, choking his words from the aching thirst which clenched at his throat. Anguish enveloped him like the warm sour sweat prickling upon the skin beneath his robes, for he was unable to grasp who he was as though he had been robbed of his memories.

One word echoed from his parched lips, revealing the misery that wallowed within his troubled mind, a single phrase he struggled to recall, "Ah'z ...Az-ra."

The hot sun dipped from sight and the shadows of the shifting dunes reached out to enfold him in their merciful embrace as the cool blanket of darkness spread upon the evening sky above. One by one a sprinkle of stars poked through the canopy of the heavens until a river of twinkling lights filled the night. The lone man sat like a forgotten statue in an empty garden lost to time as though he were a monument to sorrow. He raised his head to gaze upon the beautiful mystery of the stars as his ears beheld the faint calling of a distant flute.

He sat motionless in surrender and listened to the sad melody as it drifted upon the desert wind while the tide of sand from the dunes slowly washed over him, grain by grain, until he was eventually consumed whole beneath its weight. The tune of the flute faded away, and a gentle peace fell across the desert washed in silken moonlight under a star-filled sky.

Michel Savage

About the Author

Michel Savage has been devoted to writing throughout his career. If one reads between the lines they will find his novels revolve around the reminder that we are only borrowing our small place in nature but for a brief period of time, and to take responsibility for the environment, for one another, and all other living creatures with which we share this world; and hopefully planting a seed in our conscience of the importance to preserve what is left of the wilds, our untainted woodlands and ever-dwindling rainforests.

He has had the blessing of sharing his stories and artwork around the globe, which is a gift in itself, and would encourage others not to waste too much of their lives chasing someone else's dreams but to follow their own.

And as a final word, one of the most valuable lessons he has learned in his years is that there are more far important things in life than power and money, such as kindness, compassion, and consideration towards others.

...share that thought if you will.

*"When the winds of fate flickers our candle,
only then do we to realize how easily
we can be left in the dark."*

Michelangelo Savage
ഔകൃ

Ubar ~ the Lost City

Be it Medina, Shaddād, Iram of the Pilars, the fabled city of Ubar was known by many names in ancient Arabia, which was once the center of the vast frankincense trade. This legendary outpost existed from 2800 B.C. to 300 A.D., which was known throughout the region as the Atlantis of the Sands; a remote fortress which had mysteriously disappeared.

Its ruins were rediscovered by accident in 1992 through the collection of remote sensing data acquired by NASA satellites scanning the southern deserts of Oman. Little is left of this lost city which was built upon a solitary spring atop a vast cavern. Reports of earthquakes from that period were cross referenced and confirmed by site excavations of the fortress that a tremor had cracked the fragile bedrock and swallowed the entire city and all its inhabitants in a single night.

It is but an example of places long forgotten where such tales and tragedies retold turn from legends into myth, and are all but forgotten until their ghosts resurface to be remembered once again.

This story is dedicated to those who lost their lives that fateful night; may their dreams forever live as whispers in the wind upon the desert sands.

Also by
Michel Savage

Shadoworld
Shadow of the Sun

On a distant, slowly rotating world, Bronze Age tribes must migrate thought their lives to avoid the long cold death of nightfall. As of late, strange events have been deeply troubling the tribal elders; revealing evidence perhaps, that something is lurking on the dark side.

As for a pair of young misfits, the ancient mystery is about to unfold; to reveal their peoples forgotten past, buried deep within the underworld, shrouded in the shadow of the sun.

Shadoworld
Veil of Shadows

Ash was an orphaned street urchin who grew up in the gutters of a desolate medieval city; his bitter youth spent picking pockets and snatching trinkets from the wealthy to survive.

Over the years his art for stealth and sharpened skills had drawn the attention of the Thieves Guild who took him into their folds. Little did they know that the boys tragic past would one day find itself woven within the treacherous schemes of a mysterious spider cult.

As of late, a series of chilling murders had befallen several nobles within the privileged upper districts. Their gruesome deaths had appeared to be centered around an ancient cursed skull, which had recently found its way into the hands of a rich collector. There were few who would trespass upon the strange realms of witchcraft and dark magic ...but a master thief does not fear those who dwell in darkness, for he is one with the shadows.

Broken Mirror
Apophis 2029

Hurtling through space was an enormous tumbling rock known as MN4 our astronomers affectionately named after an ancient Egyptian god of destruction. Asteroid Apophis was the talk of the year that every scientific community on Earth was aware of, though its flyby in April 2029 was to be nothing more than a spectacular celestial event; but as warring nations were locked in global conflict, our civilization was unprepared for the devastation that followed in its wake.

Several years after governments fell and society dissolved a ragged pack of survivors stumble upon the buried truth, revealing what circumstances had led to the aftermath that ensued; leaving them to question their struggle to salvage what few splintered shards were left of our world that would forever define our bitter legacy.

Islands in the Sky

At the edge of the world an impossible relic from the fables of antiquity has risen from the frozen wastelands of Antarctica. Professor Logan and his exploration team rush to investigate this historic find, but this unique discovery puts their lives in peril when they unearth the remnants of a long forgotten civilization left buried beneath the ice.

Within the twisting labyrinths below the melting glaciers they uncover an ancient culture which had perished from a mysterious cataclysm. They soon realize that a polar shift had triggered the destruction which now threatens a global disaster that could sling our modern world back into the Dark Ages.

Outlaws of Europa

The 2nd moon of Jupiter has been turned into a prison planet where for several generations, robot drone ships have been dumping the scum of the universe and are patrolled by a ring of advanced security satellites that would destroy any vessel attempting to land. After a century of research, old core samples from the ice reveal that the frozen oceans of Europa hold the base element of an immortality drug that can extend the human lifespan several-fold. Now greedy military corporations race for the new fountain of youth, only to discover they can't disable the orbiting sentry which was programmed to protect itself at all costs.

It appears the Confederation has a problem. How do they get past a self-evolving AI that has appointed itself as Warden, and furthermore, retake a planet roaming with Earth's worst criminals who might well be immortal themselves…

Hellbot
Battle Planet

Tranquility was one of those out of the way planets in a system far out of reach from the normal space lanes. Loners, dreamers …whoever they were, chose to colonize this world. Thirty cycles ago something went terribly wrong. It was rumored their terraformer reactor went critical, and few escaped the chain reaction that clouded the atmosphere with a planet-wide sand storm. A decade of hard labor evaporated overnight. What wasn't buried under the ocean of sand was left to fry under the twin suns.

Human explorers began to wander back into the forgotten zone. No one knew of the machines that had evolved, or the war that raged beyond the edge of the universe …where mankind did not belong.

Witchwood
The Harvesting

Every day around the world hundreds of people go missing without a trace. Year after year their numbers add up to millions of lost souls who are never to be seen again; and their numbers keep climbing ...this is where many of them went.

The Faerylands Trilogy
I • The Grey Forest
II • Soulstorm Keep
III • Sorrowblade

Long, long ago the Faerie had roamed free, but for countless centuries now the fey themselves have remained unseen; hidden and withdrawn, shrouded within the boundaries of the Evermore. But just how they became imprisoned there was a mystery their own elders had forgotten or refused to speak of, and a subject of taboo among the ancients.

The Elvenborn had become a dying race, and now a strange and dreadful blight was encroaching upon their sanctuary. Ivy knew there was something terribly wrong with her world, something unspeakable her kind was hiding from. The Faerylands were vanishing, and she had to find out why.

Artwork from the Faerylands series available online

Enter the Grey Forest

www.**GreyForest**.com

Made in the USA
Columbia, SC
27 July 2019